3

A PLACE AT THE TABLE

A PLACE AT THE TABLE

Edith Konecky

RANDOM HOUSE
NEW YORK

Grateful acknowledgment is made to Farrar, Straus & Giroux, Inc.,
for permission to reprint an excerpt from "After the
Persian" from *The Blue Estuaries* by Louise Bogan.
Copyright © 1968 by Louise Bogan. Reprinted by
permission of Farrar, Straus & Giroux, Inc.

Library of Congress Cataloging-in-Publication Data

Konecky, Edith.
A place at the table.

I. Title.
PS3561.0457P5   1989   813'.54   88-26471
ISBN 0-394-57522-9

Manufactured in the United States of America

2 4 6 8 9 7 5 3

FIRST EDITION

Book design by Carole Lowenstein

*This book is dedicated
with much love to my children:
Michael, Joshua, Vicky,
Heather, and Cassie.*

A PLACE AT THE TABLE

For Suzanne Epstien
AT the instigation of her
friend Stacy
On the occasion of her
25th birthday —
tardily
With best wishes

Edith Konecky
3/22/90 NYC

"He writes nothing whose writings are not read."
　　　　　　　　　　　　　　—Martial, *c.* A.D. 95

"She who has no lover lives only half a life."
　　　　　　　　　　　　　—Rachel Levin, *c.* 1988,
　　　　　　　　　　　unless D. H. Lawrence said it first

I am Rachel Levin.

I haven't really got the time to write, what with the daily and Sunday *New York Times*, *The New Yorker*, *New York*, and *The New York Review of Books*. There is considerable required reading for New Yorkers, all these periodicals that leave little enough time to read any books, much less write them.

There are also breakfast, lunch, and dinner. They take time. I could easily devote the rest of my life to periodicals and meals. I'm talking about waking time, so there's no need to mention sleep, except for the extra sleep I do during waking time. The moment I sit down at the typewriter, I have an overwhelming passion to take a nap, even if I have recently awakened from a full night's sleep. There's nothing less refreshing, more debilitating, than sitting down at the typewriter. There must be something I could do that's more stimulating than sitting there yawning, eyelids heavy, waiting for words.

Words. Why do I never use words like frangible, plangent, gallimaufry? Under what circumstances might frangible be preferable to fragile or breakable? Oh, my frangible heart. For plangent I would need a seashore or jungle drums, perhaps a hoot owl in the trees outside my window. I could easily find a use for gallimaufry, however, since it describes my life.

As for breakfast, lunch, and dinner, why not write about each meal in the same detail that Anna and Margo and Karla describe the sexual act in their writing? This morning's poached egg. How much you can imagine about people from the way they eat eggs: those who eat all the white, leaving the yolk, like a heart, intact, then dip the point of their toast in it, blotting it up one bite of toast at a time until it's entirely erased; those who eat from the heart out; those, like me, who would not accept a poached egg with a broken yolk, yet whose first act before eating it is to stab that yolk and spread it around. And the boiled-egg eaters: those who snip or whack off the heads and eat them out of the shell; those who smite them smartly across the midriff and scoop the innards into a cup; the toast dippers; the toast tearers. This morning, fascinated, I watched the sloppy, unshaven young poet in the frayed cable-stitch sweater carefully slice his omelet into neatly matching strips before beginning to eat it. When I couldn't refrain from asking him why, he said, "Because my mother hated me."

For the past thirteen years I have spent part of most years here at Woodlake Center, an artists' colony in the northern part of New England. I came here first when I was still with Dibbs. Later, when I was trying to leave her, I cleverly arranged to stay here for almost two years, thinking not only to put miles and hours between us but to inure myself as painlessly as possible to the separation and to living alone. I had never lived alone, and I had no idea if I could survive it. This two-story cottage became a kind of halfway house, since it was a place where I could be alone without being entirely alone. I was and was not part of the Center. I had my studio, bedroom, bath, and kitchen all to myself in this funny little house that leans against a large, stately, unoccupied stone mansion filled with bedrooms, used only in the summertime. It is an amusing cottage because, though it has only three small rooms, it has fourteen windows and thirteen doors. Like a bad stage set, it is filled with entrances and exits. I think it must once have been a caretaker's lodging. It had a fireplace but no heat, and in exchange for being allowed to have it for those two years, I had it rewired, equipped with heat and storm windows and insulation, and I bought a stove and refrigerator for the kitchen. I gathered odds and ends of furniture from the Center's storage barns. I didn't eat in the communal dining room and was not officially in residence. They plowed me out and received my mail. I installed a phone, bought a cord of wood, and settled in.

At about this time, one night in our New York apartment, Dibbs fell into a drunken sleep, leaving a burning cigarette on the arm of my scarlet velvet club chair. When the firemen were finished chopping up and hosing down, and Dibbs had moved somewhere else, I came to New York to put what was more or less intact into storage, gave up the apartment, and moved my clothes up here. I loved it. I was prepared to love my solitude, too, but I didn't have much of it. Friends from the city came to visit; acquaintances at the colony were forever dropping by for gourmet meals or to while away the cocktail hour. Some of these acquaintances would ripen into friends, and on a couple of occasions into lovers, though that was later. At the end of the school year, Dibbs appeared. Surprise! She was on sabbatical and had rented a house nearby so that we could torture each other a little longer. That summer she fell in love with someone else, and, another surprise, my frangible heart broke. I never saw her again, but I've been told that she stopped drinking and that she and my replacement are even now living happily ever after.

How much of my time has been devoted to love, to pursuing it, waiting for it, soaring on the ecstasy of it, suffering the pain of it, recovering from it, ruminating on the nature of it. Has it, I often wonder, been a wasted expenditure of time and energy? Shouldn't I have been doing something better? Larger, more selfless work? Would my *oeuvre* have been greater? Might a less hectic emotional life have kept me younger longer? How much of it do I regret?

Not much, really.

Therefore, I am waiting for my next lover as I am waiting for my next book. Empty, drained, aching to fill up again, I am in Limbo Land. The last book may never make it into print, the next lover may never materialize. Lisa says she misses me, and I miss her, but it is not the missing of lovers. There is no yearning in it.

According to my horoscope, there are very few days this year when I will meet anyone romantically of whom I don't have to be wary or with whom it will be possible to be happy. Still, I am dying to fall in love, as I am dying to have a book in me that is dying to force its way out. Last night I dreamed that I was eating from a platter of dried afterbirth, blackish strips of tough, dry, horrible-tasting stuff, because it was supposed to be good for me. Then, the implication of cannibalism made me deathly sick and I began to retch, wanting to get every last bit of it out before I strangled on it, and I couldn't. I woke myself up, nauseated, and thought about writing and why I do it and why we do it.

A new friend here, a tall and passionately intellectual woman though outwardly cool and self-contained, says that part of her need to write is an insistence on being understood—properly, accurately known. I've been reading her work, and it's true; she has to restrain herself from overexplaining. Sometimes I see her as a child, black hair flying, stamping her foot, howling into the void, the void in which she doesn't want to be lost. This is what, this is why, this is how, and, especially, this is who. But to whom, to what out there? Who cares? The world? The mother who died too early, whose absence was so much more intense than her presence might have been? It can only be to herself. When the mother is lost, the child of that mother is also lost. The one who knew me best knows me not at all; her knowing of me has died with her, leaving me perhaps forever insufficiently known. Those of us whose mothers stayed have been able to come to understand the full meaning of birth and of separateness, and have stopped trying to explain. No one, not even mothers—perhaps especially not mothers—is ever sufficiently selfless to know us as well as we might wish, or we to know others. We try and we try. We name the parts. The shapes, smells, sounds, language, habits, feel of the Other can become so familiar that we cease to think about them, yet we are separate. Though we give our love to another, that love is our own. What the beloved receives of our love is his and may have very little to do with what we think we have given. What we share may be mutually dependent, but it is not the same, and it is separate. This is something I cannot emphasize strongly enough.

It never occurred to me, though, that my writing was an insistence on being understood. Rather, it is an insistence on understanding. It is my way of digesting experience in order to discover what it means, what I think, what I think it means. Alchemy. I take the dross, give it some sort of shape, find its metaphor, report it, refine it, rehash it, renew it, give it order within some context, as though it is not random and meaningless, as though it matters.

"We would rather speak ill of ourselves than not talk of ourselves at all."—La Rochefoucauld

When I finished that last book, though, the one that took five years, I felt as Huck Finn did when he said, "There ain't nothing more to write about, and I am rotten glad of it, because if I'd a knowed what a trouble it was to make a book I wouldn't a tackled it, and ain't agoing to no more." I felt that way for two weeks.

You'd think it would be the other way around, but the fact is that the longer you live, the less there is to write about. It isn't a loss of energy or a diminution of present experience. It's that more and more, things seem self-evident and less worthy of mention. Oh, that, you think, everyone knows that!

Also, *So what?*

When I discovered early in my marriage that Peter told lies, and Dr. Dresher, my psychoanalyst, insisted from the evidence I brought him that the lying was pathological, a character disorder, it was as if I'd been struck by a thunderbolt. I couldn't take it in. I spent enormous amounts of time and energy trying to understand what it meant, why Peter lied, what really went on in his head, how it might affect Jed and Henry, our sons, how it affected me, how much of what I thought existed between Peter and me was actually there, whether when I spoke to Peter he was able to hear what I said, how much of his behavior was predicated on his own invention, not only within our family but in all his dealings and associations. Although he looked and sounded so familiar, so known, to me, he had become a stranger; he could as well have come from another planet. His was an immutable character disorder that, once it had been named for me, explained and changed everything. The way I listened to Peter began to be unlike the way I had ever listened before to anyone, and the things I said to him were different, too, except on the most superficial level. But for years I tried and tried. "Tell me," I would say to Peter when it was inescapably apparent that he had lied about an unpaid bill, the reason he had lost his job, or something even more important because it was so trivial, "tell me why you told it *that* way instead of *this* way, the way it *was*. Tell me how you really saw it, at what point you decided to add this detail or subtract that one. Tell me *truly* from your deepest center." But all I was doing was demonstrating my failure to grasp the essential nature of his malfunction, unable to understand that it was not subject to will, that it was out of control. Peter, of course, had no idea what I was talking about, since he never believed that he lied. The current of his fantasy carried its own logic and swept everything in its path along with it.

What was out of control was his need to control, to reshape and reorder a detail here, a word there, a sequence, to make it fit God knows what inner need, what inner ear and eye. He was doing what a writer does: reorganizing experience to fit the story. Often, I marveled at his creativity and wished he would use it somewhere appropriate, outside our actual life.

When, after the years of trying, after my breakdown, when the kids were half-grown, I realized that I was no longer listening to him, because what was the point, or saying anything to him much more than "pass the salt," I understood that the marriage was at an end.

When I told my father that I was thinking of getting a divorce and why, he said, "What's so terrible? He makes a good living. He doesn't fool around with other women. He doesn't gamble. He doesn't drink." My astonishment lasted only a few seconds. My father's was a natural Jewish businessman's response: everything in life is a trade-off. You weigh. You measure. If it's not such a bad bargain, you settle.

Not me. How could I explain to my father something so obvious: that any exchange between one person and another must begin with trust? Even with strangers, even in the most impersonal transactions, you must assume that people are trying to tell the truth, that they have some integrity. You have time to decide if you are wrong, but you can't start out believing in the deceitfulness of others, or you would never start out at all. Oh, I know there are misanthropic, untrusting people who expect nothing but the worst from others, but they are the flip side of the liars, as diseased in their own way. I am talking about normal intercourse.

But now, years later, I sometimes wonder if my father was so wrong. Peter is happily remarried to a dark, slim beauty—a former fashion model. His wife is loving and protective of him, and I know why. He is an attractive, warm, loving man. He is generous. He is a good and considerate lover. He never loses his temper. He is sweet. His wife's first husband, killed in an automobile crash, left her with four young daughters and the shock of his sudden absence. Peter took on the role of the lost father, assumed it with loving alacrity. When he lies to her, I wonder if she even notices. If she does, I'm sure she brushes it aside as unimportant. Indeed, he has probably brought so much to her life that she values that his lying must seem to her like some rather sweetly inexplicable eccentricity. Peter is perfect enough, she would think, without being *that* perfect.

When people ask me what my marriage was like, what my husband was like, and I describe Peter fairly, they wonder why I ever divorced him. "He lied," I say. "Pathologically." I have to add that label, supplied by Dr. Dresher, to give the lying its full weight. Still, it fails to hint at the agonies of frustration and despair I suffered, and of which I must remind myself in order to give my renunciation credence even to myself, now. An important part of Peter was absent. If he were truly there, would he have needed to make all those alterations? Part of his dishonesty lay in his inability to voice an opinion, to take a position, to have a conviction of his own. He would wait to see where I stood, and then he would stand there, too. Was this out of fear of me? Was I so intimidating? Is he still this way? Or does he dwell in a world now where everyone thinks alike and no one bothers with stupid questions like these?

If I met Peter now, at this point in my life, and we were to fall in love and marry, and I gradually discovered that he told lies of the sort that he told then, I don't think I would react in the same way. I would lose respect for him, for part of him, but I would still respect his consistent, enduring niceness, which then seemed worthless to me, coming, as it must, from the same place as the lies. I might very well at this point in my life manage to make some accommodation, as my father expected me to do all those years ago, when it was absolutely out of the question. I would be angry, I would be curious, I would be disappointed,

I would be interested. But I would be more detached. My own integrity would not be threatened. This is what aging does, why there is less and less to write about: the terrible importance of things abates.

Once again, I am back in this little writing house, perhaps for the last time, my stay nearly over. In a few day I return home. The cat and I are looking out at the falling snow and the chickadees on the tree outside the window, where I have hung a feeder. The chickadees are decoration, like Christmas ornaments, fat popcorn balls, and I am remembering other times and other words while I wait for new ones.

"Which do you think it is?" my new friend asked the other day when we were walking in the woods, telling each other our lives. "Love or work?"

"Oh, love *and* work," I said, without having to give it a moment's thought. "I can't imagine one without the other." They are the two ways by which I know I am alive. I have been made to feel that there is something shameful about this, that if my ego were solid, I wouldn't depend on "outside" things to make me feel alive, I would always feel alive and whole because I would *be* alive and whole, but I am so deficient that I cannot understand what people mean by this. What they mean, I suppose, is my dependence on acceptance and approval and validation from others. And it's true, nothing makes me happier than success. And love, which is also success. It's hard for me to believe this isn't true of everyone. William James said that we are what we cause others to experience.

It's a wonder to me that all old people aren't depressed or insane. All those losses! My new friend said that she couldn't understand why people think of aging with fear rather than with annoyance. "It's so inconvenient," she said. "And *boring*."

Last summer I took one of those organized tours, with my mother, whose guest and porter I was, and a group of about thirty widows in their seventies and beyond. It was an arduous trip for women their age, and there was considerable quarreling among them when they weren't too stupefied with weariness. Still, they were game. Bravely, they put on their little costumes and suites of matching jewelry and, wherever we went, shopped for costumes and jewelry in other languages, and at night they gathered in their hats and scarves and bangles in hotel lobbies and followed our leader to restaurants with timid, tottering steps, conspicuous because of their number and a certain sameness, the size, the bouffant pink hair, the age. People were cruel. Restaurateurs banished us to back rooms, and waiters were impatient. Hoteliers were rude. Unkind children sniggered at us at Napoleon's Tomb in Paris, and I scolded them in broken French. In Vienna, the shopkeepers were impatient, their manner implying that they were accustomed to catering only to those capable of making instant, expensive decisions. In Innsbruck, a large party of Argentine male tourists were convulsed by us and took pictures, eager never to forget us. I forced myself to scold them, too, in English, and in broken English they denied everything. I am normally too timid to rebuke strangers, but I suspect they were echoing my own terribly mixed feelings and I couldn't bear it.

The trip frightened me, I suppose because I feel myself teetering on the brink of old age, that slow, inexorable ebb tide. I had always been heartened by the example of my mother and a few of her friends who have aged gracefully, who are still able to enjoy themselves, to laugh. But these women seemed repetitively empty of everything, and especially of hope. They bickered in the wagons-lits about who would take the upper berths, in buses about who would sit next to whom, in theaters about which of them were given the worst seats. In Salzburg, nobody cared that we couldn't get tickets to the festival and that we weren't going to hear music. It was enough to be given *The Sound of Music* bus tour, to be shown the hillside where Julie Andrews this, and the castle where Christopher Plummer that, while on the bus's P.A. system the original-film-cast album music played deafeningly. I am ashamed to admit that I went along on that bus, unable to believe that this was really happening.

Most of those women were depressed, and some of them were actually insane. Most of them at one time had been pretty, you could see that, and that was gone. They had all been married, and that was gone. Some of them talked of children and grandchildren, but they sounded as if they were hanging on by their fingernails. Some of them had had businesses or jobs. That was gone. Their teeth were gone. Some of them could barely see, others were deaf. They all walked slowly. Many of them hurt or ached in one place or another almost all the time and tried not to think about it. They were intensely lonely. This trip was supposed to cause them, for a while at least, not to feel their loneliness, but they carried it along with them in their sad eyes, in their downcurved mouths, in their drooped posture, in their little outbursts of temper, in the aura of their despair. Some nights I cried myself to sleep.

My mother, with whom I occasionally discuss these things, told me not to be silly. "You're making most of it up. It's *your* imagination, not theirs. You've always done that." And I was that child again, suffering everyone else's misfortune, nearly hysterical with imagined and borrowed pain.

My horoscope for this past week promised something unique: four consecutive *good* days. Those were the days I was sick in bed with a stomach virus. I suppose I could have been sicker. My fever never rose above 101 degrees. I threw up only twice. On two of those days it poured, and gale warnings were posted along the coast. I lost five pounds.

Karla and Anna were here Thursday for dinner. With Margo, who's away, we're a sort of writing group, or what remains of it. Margo is new to the group, by way of me. Karla and Anna knew each other long before I met either of them. They couldn't be more dissimilar. Anna, who is childlike, is always a little disheveled, both in her appearance and thinking. Karla is careful and cool and intellectual. Still, they are both passionate women, drawn to each other by an abiding and deep-seated mutual respect. I don't know Karla very well yet, but I feel that she is my friend, probably for life.

I made a delicious lamb stew. Perhaps once a year I get an overwhelming urge to make lamb stew. This must be a reference to something in my past that is too elusive for me to recall. Some kitchen, perhaps, where for a moment I felt comforted.

The lamb stew could only have been incidental, because I'm not that crazy about lamb stew.

Karla had just finished reading the first three hundred pages of Anna's new novel and she was supposed to bring it to me, but she forgot. Anna was upset that Karla remembered to bring a cake but not her book. Actually, she was upset because Karla's reaction to her book was negative. "It was worse than negative," Anna told me later. "Not that she said anything bad. When she talked about it, her tone of voice was kind and reasonable, but I could tell that she was repressing *anger*. She's *angry* at my book."

I don't know why I bother to read those stupid mass-market horoscope paperbacks that, every December, I buy with an ashamed lifting of the heart, a furtive sense of hope. I am a Leo and my father was a Leo and my son Henry is a Leo, and it's perfectly clear to me that Friday, June 14, or some Tuesday in October, couldn't possibly be the same for me, my father (if he were still alive), Henry, and every other Leo in this world. Of course I don't believe a word of it, so what am I doing? Do I really want some higher authority to speak to *me*, to be paying attention to me? Stars, planets, the sun and moon. How sincere, then, is my atheism? Even if I know with at least 99 percent of my rational being that I am merely playing, what is that other errant agnostic whimsical one percent, and who let it in?

It's possible that I will be angry with Anna's book, too. Anna is wildly imaginative in her writing, in her tangled hennaed hair, in the outrageous thrift-shop clothes she wears, in her attitudes. There's a lot of weird fantasy in her fiction that serves to accentuate the absurdity and irony of the lives and attitudes of her characters. It's this freedom that she allows herself that gives rise to what is best in her work, but it's also responsible for what sometimes flaws it. The unrestrained outrageousness of her creativity often spills over into the mechanics of her writing. Writing fiction is in itself a most extreme form of self-indulgence. To raise it to the level of art obviously requires the imposition of the intellect on the imagination, the discipline of making choices. At heart, Anna is an anarchist. Anarchy is lovely in theory, but how can it possibly work, people being what they are? For Anna, spontaneity is all, and she has enough faith in her artistic self to be saddened but unmoved by those editors and agents and publishers who fail to perceive the heart of her work because of their inability to penetrate the tangled vines of prose, punctuation, and errant vocabulary that frequently obscure it.

The other person in the cast of characters for my four consecutive *good* days is Lisa, my lover, and therefore the closest member of my family for the past five years, although we have never actually lived together. On Friday morning she asked me what I'd like to do that night that would make me happy. *"Happy!"* I said.

So last night Lisa and I went to a costume party given by a suburban lawyer friend of hers who lives in a new Connecticut condo complex built of cedar shakes, with a communal building that has a silo—the barn effect. You're supposed to imagine that you're on a sheep farm, some croft, though what it really is is a rec hall with showers and lockers and a sauna and a pool outside. The party was in the rec hall, and about a hundred people came, dressed as Pilgrims and Miss Piggy and chickens. There were two flashers in raincoats and a smattering of Central American guerrillas wearing berets. Because of the clothes I bought in Hong Kong, the black silk pants and the white silk jacket with the orange dragons, I went as the dowager empress, though I also wore a coolie hat, since I happen to have one. Lisa wore chinos and a corduroy jacket, but she made her face green and pustulent with gumwax and multicolored glitter that she bought at a theatrical makeup shop, and she silvered her hair with something out of a spray can. She looked weird and sensational. At the party a woman asked her what she was supposed to be, and she said, "A preppy monster," and the woman felt Lisa's stomach and said, "So you are." "*Preppy*, not preggy," her boyfriend corrected, and the woman looked embarrassed and Lisa began to pout. "Don't be silly," I told her, "it's just so noisy in here. You haven't got a stomach." "I'm not exactly concave," she said, close to tears. "No, you're not concave. You've got just the right amount of stomach for a gorgeous thirty-two-year-old woman with a perfect body." She smiled at me through her spangled green face.

This didn't prevent our having a dreadful fight on the drive home. It was because I knew when it was time to leave, which was long before Lisa was ready. I was having a terrible time. The music was deafening and there was no room to dance, except in the tiny space where you happened to be standing. You could merely undulate in place, not moving your feet at all, which a few people were doing self-consciously. Even if I could have been heard over the music, I couldn't think of anything to say to anyone, and it was clear that nobody had anything to say to me. "Who makes your shirts?" I forced myself to ask an early-American dandy. It was a beautiful shirt, with fine details—jabots, wrist ruffles, eyelet lace, that sort of thing. "A friend of my *wife's*," he said, backing away, as though I had threatened rape. "She made my *wife's* costume, too." He pointed to a woman in a mobcap. I'd have asked where people get friends like that, but he was gone. From the degree of my unhappiness, I realized that I was in the middle of one of my chronic identity crises. Very soon I'll be a grandmother, by way of Henry; I'm pushing sixty; what was I doing there?

Today, according to the zodiac, is a *quiet* day, when I will not have any serious problems with in-laws. I once had so many in-laws that I could hardly keep them straight, but they all fell away with the same ax-stroke that severed my marriage. In-laws. Relatives by marriage. In the eyes of the law. Once were, by law, now freed of that. Law. Lisa is now a lawyer. When I met her four years ago, she was twenty-eight and still trying to decide what she wanted to be when she grew up. She seemed to have so many options: baseball player, singer-guitarist, poet. She's a natural athlete, a pleasure to watch playing softball, tennis, basketball, anything on land except golf. She has a lovely rich, true, velvety singing voice, but she's temperamental about using it; mostly she sings in the car. She might have been a poet, but she joined a poetry group led by a hostile, aging, insufficiently recognized man who convinced her that sound was all and the less said in a poem the better. My own passionate feeling about words is that they were painstakingly crafted (and in all those languages!) for the purpose of conveying meaning, no matter how banal or unnecessary, and that, while some do sound more pleasing than others, if it's sound you're after, listen to a string quartet. After I expressed this opinion at some length, Lisa never wrote another poem. I didn't mean to quash a talent, only to give it more latitude. I may be protesting too much, but poets I have known, while sensitive, are not that vulnerable; they do go on writing poems. Poets write poems, with or without my approval. Writers write. Singers sing. Darryl Strawberry goes on swinging his bat even if he does strike out a lot. I'm sorry, Lisa, but that's the way it is.

How Lisa became a lawyer: Lisa was making a scant living as a free-lance copy editor. In spite of her attitude toward language in poems, she does have a feeling for words, their precise meaning, their derivation, usage, spelling, and for punctuation. Surprising in one who reads so little. She read in school, of course, but she isn't a natural reader, not someone who has to be in the middle of a book *all the time*, who takes *The New Yorker* to the bathroom, who will read anything that happens to be lying around, even other people's mail. She is not naturally curious about *what the writing says*. So it always surprises me to discover how good she is with words, even more so than I in crossword puzzles, in copy editing, though less so in conversation. She has an excellent memory for whatever she needs, rules about commas, words she once looked up, law. But she doesn't remember conversations or the punch lines of jokes. It drives me crazy when I want her to tell what someone said, to repeat it exactly, and she can't.

Lisa was a paralegal for a few years after college, making good money and having a rich, full life in New York City with lovers and tennis and a cat and her poetry group and her therapy group and eating out in various restaurants trying out all the ethnics. And then, one day, she quit her job, probably out of pique, and began to do free-lance copy editing. She says, "I started this copy-editing business." Business. It's as if I were to say, "I started this little writing business." Why business? Measured by income, though, I'd have to admit that Lisa's business, insufficient though it may have been, was bigger than mine. All businesses are bigger than mine. I say that with unfeigned bitterness.

When I met Lisa, she was in the business, and if we went to

a restaurant or to Maine, I'd sometimes have to pay for her, or lend her the money, since fortunately I have a small independent income. That is, the income is independent of any effort on my part, enough to keep me from having to go to work in an office, and to allow me to indulge my writing habit. But Lisa, before we met, was practically indigent. Then I came along and ruined her life. She made the mistake of telling me that while she was a paralegal she took the tests for law school and scored very high on them. One of Lisa's friends, a pert little redhead named Tuesday, was in her first year of law school. We arranged to spend an evening with her.

"Tell Lisa about law school," I said, and Tuesday talked for half the night about moot court, et cetera. Summer was ending. Lisa and I stayed up the rest of the night talking, and the next morning she went downtown to NYU and filled out an application. She was highly qualified. Wellesley, grades, those test scores, the few years of paralegal work. When she got home from the interview, the telephone was ringing. She had been accepted.

Now, she's a lawyer. Now, she wears her sneakers and blue jeans—tight blue jeans molded to her splendid figure—only on weekends. During the week she wears dresses with pleats and little buttons. She wears high heels. She walks differently. Instead of swinging, she sways. She looks into mirrors for long moments, her expression blank, trying to see what strangers see. She spends ten or eleven hours a day in an office working for a sarcastic man. She gets up at six-thirty so that she'll have time to wash and blow-dry her long, beautiful hair, and at night she's too tired to stay awake for Joan Rivers. She spends her days pursuing her way through the dusty corridors of contracts and estates and trusts and negligence. If she can conquer sloth, she will make a good lawyer. She is stubborn and aggressive. I know this because of the car she drives, a Triumph that's as old as she is and has much more mileage. What keeps it running is Lisa's stubbornness and aggressiveness, her blind devotion and faith.

It's surprising how much of life touches law, or the other way around. You don't think about it much, the law, in the natural course of things, except maybe while you're driving, although even then, if you're stopped by a light, you don't really think that you're involved in the law any more than you think about it when you fail to kill someone you're furious at. You think about it when you're speeding or closing on a house, or when you're getting a divorce, but those are exceptional occasions. Having been with Lisa through the grueling years of law school, and having listened so much to talk about cases and precedents, when I read the morning paper I'm aware of how much that's in it has to do with law. Almost everything, really. Government, politics, business, crime, baseball-player trades, writers being sued. How necessary it is, really, to bind ourselves, to impose limitations, in order to function as a complicated society. My feeling about laws is that in an ideal society they arise, like language, with the need for them, and that they should be more freeing than binding. One doesn't particularly like being stopped by a red light, but it's better than being banged into at every intersection. Still, there is always the danger that "Laws grind the poor, and rich men rule the law" (Oliver Goldsmith), yet I don't believe that makes a case for anarchy; it makes a case for better law. Alas, one can quote Oliver Goldsmith indefinitely and circularly. He also said, "Those that think must govern those that toil."

Today is *disquieting*, a difficult and tedious day for Leos who are intent on carrying out their more personal plans. Emotions can run high. Requests for favors from influential people may be ignored.

Deirdre sits on the convertible sofa bed in the living room alcove that I have made over to her. I am trying to read Kundera. She is doing nothing. It's unnerving, and spoils my concentration. Her hands, tight against her sides, are curled into fists, the knuckles white. Her mouth is pressed into itself. Behind it, her teeth are grinding. She is hardly a picture of repose. I try to ignore her. I don't know how I'm going to get through the days until she can move into the apartment she's finally found. It's like living with a time bomb; I can hear her ticking away.

"Rachel," she says, pronouncing it Ray-chelle, breaking the two syllables as though they were hyphenated, rising sharply on the second. She has never lost the rhythm of Ireland, though she left there at seventeen and has recently turned sixty.

"Yes?" I say, looking up from my book.

"The thing of it is, Rachel," she says and pauses. "What I am afraid of, you see"—pause—"is that I am going mad. You know what I mean?"

I stare at her for a moment, and then I don't say what burns on my tongue to be said. I say the truth. "Yes."

There is a long pause.

"And," she says, "I am losing my teeth." Pause. "Not that the two events are necessarily unconnected."

Apart from grief, there are two things that move me to tears: self-pity (my own), and genius. When I read Deirdre's stories, in anthologies and in her own books, I cry, they are so perfect. There is never an imprecise word, a sentence that is less than elegant, a thought that is not startling in its unexpectedness, its originality. Her metaphors do not flow, they are quantum leaps. Yet they work, they are marvels. But Deirdre cannot write anymore. When I ask her why, she tells me, "I have written all I was supposed to write." She stares into space. "Oscar Wilde said that. Of course, he said more. He always did. He said, 'I wrote when I was ignorant of life. Now that I know life, I no longer write. I have lived.' "

"Balderdash," I say. "Oscar Wilde always lived. By the time he was thirty, he'd lived more than you or I. And all his best work lay ahead of him."

"Ah, Rachel, you are so simpleminded. You think to have had sexual adventures is to have lived. You are, if I may say so, a slave of passion."

I smile at the phrase; it's so old-fashioned. But what does it mean. And am I?

"I don't see how one can be a master of passion," I say. "What do you mean?"

"You let Dibbs dominate your life," she says. Her fists have moved into her lap and slowly begun to uncurl. She has distracted herself, briefly, from herself. "Not *you*, your *life*. See what I mean?"

Dibbs antedated Lisa. She hasn't been in my life for some years, though I still often mourn her. One of the many things that drove her from my life was my letting Deirdre into it,

Deirdre and her four surviving cats. It was another crisis time when, needing a place to stay, she moved in for two weeks. Not that there was ever anything like that between Deirdre and me. I was merely trying once again to save her. Intermittently. Because how could one not? I mean, I love Deirdre, and I care about her, apart from her being one of my causes—probably, from all the signs, a lost one, as they all are. It was impossible not to do what I could for Deirdre, if only because she was such a good writer. "She wrote, *The Man Who Couldn't Cry*," I told Dibbs, believing that that explained everything. But Dibbs by then no longer believed me. She was, with no justification whatever, convinced of my promiscuity. She flattered me. I have always had close women friends, with most of whom there has never been a hint of sexuality, not a thought of it. I am a perfectly ordinary woman who sometimes falls in love with another woman.

Deirdre occasionally still wrote in the Dibbs days, but no more, although she sometimes sits with a notebook in her lap, gripping a pencil, gazing into some interior distance. But though I hold my breath, the pencil never moves.

"Anyhow, there are slaves of passion," I say, "and slaves of passion. If you see what *I* mean."

"I am not a slave, I am a victim," she hints darkly. "And not of passion. Ah, Rachel, if you only knew."

But I don't want to hear her paranoid fantasies, so real to her. We have tried, her friend Marcus and I, to get help for her. Following her last episode, when she took to spending the night in the women's lavatory at *Tempus* (the magazine where she spent the best part of her adult life), and then to breaking windows, and they had the police come and take her off to prison, hoping to shock her back to reality, since they are nothing if not benevolent, Marcus persuaded her to see his ex-psychoanalyst. Marcus and I are both alumni of excruciatingly protracted Freudian psychoanalysis, and while this hasn't made either of us true believers, we couldn't think of anything else to do. The wonder of it was that Deirdre agreed to see him at all, and, for a while, went on doing it. She was on some kind of drug therapy, and I suppose it made her pliant.

"He's a decent man," she told me. "Very kind." I knew, then, that nothing would come of it. You don't talk about your analyst that way if anything is going to come of it.

Lisa doesn't mind Deirdre. She's too arrogant and fair-minded and unliterary to feel anything but suppressed ennui and, occasionally, indulgence—of me, not Deirdre—for my folly. Lisa is so young. Only the summer before last, she was playing softball with a "women's" team, most of whose members were about seventeen. When she was with them, she was certainly one of them. And, like the mother of what is known in my business as a young adult, I went to some of the games to cheer her on and to smile fondly at her sweet fierceness and at the way her large, womanly bosom swayed in her numbered gray T-shirt. How foolish I felt, sitting on the sidelines with the mothers, pretending to be one of them. No, that's not really true. If one of them asked me which was mine I said, "Number eight. I'm not her mother." And said no more.

"And with Lisa, too," Deirdre says. "She subsumes your life, although of course she is entirely unsuitable for you." How can I deny it? Though I'm more inclined to think that I am the one who is unsuitable for her.

Deirdre has another woman friend, Germaine. In her day, Deirdre had many friends, of all sexes, but the progress of her paranoia eliminated them one by one, as each became a part of the Plot, until only Marcus, Germaine, and I are left. Germaine is useless, however, being almost as needy as Deirdre. She is in some pastoral retreat, drying out again.

I first met Deirdre at Woodlake Center. I was writing a book, and Deirdre was taking care of her cats. She had been permitted to bring six of them with her and had then acquired another. Germaine had just been carted off to the drying-out place, and so I didn't meet her. Deirdre had assumed the role of Germaine's caretaker. I didn't know, then, how sad that was. Deirdre seemed feisty and determined and no more than eccentric. She had a modest reputation, but her work was so well known to me, I had studied the stories so carefully, that I was in awe of her. In fact, I all but threw myself at her feet trying to ingratiate myself. I had my Volvo then, and she had only her tiny, mukluk-shod feet against all that snow, and her countless errands, her needs that could not be met in our isolated retreat: Parliament cigarettes, Friskies, Beefeater gin, and her night-black hair that needed frequent rescorching. I made myself useful, and in due course we became friends. I was enchanted by her, by that falsely ebony hair of which she was so vain, by the green slits of eyes that, impossible though it seemed, she narrowed even further when she was about to pounce, by her carelessness with money (it was always falling out of her pockets), by her unpredictability, by her ferocious will. She was a little bit of a thing, a wisp, no larger than an undernourished child, really, yet her presence was commanding.

"I *liked* Germaine," she told me one late afternoon in the sitting room of the old farmhouse where some of the residents had their bedrooms. I was just back from my studio, exhausted by an unprofitable day, and Deirdre was there drinking tea in the waning light, two of the cats on her lap. "Not like that dreadful woman, Hilary. I disliked *her* so much that I couldn't do enough for her." She leered at me, then said, wickedly, "Would you like a cup of tea, Rachel?"

I laughed. I had already made myself a martini.

"But what a trial Germaine was," Deirdre said. "Her room was just above mine. I don't believe I had a single night of uninterrupted sleep, not that I ever do anyway, but those horrendous crashes in the night! I would run up, never knowing what I would find, though I can't imagine why, since she was always there, lying on the floor, usually bleeding, surrounded by a litter of shattered glass, and I would have to fetch bandages and sweep up the shards and get her back into bed though she was dead weight and twice my size, as who is not."

"Why did you do it?"

"I just told you, I liked her," she said, impatient with me. "She could be funny and charming when she was relatively sober. She always managed to come to dinner, you know. But how incredibly dismal she let herself look. Her face. As though she'd forgotten to take it with her and had run back for it at the last minute." She sighed. "The longer I live, the more I want to live only with cats."

I sipped my drink, wondering if I would ever be able to use Deirdre in a book. How cold-blooded I felt.

"She had a sweater that I found unbearable," she went on, her little eyes twinkling with sly malice. "In two shades of coffee, both of them dreadful. I swept it up one night with the broken bottles so that I would never have to see it again, and neither of us ever did. On the whole, though, Germaine was chic. That sweater must have been a mark of self-punishment or self-loathing. It was not in character. Still, we mustn't speculate. I

can't tell you how acutely uncomfortable other people's uncon-
sciouses make me."

"Then did you save her?" I asked.

"Save her? How could I save her?" she said with scorn.
"Really, Rachel. I was lucky to postpone her." Deirdre looked
off, memory melting her severity into a smile. "One night she
ran out naked in the snow to dance. She had a beautiful, rosy
body. There was a moon and I saw her from my window and
went out to fetch her, though I hated to do it, she was so happy.
Still, I was impatient with her. After all, I have my hands full
with the cats, who are constantly escaping from the studio looking for love. 'Germaine,' I said, 'it's all so tiring. Couldn't you
be something that's less trouble? Couldn't you be a nymphomaniac?' Germaine considered it for about one second, and
then she said, 'I've always thought I *was* a nymphomaniac,
Deirdre. But sex really doesn't interest me that much, does it
you?' It was a great discovery for her."

I have since met Germaine, and I could imagine the clashing
accents of their dialogue, the lilt of Deirdre's Irish with the slur
of Germaine's French. The two of them together, what class
they must have lent that otherwise humdrum place with its
intense bearded young men and wild-haired women pursuing
their arts and crafts like demonic children in their hidden cot-
tages, totally self-involved, which, to be fair, was what we were
all there to be.

"Under the spreading chestnut tree, I sold you and you sold
me," Deirdre mutters from her perch on the sofa bed these
years later. "Who said that?"

It takes me a minute. My retrieval system has slowed as the
material I feed into the storage tank increases. Or so I choose
to think. "Orwell?" I ask tentatively.

"*I* said it," she barks, her eyes almost disappearing. At this moment, she hates me. Briefly, I am frightened. Perhaps she has always hated me. Perhaps I don't take her seriously enough.

"Bedtime," I say, getting up and turning toward my bedroom. Then I remember the convertible sofa hunkering beneath her like a folded hippopotamus. "You want help with that thing?"

She shakes her head. "Ah, what a bed I could unfold," she says darkly.

Another time. And yet another place, a country house I've rented. It is summer and today is *variable*. The pleasant surprises that might have come in the mail for me didn't. I am being careful with machinery, as I always am, the toaster this morning, this typewriter. I don't plan to use the car today, though if the sky clears I may go out on the lake with the canoe the owner threw in with the cottage. A canoe is not machinery. It is the exact opposite of machinery. If all life were like a canoe, how much better off we'd be.

My desk is on the second floor. When I look up from the page and out the window, I see the lawn and the lake and the hills beyond the lake. The lawn is interrupted by trees, maple and birch, furry pines and conical cedars. The sun is shining, and the blue of the lake reflects the paler blue of the sky. Twittering swallows dart past my windows, into the eaves where their ravenous babies wait. Robins hop on the lawn, flocks of cedar waxwings light in the branches of the maple and break into song. In the early morning mist, and again at dusk, deer cross the lower part of the lawn, pausing to graze, tame as sheep. There's a walk I take where, at a bend in the path through the woods, I am accosted by a goshawk who berates me raucously. I take another step and she dives at me like a kamikaze, just grazing the top of my head. I stand still, looking for the nest, and then I see it. There are two baby goshawks as tall as chickens, big enough, surely, to fend for themselves. I sit on a rock and make a whistle with a flat blade of grass, and the mother and I carry on a long conversation.

There has been a succession of beautiful days. Every day I swim in the pure, cold lake. I smell the air, the trees, the mown grass, hear the birds and squirrels, see the greens and blues and saffron and gold. All my senses are marvelously engaged. Surely this is happiness, I tell myself. But I am only a little happy. I am here to work and I am alone. Time is passing, and nothing is settled. Nothing is ever settled.

Last night I dreamed of my grandchild, who is known to be a girlchild, blood of my blood, flesh of my flesh, lying in her mother's womb. She took her thumb out of her mouth and told me in an adult voice that she was my future. I shivered and sang, "You in your womb, I in my tomb," and then felt strangely happy. The dream shifted to Peter. In the dream all the feelings were there, the feelings from the marriage, feelings I thought I was long since finished with, and today I have the dream's hangover.

It took me forever to fall asleep. Outside the open windows, several million cicadas were rubbing their hind legs together in an ecstasy of sexual invitation, their collective yearning transforming my gentle pastoral surround into a jungle. Feverish for the light, moths hurled their chunky bodies against the screens, while insects small enough to make it through drowned beside me in the glass of water I keep on the night table in case I wake in the night choking. I know, from all those little holes in the lawn, at the base of the trees, under the rocks, that small furry creatures were emerging in search of nutrition. How peculiar, in the midst of so much activity, to be feeling my solitude so acutely.

Then I slept, my mouth open, gargling air.

It makes me furious when, in a dream, I can't quite catch what someone is saying. This began to occur only in the past year, but lately it is happening more and more. This is *my* dream, I rage. *I* am writing all the parts. Yet, strain as I do to hear, I have missed some crucial lines of dialogue. I wake from these dreams deeply puzzled. I may never have been perfect in my dreams, but I was certainly not hard of hearing. Why put myself at such a disadvantage? Are the lines spoken by the character who has mumbled, the lines I haven't heard, really there, unheard by me, or have I merely supplied the mumble? My frustration at not having heard is profound in the dream, as it is in my conscious life, though in the latter I often feel I haven't missed anything important, anything I can't guess at. My hearing was impaired during some illness in infancy, a marginal loss, undiscovered until I was nearly ten years old. I had a tendency to daydream, and my not hearing was attributed to this. It's likely that when my attention strayed I drifted into fantasy *because* I couldn't hear. It's also possible that writing seemed so easy to me because I was in the habit of inventing, when I failed to hear it, what other people said. I liked doing both ends of a dialogue. Occasionally, responding to what I *thought* had been said, I found by the ensuing hilarity that I was embarrassingly wrong, but on the whole my average was not bad.

Deafness in a dream is much more disturbing, because of the implication that I am drifting away from my own unconscious. Perhaps it also indicates an increasing diminution of inventiveness. Will I have to begin wearing a hearing aid in my dreams? Will my annoyance with the hearing aid match my waking annoyance with the static, the lack of discretion, the death of the battery at the most exasperatingly inappropriate moment? If all this is going to happen in my dreams, what will be the point of going to sleep?

You couldn't describe a blind man and omit his blindness, nor even a very nearsighted one. Yet it occurs to me that I have never considered my deafness part of my persona, never written about it, never made it part of the characters who sometimes play me in my fiction. I rarely think about it, never unless it's during a moment of inconvenience, trying to buy theater tickets and finding there are none available within hearing range, seeing a movie where the sound track is weak, being in the company of someone new whose voice is too soft, too low. Dibbs had such a voice, and when I was falling in love with her, it drove me mad. It was so hard to be sure what I was falling in love with; perhaps she wasn't as brilliant, as exciting, as exotic as I thought.

People are rarely kind about deafness as they are about blindness; it evokes laughter and impatience. It's as if the person who has failed to hear has done so deliberately, could have heard if she had really tried. And no matter how considerate they may be of others, people rarely adjust the volume of their speech to accommodate the hard-of-hearing. If they do it in one sentence, they will have forgotten by the next and lapsed into their normal speaking range. Unless you are deaf yourself. I always talked at the top of my lungs to a friend who was very old and very deaf, sometimes until I was quite breathless, but this may have been because I wanted to forestall one of her monologues. Because she couldn't hear, she had a repertoire of long and polished stories, stories from her life. They were good stories, but not after the first few tellings.

It was Dibbs who made me get my first hearing aid. Until then, I hadn't believed I was deaf enough. When I first wore it, leaving the clinic, I was sure it was going to change my life. When I dropped my cigarette to the sidewalk to step on it, I *heard* it hit the sidewalk. It *thunked*! I couldn't believe it, that a cigarette falling to the ground could be heard, and unknown to me, had been making that sound all the years of my smoking life. And how the birds sounded in the trees that spring! I had heard birds, but never before had they made such a racket. It was suddenly obvious to me that the normal-eared experience life differently from me, and had always done so.

Still, after the novelty wore off, I began to hate my hearing aid. I wear it when I must, but taking it off when I'm alone is as much a relief as taking off a girdle used to be in those dark ages when girdles were mandatory. So I'm sure I wasn't wearing it in my dream last night, and besides, I was in a time when I was less deaf. I was in my marriage. Peter was trying to swing one of his deals, and a few people were coming over to talk about it. A few people came, then a few more, and a few more, until there were 250, all nicely dressed and looking faintly bored. I missed a little of what they said, but I understood that most of them didn't know one another and didn't seem to know exactly why they were there.

"These people are bored," I told Peter, who was happily moving from group to group being affable. He denied it. Then I realized that they were hungry. They were waiting for the refreshments. "These people expect to be *fed!*" I howled at Peter. "I didn't even know they were coming. There are two hundred and fifty of them! I don't even *know* them. My God!"

He was so irresponsible. Although he usually managed to make a good living, I only gradually realized what a tightrope he always walked. He spent money he didn't have, ran up bills he never meant to pay, made promises he couldn't keep. Smiling sweetly all the while. We were always on the edge of bankruptcy, saved only by his fancy footwork leaping from agency to agency. He was in the advertising business, but it could have been any business, because at heart he was a salesman. Although he knew the business well, he depended not on the nuts and bolts but on bullshit and charm. Fantasy, as I've said, was his forte, and in his chosen business it served him well.

Since the divorce, my life has been picaresque and, on the whole, more interesting, though less crowded. But now that I've passed fifty, I tend more and more toward anxiety, an anxiety that sometimes induces catatonia. I would feel safer living with someone, a permanent person who adores me and is willing to grow old with me, who will think it perfectly natural when my mind begins to go. Lisa and I are in the slow throes of breaking up, and I suppose this has a lot to do with my uneasiness. With good reason, I grow less and less eager to take off my clothes in front of strangers, or even to get into a bathing suit, and perhaps that means that my love life is winding down. You have to like yourself a lot, at this age, to embark on a new love affair.

The chief reason Lisa and I are splitting up is the difference in our ages. I have never found youth particularly attractive; there is too much missing. However, in Lisa's case I have made allowances, surprised at myself. She is brash, angry, arrogant, but she is fiercely loyal to whatever is hers: her car, her one-room apartment, her bed, her cat, her coffeepot, her brown boots. Because these things are her own, they are the best of all possible things in their category. Nevertheless, being a Libra, she is fair and reasonable, and in most things she balances those scales that have fallen from her eyes. This is more than I can say for myself.

The phone rings. Certain that it is Lisa, I hesitate before answering. She will tell me something I probably don't need to hear, and she will talk to me as if I am her aunt. It will enrage and depress me even more. Instead of making me feel youthful, which is why I imagine people think she is in my life, she will make me feel even more ancient than I am.

But it isn't Lisa. It's an operator. She has a collect call for me from my son Henry.

"Congratulations, Mom," he says. "You're a grandma."

"Oh, wow," I say. "Who? What? When?"

But at this moment, perhaps because I'm his mother and the symmetry is borne in on him, he breaks down. He begins to sob with exhaustion and happiness, and it's a while before he can speak.

I am holding my new granddaughter in my arms, a little awkwardly, trying to summon the passion grandmothers are notorious for, but falling slightly short. This baby is still too new for me to know what I feel, apart from the usual awe about the miracle of life, et cetera. The baby is crying. I search her contorted face for evidence of that fraction of my genes that is supposed to have passed to her, but nowhere do I find it. The lower part of her face is her mother's, the upper is almost Henry's. I never saw the least part of me in Henry, either. Long and lanky, with brilliant blue eyes and a tousled mop of yellow curls, he is Peter's alone. I can't imagine why my genes should all be recessive. I don't look particularly recessive. I'm a tall, strong woman, with a certain amount of presence. Perhaps I have given her something hidden: my greed, my lust, my weak stomach. As if on cue, the baby hiccups and spits up, and Patti takes her from me.

The baby is ten days old, and her name is Alexandra, though I now see on the coffee table before me where the newly printed birth announcements are scattered, while Patti has been addressing and stuffing envelopes, that the printer has made an inexcusable error. According to him, this innocent infant's name is Alex*o*ndra.

"There's a typo," I tell Patti. "They've misspelled the baby's name."

"Where?"

"Here. They've got an *o* instead of an *a*. In the middle."

Patti laughs indulgently. "*That*," she says. "We spelled it that way on purpose so that the New York contingent"—she means me; she means my and Peter's Jewish relatives, all of them— "won't pronounce it Alex*aaaaa*ndra." She flattens the vowel so that you could walk on it and never feel it underfoot. I am amazed. We may talk like New Yorkers, but we don't talk like *that*.

"You can't do it," I say. "You can't do that to this child."

"Why not?" Patti says, and because she believes that she can do anything she pleases, she can.

"It's incorrect," I say, trying to keep calm. "It's embarrassing. If it doesn't embarrass you, I hope to God it will embarrass this child by the time she's six."

I turn to Henry, who, smiling benignly, has remained silent throughout this exchange. Not surprisingly. Small, wiry, energetic, Patti is a strong, controlling woman, rendered so insecure by who knows what childhood trauma that she can never admit to being wrong about anything. I have always tried to give her the benefit of every doubt. For one thing, I believe in sisterhood, and I love the women who are my friends. For another, Patti took on the responsibility for Henry, one of this nation's pioneer hippies, who stayed stoned for fifteen years and almost blew his mind. I think he married Patti for motivation. He didn't know what to do, and she could be counted on to tell him, in no uncertain terms. Live here, she said, with me. Marry me. Now let's go back to school to get the degrees we dropped out on. Study. Pass. Fertilize me. The only thing she didn't tell him to do and that surprised us, himself most of all, since he had never been much of a student, was to graduate at the top of his class. He has a degree in bugs. Beetles, primarily. Desert beetles. They are pinned and mounted everywhere. Patti has been good for Henry, and I'm grateful. Nonetheless, I turn to Henry and say, "Where were you when all this was going on? Surely *you* know you can't take a classical name like Alexandra and misspell it just to outwit some New York Jews." And because I am really angry, I cannot forbear to add, "Not without sounding completely illiterate."

Now I've insulted them both, but Henry smiles his sweet, affable smile at me. He is terribly good-looking. "As you've pointed out," he says reasonably, "if the baby doesn't like the way we've spelled her name, she can change it."

"Besides," Patti says, "nobody ever spells *my* name right. They always spell it with a *y* at the end."

"Because that's the way it *should* be spelled," I say.

"But that's not the way it *is* spelled," says this haver-of-last-words.

"School is okay," Sherry says, "but the girls are snobs." Sherry is Patti's daughter from a brief, disastrous first marriage, though I credit the missing father for not allowing *her* name to be misspelled, even if they did name her for an aperitif. She is, nonetheless, a perfect child, everyone's darling. At ten, she is ahead of herself in brains, in size, in poise. She's at an awkward age now, also precociously, but she has been and will again be beautiful, with hair the color of high noon, worn now in a Dutch braid around her head, and with gray blue eyes and skin all gold and roses. I've known her since she was three, not quite a year after Henry fell in love with her, when she was utterly charming. He is in the process of legally adopting her, and when he does, she'll be my elder granddaughter. I'm tickled to have her.

Sherry is in a rocking chair, and the baby has been deposited in her lap, freeing Patti to go on with her envelopes. Sherry has her arms around the baby and she's rocking hard, trying to quiet her. Since Sherry was an only child, utterly doted on until ten days ago, her whole life, I imagine, has been changed by the advent of this baby. So far, she's very good about it, but I think I see a sadness in her eyes. Perhaps I only imagine it.

"What do you mean, the girls are snobs?"

"If you don't wear designer jeans, they think you're some kind of freak. Dumb things like that."

Sherry wears dresses that have been lovingly, painstakingly made for her by Patti's mother. They are always a little too long, a little too large. She will grow into them. But by the time she does, there are new dresses, again too long, a size too large. They are beautifully detailed dresses, and Sherry looks, always, as though she is going to a birthday party. When she comes to visit me in New York, I will buy her designer jeans.

"Kids your age can be cruel," I say. "They're cliquish. It's hard to be the new girl."

"Sherry doesn't care about people any more than I do," Patti says. "She doesn't need friends."

"Everyone needs friends," I say, shocked. I look at Sherry, but her eyes are downcast and her face reveals nothing.

"What for?" Patti asks. "They waste your time."

"They enrich you," I say. "They keep you sane."

"I don't need anyone to keep *me* sane," Patti says. I bite my tongue, vowing to get Sherry's ear later if we're ever alone. Should I meddle? How can I not?

Sherry has slipped back inside the earphones of her portable cassette player, my birthday present to her. My son Jed, Henry's brother, had put the complete Beatles on cassettes for her. Thinking that she might like her own access to them instead of having to play them on the family stereo, I decided it would be the perfect gift. And indeed, Sherry has scarcely been unconnected to it since yesterday, when I gave it to her. Patti now rises from her labors and strides across the room to Sherry and removes the earphones from her head.

"Have you got this thing on too loud?" she says, her voice irritated. "You'll make yourself deaf with this thing." She puts "this thing" to her own ears to listen.

"It's not too loud," Sherry says patiently. "It's quite soft, in fact."

"Well, all right," Patti says after listening for a moment. Her face shows disappointment as she hands the headset back to Sherry. My gift has been acknowledged by Patti.

The third morning. Sherry and Henry have left for the day. For the third time, I've watched them prepare and pack their lunches, a slab of processed American cheese between two slices of whole-wheat bread. Sherry puts hers in the microwave oven and removes it a few seconds later, the bread intact but the cheese runny. Since she won't eat the sandwich for another four hours, I wonder what difference it makes that the cheese is melted. I hate the microwave oven. I've been putting my morning bagel in it, sliced, but it will not toast. This morning I discover inside one of the dozens of cozies an ordinary, old-fashioned pop-up toaster. I de-cozy it, plug it in, pop in my split bagel, press the lever, and in a few minutes the smell of burning flows from it, along with threads of smoke. I extract the bagel, which is not, after all, on fire, to find that old crumbs at the bottom of the toaster are burning. I upend the toaster over the sink and shake out the crumbs, put back the bagel, and continue toasting it.

Patti comes into the kitchen sniffing, the baby on her shoulder. She sits down across from me, puts the baby into a molded plastic container that sits on a chair next to the table, picks up her interrupted mug of coffee and the newspaper. The baby is sleeping. The house is silent. It's a nice, companionable moment. Hope fills my breast.

Until now, Patti and I have always managed to get along all right, and I am surprised at what a disaster this visit has been so far. Maybe I've come too soon after the baby's birth, an interesting one, since it was a family project, a natural childbirth performed with the assistance of a pair of midwives plus Sherry and Henry, who took classes throughout the pregnancy, and not least of all, Patti herself, breathing knowledgeably, undrugged and undoped. Unlike me. I'd have sold my soul to have been unconscious throughout the whole procedure and, in fact, spent most of the time screaming for help. I was not, for seven months prior to Henry's birth, in training, nor was Peter, who went to work as usual. Those were still the dark ages when women fell in love with their obstetricians, probably because of their total passivity and dependency in the relationship, that frightened state so often confused with love by masochistic women. I hoped that at the crucial moment Dr. Hellman would prove to be a kinder father than the one I had, or a stronger, more competent husband than Peter. As it turned out, he was different from both of them; he never showed up at all.

It took me seven years to get up the courage to have Jed.

Henry and Patti have just moved into this house, which her father has financed for them. It's a nice ordinary ranch-type house, one that moves them, for the first time, up the ladder and solidly into the middle class. The last time I saw them, they were living in what's called a mobile home, although it was firmly rooted to the ground it stood on. There was a lean-to greenhouse, built by Henry to house his proliferating cactus collection, two large dogs, two medium-sized cats, and a piano. The animals wandered in and out freely by way of the plastic greenhouse, as did flies, though once inside, the flies tended not to wander out again. Because of them, Patti encouraged spiders, leaving their webs to dangle from all the corners, a macabre touch that belonged more to a haunted Victorian house than to this relentlessly all-American trailer home with its plastic early-American kitchen. Startled though I was by the cobwebs, I saw the ecological logic and never said a word. At least, I don't recall if I said a word; perhaps I did. Oh, I'm sure I must have. The flies were everywhere, the spiders far from efficient, probably glutted. Also, it rarely occurs to me not to say a word. Why should I be different with my children than with others? They aren't invalids.

Though Henry hasn't yet put up his greenhouse, there are flies in this house, too. The kitchen door, which opens onto the big, fenced backyard where the dogs and cats live, is always ajar. The flies, drawn to the yard by the mounds of dogshit that have already collected everywhere, as I soon unhappily discovered, come straight from their alfresco feasting to the kitchen table for dessert. I can't help feeling that this is unsanitary, especially since Alexondra, when not at her mother's breast, is asleep in that carrier on the kitchen chair next to the table, and I am kept busy whisking flies, drawn by the sweet residue of mother's milk, from her face. I try not to say anything, and once again fail. This is not, after all, Appalachia.

"We have a screen door," Patti says. "Henry hasn't had time yet to install it. He'll get to it this weekend."

"How about keeping the kitchen door closed meanwhile?" I suggest.

"I prefer to keep it open."

That settled, I look around for other ways to be helpful. There are still cartons everywhere, not yet unpacked.

"Why don't we unpack some of these cartons?" I say.

"I'm too tired."

"I'll do it." I'm bursting with boredom and energy. I need an activity. "Just sit quietly there and tell me where to put things."

"I don't know where to put things." Her voice is dry and exasperated. "The kitchen cabinets are full. Henry will be putting up more cabinets when we've replanned the kitchen."

I sit on, immobilized. "It's a lovely big kitchen," I remark. And it is. Filled with sunlight, too. Apart from flies and cartons, and all Patti's sewing paraphernalia and ceramics equipment, which is scattered about, it's a cheerful room. I often yearn for a kitchen like this. One of my few regrets about the divorce isn't the loss of the house but of its kitchen. All my kitchens since have been spaces carved out of apartment living rooms. "The space is wonderful," I say.

"It used to be two rooms," Patti says. "The wall they took down was right there."

"Ah," I say, nodding approvingly.

"*We*'re going to put the wall back," she says. "As soon as Henry can get to it."

There are three bedrooms and two baths and a big den with a fireplace and the TV set, and there's also a living room, unused and empty except for carpeting and drawn blinds that cover the picture window.

"Why?" I say. "Don't you have enough rooms?"

"I want it for my workroom," Patti says. "And I don't want to have to keep it neat. I want to be able to close the door on it."

I nod understandingly, or so I hope. Alexondra is again at Patti's breast, and Patti's eyes have begun to glaze, either from sleepiness or sensual pleasure. Patti is a member of something called the La Leche League and plans to nurse the baby until she's old enough to tell Patti she would prefer her milk from a cow.

"I think I'll rake up that stuff on the front lawn," I say, desperate to do something. "Before it kills all the grass." What lies on the lawn is moribund ivy that recently covered the house, from where it was ripped only a few days before my arrival. Something about weakening the structure of the house, they told me. "Where can I find a rake?"

"Don't bother," Patti says. "We want the grass to die."

"You want the grass to die."

"We're going to put a circular driveway there."

I stare at her in disbelief. The front yard is only a few feet deeper than the length of the family car, a pickup truck, which is neatly parked in the perfectly adequate driveway at the side of the house. A circular drive in front of this modest ranch-type house will be as functional and meaningful as a widow's walk on a chicken coop, and it will cause the truck to be parked squarely in front of the picture window, providing whatever view there might be, should the blinds ever be raised.

"What about the trees?" I ask, grasping at straws. "Those three *lovely* mulberry trees you are so *lucky* to have?"

"Oh, they have to come down anyway," Patti says. "They're sick."

I look out at the trees. They are in full leaf. They give shade against the hot desert sun. They are interesting trees, twisted, gnarled, Oriental. If they're sick, I think, why not minister to them instead of committing euthanasia? But I give up, defeated.

"I'm going outside," I say, grabbing my book. "It's too beautiful to sit in here all day." I wash my dish, my cup. There's a dishwasher, but Patti won't allow it to be used. It will be removed entirely when Henry gets to the kitchen. "We already have a dishwasher," Patti says. "Sherry."

I pick up the straight-backed wooden chair I've been using for three days, since there is nothing outside to sit on that isn't broken and waiting, I assume, to be taken to the dump. I lug the chair outside through the open kitchen doorway and place it beneath the one tree out back. As soon as I'm seated, the dogs lope over to greet me. They are large dogs with small charms. The larger of the two smiles at me and wags his tail, then sits abruptly down to scratch his fleas. The smaller dog rests his head in my lap and looks up at me soulfully. I scratch his ears. The odor of dogshit, baked by the hot sun, is strong on the desert air, and although it's still early, it's already hot, even in the shade of this tree, which I'd better not grow fond of, since in all likelihood it, too, is doomed. The backyard, a good big, deep one, is expensively enclosed by five-foot-high steel fencing. Were it not for the lush growth of pyracantha that covers much of it, with its shiny deep green leaves and bright orange berries, the place might have the harsh feel of a prison yard. As it is, still littered with the leavings of the former tenants as well as the not-yet-unsorted possessions of its present owners, it looks like the cover for a paperback edition of *Tobacco Road*. Poor Henry. There is so much to be done here, and only he to do it: redo the kitchen, put up that wall, install his greenhouse so that he can put all those cacti where they belong, install the screen door, slay those trees, kill that lawn and pave it over. He has already built the rabbit hutch (rabbits are Sherry's 4-H project), and his bees are in place in their drawers. He has put up the steel shed and his tools are in the toolshed. But he is going to have to gather up these broken appliances and dead tires and other bric-a-brac, and the clutter of dying ivy out front, and haul it all to the dump. The grass in back needs cutting, but first he'll have to do something about all those turds. He has a stiff sentence ahead of him, months of hard labor.

"Why are you sitting on that hard, uncomfortable chair?" Henry asks, leaning to kiss me. I've had a walk and a nap and another walk, and I'm back under the tree with Iris Murdoch. It's a little past five, and Henry has just come home. "There are comfortable lawn chairs in the steel shed."

"It's locked," I say, having tried the door earlier.

"The key's on a hook right next to the kitchen door," he says, surprised that I don't know this. I am really angry now. I truly believe I'm a feminist, but where do I put Patti, how do I fit her in, what are these primitive feelings that elude my elevated consciousness?

"I'll bring a couple of chairs out," Henry says.

"Don't bother. I've finished my book." (Alas). "I'm going to have a drink now. Can I make one for you?"

"All we have is beer."

"I bought vodka."

"Out of sight," he says archaically. "A Bloody Mary?"

In the kitchen we scout around for the makings. Henry finds a can of tomato juice, a lemon, Tabasco, Worcestershire sauce. Patti comes in, burping the baby. "Can I fix you a Bloody Mary?" I ask her.

"I can't drink while I'm nursing," she says. "I don't drink anyway."

I know this. I'm just being polite. Patti sits down and stares disconsolately at the package of defrosting pork chops she has taken out of the freezer. Every night since my arrival I have taken the family out to dinner, the baby, too, in her plastic package, waking in midmeal to demand the breast and getting it. Tonight, Patti has offered to cook dinner, though I have said, truthfully, that I would be happy to do it. More and more, I find myself sounding like the mother-in-law I have turned into right before my eyes.

"It's not going to be enough," Patti says. There are four dispirited, wafer-thin chops in the soggy package. They wouldn't have been enough for even one of these trencherpersons. "Henry, you'll have to go to the store for more."

"I'll go with you," I instantly offer, abandoning the drinks. I happen to love supermarkets.

"So? What do you think of my baby?" Henry asks, when we're in the pickup, driving to the market.

"She's terrific," I say, trying again to feel what I know I should be feeling, what I am sure I will soon be feeling. I'm glad that Henry has a baby; he's so happy to have her. Still, I wonder if I will ever really know this baby, or have a genuine sense of kinship, partly because of the distance between New York and Albuquerque, but more because of the increasing distance I feel between Patti and me.

If I'd had a daughter and this were her baby, would it be different? Men are so incidental. Here is Henry adopting Sherry although her flesh-and-blood father is alive and well and living not five miles away. He hasn't seen Sherry since she was three and is perfectly willing to sign whatever documents are required to allow the adoption to go through. How easily some men slip in and out of their roles. How Patti and that first husband must have hated each other. I look at Henry's serene, handsome profile. He looks so strong, so confident. He is not strong. He is not confident.

I remind myself, as I so often must, that the things that are important to me aren't necessarily those that are important to others.

"Are you happy, Henry?" I ask. He takes his eyes off the road and looks at me solemnly. Then he smiles sweetly and says, "Yes. I'm happy."

We buy eight fat loin pork chops and baking potatoes and milk and tomatoes and salad greens, and then, at the delicatessen counter, I buy sliced ham and turkey breast and Swiss cheese and pickles, while Henry scuttles back and forth collecting other goodies, a six-pack of beer, cans of tuna fish and sardines and frozen orange juice, maple syrup, anchovies, boxes of crackers. This has nothing to do with the way they ordinarily shop; it's the way I shop, a spree, a binge, what visiting mothers are for.

At breakfast the next morning Sherry takes out the dwindling loaf of American cheese and the bread for her lunch.

"There's some ham in there," I say. "And turkey and Swiss cheese, if you'd like a change."

"Oh, *good*," Sherry says, putting the orange brick back.

Patti puts down her coffee cup and looks at me accusingly. "We don't ususally make much of a fuss about lunch," she informs me. "We usually just have leftovers. Of course, with an extra person, there aren't any leftovers."

I can't believe she has really said this. Last night was the first dinner we have had at home. I look at Henry, waiting for him to react, to speak. His expression is placid, serene, unruffled. He does not speak. He is not a stupid or insensitive man. Almost, I begin to understand how it was possible for ordinary German citizens to have stood by while those terrible things were done. I feel utterly alienated, and at this moment I thoroughly dislike my son, but in the next moment I am awash with guilt. I think of the exceptional, adorable, intensely busy little boy he was, and I think of how crazy about him I was, about every morsel of him, and I think of all the mistakes I made.

Henry and I are out in the backyard. It is the first day of Henry's weekend. We've put up the kitchen screen door, flushed out the rooftop cooler, and he has just informed me that the pyracantha, whose lushness I have praised, must come out because it is a "hostile" plant.

"The dogshit is friendly?" I don't refrain from saying, my syntax suddenly, unexpectedly, Jewish.

"The berries are poisonous," he explains. "The baby. And they're useless. We're going to plant grapes there."

We are gathering up some of the trash, piling it into the back of the truck, preparatory to the first trip to the dump. Sherry comes out the back door holding the toaster in her arms.

"Mom says to throw this out," she says, in a nervous voice. "She says it's no good anymore."

"So why the announcement?" Henry asks, but I know. "Throw it out. What's the matter with it?"

"*I* don't know," Sherry says, close to tears. Obviously, there has been a scene inside, or perhaps Sherry has been overworked. "Mom says it's broken."

"Put it on my workbench," Henry says. "I'll take a look at it."

When Sherry has gone back inside to resume her duties, I go to the workbench and plug in the toaster and depress the lever. In a few seconds, all the elements are aglow. "The toaster seems to be working fine," I tell Henry. "I shouldn't have come. It's too soon."

"Don't pay any attention to her," Henry says. "She's always like this. Besides, *I* wanted you to come."

"I called the airline. They said I can't leave before my seven days are up, since I'm on Apex. I asked them what would happen if I *do* leave early, would they take away my apartment or what? They looked it up and figured out that I'd have to pay an additional eight hundred dollars. I could have gone to Australia."

"You'll have to stick it out," Henry says cheerfully. "I'll be around all weekend, and on Monday you can come down to school. We'll have lunch."

Monday: the day I am going to give Patti a rest from me. I can't wait, and I'm pretty sure she can't, either. I'll have lunch with Henry and then wander around the campus. There are a couple of museums, and if I get tired I can go to the library and read. At five o'clock Henry and I will go home, have a couple of drinks, and then we'll all go out to dinner.

There's a knock on my door. "Telephone for you," Patti says.

"For me? Who would be calling me here?"

"It's Henry," she says. "He wants to talk to you."

I go into the kitchen, where the receiver is dangling from the wall phone like the not-quite-severed head of a chicken.

"Mom?" Henry says. "Listen." He sounds small and uncomfortable. "How would it be if you asked Patti to join us for lunch?"

"What? The whole point was . . ." But I know what has happened. Patti has made a scene. It's not that she doesn't want to be free of me; she doesn't want to miss anything either, and the latter weighs more than the former.

"All right, sure," I say, and when, a few minutes later, I ask Patti if she'd like to join us for lunch, she doesn't pretend surprise or pleasure. She's ready to go.

Patti drives the truck, the baby asleep between us on the seat, wrapped and tied into the plastic carrying case. How jaded this baby must already be; I doubt if anyone as brand new as she has been to so many restaurants.

"Well, Alexo," I say to her, "all set for a terrific lunchy-poo?"

Henry is waiting at the appointed place outside the gates. Sheepishly, he gives me a meaningful look of thanks. He is wearing a fishing cap with a bill, the kind of cap I used to see in camping grounds on the heads of men who had John Birch bumper stickers and who put up signs in front of their Winnebagos saying ED AND FLO. This cap has a legend printed on it: THE THING I HATE ABOUT SEAGULLS IS THEIR SENSE OF HUMOR.

Henry leans into the window of the truck on Patti's side. "Where should we go for lunch, hon?" he asks.

"What do you feel like?" Patti asks me, deferring.

"I don't care. Anything but Mexican." I've never been able to cultivate a taste for either Mexican or Indian food; both, in their native countries, have made me deathly ill.

They decide on a restaurant called Paul's Place. Henry leaps into the open back of the truck, 6'2" of cargo, and Patti rolls the truck down the street and into one of the wide six-lane avenues that grid the city. Ten blocks later, we pull up in front of Paul's Place. It's closed.

"Damn," Henry says. "It's Monday."

"It'll have to be Tia Miranda then," Patti says happily. I have had my chance and flubbed it; Mexican it is.

"Is that all right with you, Mom?" Henry asks anxiously. "You sure you don't mind?"

I shrug. I can always get a couple of huevos, hold the ranchero.

"Oops!" Henry shouts from the back of the truck. "There goes my hat." We are in the middle of the same business thoroughfare, three lanes of traffic coming and three lanes going. Patti maneuvers the truck over to the curb. Through the mirror I can see the cap a block and a half back, wheeling away from us like tumbleweed.

"Go get it," Patti says.

"Are you kidding? I can't even see it anymore," Henry says.

"*Get* it, Henry!"

Without another word, my gorgeous son vaults over the side of the truck and begins to bound like an antelope through the traffic. I think of all the years of his growing up when I couldn't get him to pick up his room or put anything away. I would plead, cajole, scream, bribe. Nothing. "Watch me, Henry," I would say. "Look at what I'm doing. See all these crumpled papers on the floor? I am taking them in my hands and lifting them off the floor. See this basket? It's always been here. It's a trash basket. I am putting these crumpled papers into it. Did that look hard? That wasn't hard. Now, see that jacket rolled up and tossed under your desk, under your feet? I'm picking it up now and walking over to the closet with it. See these items in the closet? They're called hangers. As their name implies, the purpose of hangers is . . ."

On and on, year after year. To no avail. He would sit and watch me with either a smirk or dazed bafflement, as if I were crazy. What was all this about? What possible difference could it make if the jacket was on the floor or in the closet?

But this woman, this absolute monarch, has given him his orders and off he goes, tearing down a busy six-lane divided (thank God) highway, dodging traffic in pursuit of a dollar-fifty duckbilled cap. I want to kill him even more than I want to kill Patti. He'll be run over, not killed but maimed and crippled for life, and it will serve them both right. She will have to do everything for him, bedpans, bedsores, spoon-feed him, chop down the trees, put on his socks and shoes, comb his hair, take him to the dentist, cut his toenails, wheel him out for a little air, do something makeshift for sex.

"Was there something special about that hat?" I ask. "Did it have sentimental value?"

"My father gave it to him. *I* think it's funny, but most people don't get it."

"The joke? You mean that hat is over their heads?"

"I suppose if it were pigeons instead of seagulls," Patti says, "people would get it."

Henry is sprinting back, hat in hand. "Okay," he says, hurling himself back into the truck. "Onward and upward."

I remind myself that I am crazy about Henry, and I am, even when it isn't easy, and I tell myself that Patti is a good, hard-working mother who has given Henry a life that he was incapable of giving himself, that whatever I think or feel is, in the context of their marriage, irrelevant, and that in a year or two, if I see her from time to time, I'm really going to love this baby no matter how she's spelled, and that tomorrow morning I'll be upward and onward. By the time we reach Tia Miranda and my huevos, I am calm and smiling, that incidental and totally expendable bystander, the mother-in-law.

"Love means that I want you to be." Saint Augustine said that.

"Aren't we lucky," I once said to Lisa, and I meant it, the wonder of it. "To be alive at the same time in virtually the same place? Just think, one of us might have been born in the thirteenth century, or in Thailand. What a miracle."

But despite all the chanciness, not only of time and place but of having met at all and, having met, of having discovered each other (I think I had been in the same room with Lisa three times before I really noticed her, and then only because she deliberately called herself to my attention), and then falling in love, miracles aren't enough. If I had been born two hundred years earlier among the Sara in Central Africa, I might have been thinking the same thing about some stunning Ubangi, if I had a romantic heart, while Lisa might never have thought about it at all, anywhere, the luck, the miracle. She's a pragmatist and doesn't think that way, though she *has* said that she wished she had known me when I was eighteen, and wondered if she'd have liked me. "You'd have been crazy about me," I told her. "I was lean and cocky."

But if I was attracted to women then, I didn't dwell on it. I was also attracted to men, as I only rarely am now, in love with one after another. One of them, the last before I married Peter, the one I probably loved best, was Amos. I missed him for years, and I still occasionally wonder what my life would have been like if I'd had the courage to wait for him. A fragile reed waiting to break, I was at the mercy then of forces and impulses that I would spend years sifting through for nuggets of understanding. I was very young. Peter seemed safe to me, recognizable. Amos, of whom my parents disapproved—he was penniless, an intellectual, it was wartime and he was about to be shipped to Germany—was too risky.

So that this morning when Rebecca, my oldest and closest friend, calls to say that Amos is coming to New York (he is Rebecca and Paul's good friend; we met at their wedding), without Angela, his wife, I'm not surprised by the small anguish in my voice when I tell her no, I will not come to dinner next Friday when he will be there.

"Oh, no," I say, my heart beating. "I couldn't."

"Don't be silly," Rebecca says. She is the most reasonable of women. We have been friends since childhood, when I began to make her into my superego, a role she would never have asked for. But I needed a decent superego badly then, no one else being stern enough, least of all me. I trusted Rebecca's intelligence and integrity more than anyone else's, and I still do. We met early in high school and became friends at once, never having to go through that tentative circling about. We spoke the same language, we were both crazy about what was then brand-new food to us: chow mein. We found the same things hysterically funny, and we laughed a lot. We were readers, and almost never did we have to explain and explain. Who could ask for anything more?

So when Becky says, "Don't be silly," it's probably more than a figure of speech; it probably means that I'm being silly. During most of our years, Becky and I were each other's closest confidantes and advisers. Nothing then was ever entirely settled or understood until we had talked it over with each other ad nauseam.

"What's the worst that could happen?" she asks.

"Let me think about it."

What I mean is, let me think about what the worst that can happen could be, not whether I'll come to dinner. I won't come to dinner. How could I? And why would I?

I was in the third month of my pregnancy with Henry the last time I saw Amos, telling him over lunch in a little French bistro that I still loved him and that marrying Peter instead of him was probably a mistake. I wasn't at all sure if that was true, but I was crying. He was still in uniform, hideous coarse winter khaki like the stuff of a horse blanket, a private first class, a rank he'd risen to despite those pure revolutionary principles that had kept him from seeking a commission. He took my hand and said, "Come with me." "I can't," I wailed, "I'm pregnant." "That doesn't matter," he said, not hesitating but turning pale. "I'll love your baby."

But I couldn't. I couldn't do that to Peter. Or to Amos. I loved them both.

Amos was on his way to Berkeley to get his doctorate, become a professor of eighteenth-century English literature, and write more poems. That was thirty years ago. He did all those things. He also married Angela, fathered five "interesting" (Becky's word) children, became a full professor, and has been having, according to my informant, a perfectly marvelous life. Thirty years! I was young, willowy, gorgeous, the three most important things that I no longer am. He, of course, would be exactly as

I remembered him: young, solemn, proud of his neat, compact body (he was shorter than I, another drawback then), with that sweet mouth and those dreamy, bottomless eyes with their long, curling black lashes. I thought him the gentlest of men, sensitive and profoundly intelligent, so unlike my crass, tyrannical father that I was both attracted to him and frightened of him. Was this really the way a man should be . . . *understanding*? Someone I could talk to? Someone I could listen to? Someone who listened to me? Could I respect someone like that? Could I really *trust* him? How hard it is to be young and stupid and yet have to make serious choices.

"Let me know about Friday," Rebecca says when we have finished chatting about other things. "Aren't you curious, at least?"

When we have hung up, I go down for the mail. This is a trip not to be taken lightly in the apartment building which is my principal dwelling, a rent-stabilized building in a large complex a few steps from the East River. The apartments are bright and spacious, and everything works. The hot water is always hot, the water pressure is strong, the oven is reliable, and I fit in the bathtub. The rent, by New York standards, is so reasonable that nobody ever moves out except horizontally. There is a ten-year waiting list for apartments here. Most of the survivors, my neighbors, are widows, or couples who hold each other's arms for support. Going down for the mail is the high point of the day. Mail is the outside world, the only channel through which the unexpected could happen, though it so rarely does. And, too, the trip is an occasion to see others, exchange a few words, tell someone to have a good day, be seen, no matter how peripherally, how superficially. For some, it's the equivalent of the cocktail hour. Lonely, lonely. It's so sad and sweet that I can't bear to go prematurely, to go through it more than once. On the way down, I offer a few words of sympathy for Mrs. Goldfein's swollen feet, and at the seventh floor Mrs. Condon comes aboard, small and plump and smiling, as always, and tells me for the dozenth time that her son and daughter-in-law, who are economists, are writing a book, too. Why don't I stop in at her apartment when I have a few minutes so that she can show me a photograph of them and some other treasures. Since I have already done this twice, I smile and say some lying thing, hardly hearing myself, then hold the door open when we have arrived, while they precede me out of the elevator. We don't have a lobby, only an entryway lined with mailboxes, all business. There's no doorman, either. If there were, there would be someone else to kibitz with besides Freddie, the mailman, who is still shooting white rectangles of hope into our small brass cubbyholes. My section is finished, however, and I extract my mail and hasten back to the elevator and up, alone this trip. There are eight appeals for money, a fair daily average, for worthy causes in which I believe passionately. I wish I could afford to support them all with more than my heart, but as fast as I contribute, even faster do they ask for more, and even faster do I get added to new mailing lists. How I wish they would consolidate, all these organizations that want to do the important thing, save the earth, stop the bomb, avert the end of everything, instead of being so factionalized and wasting all that money on printing, paper, postage, in competition for my few dollars.

Among the not-for-profits is one envelope stamped first class. For a moment my heart lifts; then I see that it is from my agent, and my heart plummets. If it were good news, it would have come to me over the telephone. I've been waiting nearly six months for Grenville & Wyatt to make up their minds about *All the Things You Are*, my last novel, which for two years has been crawling from publisher to publisher, rebuffed by all, though mostly with raves. "It's the state of the industry," I am repeatedly assured, and I know it's true; I read newspapers, I know what's going on. Still. Books do get published, and I know without a quiver of doubt that mine is better than many of them. It's my misfortune to have written what the industry calls a "midlist" book. I spent close to five years writing it, and at no time was I ever aware that what I was wasting those years on was a "midlist" book.

Back in the safety of my four-room enclave, I walk to the bedroom, remove my sneakers, and lie down on top of my carefully made-up queen-sized bed. The sun streams through the windows, brightening all the color in the room: the wild, profuse coleus on the windowsill, the paintings on the walls, the bright-spined books on the shelves beside my bed. I close my eyes and drop all my mail onto the floor except for the one that does not ask but tells, thinking how odd that at this moment I am more concerned with a letter of rejection than with the end of the world. Then I grit my teeth and read this latest judgment made by some anorectic WASP child of wealth who, underpaid though she may be for her enviably prestigious job, is, by any standards applied to my own endeavors, valued far more than I for her avid willingness to sit in air-conditioned judgment of me. ". . . wonderful writer . . . wit, verve, energy . . . love the humor, the ultimate sweetness . . . reveals a lot of rich, contemporary thought about the way we live our lives . . . admire her work a great deal . . . unable to get enough in-house support to make an offer . . . thank you for your patience."

She refers not to *my* patience but to my agent's. She knows nothing about *my* patience.

I stare at the ceiling. The letter falls from my hand to the floor to rest with the other bad news, and I lie in a state of deep depression, tempted to sink into sleep, away from it all, though it is not yet noon. I am jarred from my stupor by the telephone.

"Mom?"

"Hello, Jed."

"What's the matter, Mom? Are you all right?"

"I'm fine," I say, trying to brighten my voice.

"You sound awful. What's wrong?"

This son has an ear. He hears everything, spoken and unspoken. He was supposed to be a musician, but somehow he has turned into a printing salesman. He has an eye, too. When he was little, he was constantly reading my face for clues. The least sign of displeasure on my countenance, no matter who or what had evoked it, would cause his lower lip to start quivering. "I don't have to be happy every minute. Give me a break, Jed," I often said to him. "You do," he would pipe back. "You have to be happy every minute." I don't know how either of us survived his childhood.

"Nothing is wrong," I tell him. "There's no longer any need for you to be sensitive to every nuance. You're all grown up now." He even has his own apartment, though it's only a few minutes' walk from mine.

"What has age got to do with it?"

"Can we get to the point of this call?" I ask.

"You *are* in a lousy mood. There isn't any point. I just called to see how you are. You know? A Jewish son? But what's the good of being a Jewish son if you have such an un-Jewish Jewish mother? I know how you're languishing there, alone, feeling unloved, unappreciated, deserted, your life meaningless, barren, nothing to look forward to, nobody to cook for, nothing much to mend or darn. With a heart bursting with pity, I telephone, just so you'll know there's someone in this world who thinks about you once in a while, and what do I get for my trouble?"

"Oh, Jed," I say, laughing. "I'm sorry. It was just another rejection. From a publisher, I mean."

"What a relief," he says. "I thought it was something serious."

We have barely hung up when the phone rings again.

"This is Harvey Candleman. Margo gave me your number, did she tell you?"

"Margo Strasser?" I say, stupidly, since how many Margos do I know?

"She did a television treatment for me. She thought you might be interested in working with me?"

Ah, yes. At our last writer's group meeting, Margo mentioned that she had given my name to this man for whom she'd done a script before moving on to bigger and better things, the blockbuster novel for the book packager.

"Oh, Harvey *Candleman*," I say, as though my life is also spilling over with Harveys. "I can't believe your timing."

"I think I have a project that would interest you. Can we make a date to meet?"

"Yes, of course."

"How's Thursday at ten? Are you free?"

"Hold on, I'll check my calendar." I put the phone against my stomach and stare at the ceiling. "Looks good," I say after a minute.

"Fine. Ten o'clock at the Gaiety."

"Pardon?"

"The deli. You know, West Forty-seventh?"

Margo, I now recall, told me she first met him at the Carnegie Delicatessen at three in the afternoon; I thought it odd. Now I see that this is a man who conducts his business in Jewish delicatessens during off-hours. It augurs ill.

"Ten o'clock is a little early for me. Unless you mean P.M., in which case it's a little late."

"A.M."

"Can we make it a little later? Eleven forty-five?" I say, determined to get at least a pastrami sandwich for my time.

"Ye-es, I think that's all right. But, listen, make it Wolfie's then, on Fifty-seventh. You know where it is? The northwest corner?"

"I'm writing it down. How will I know you?"

"I'll be wearing amber-tinted aviator glasses," he says.

Somehow, I knew it.

"But don't worry," he says. "I'll find you."

"How?"

"Trust me."

"By the way, what's happened with Margo's, um, treatment?"

"Nothing definite yet." He has a strong, confident, friendly voice. "Lots of interest. By the time I see you, I'll know more."

We disconnect, and I lie there, studying the ceiling, wondering if I have it in me to do something called a treatment, and whether it will be therapeutic like the steam room at the Turkish bath where my grandpa used to go to *schvitz* out the poisons, or the mineral waters my grandma drank at the spa in Saratoga to clean out *her* poisons. Treatment. As with sewage, television requires not writers but treaters. Margo said she didn't know anything about Candleman, but that she liked him, which

· 63 ·

doesn't mean much, since Margo likes most men. Anyhow, she has already lost interest in Candleman and in television. Her agent has brought her together with a book packager who does for publishing what Candleman supposedly does for television, and for much more money. The book packager has a track record. Who knows about Candleman?

Margo, by the time she was twenty-five, long before I knew her, had written three novels that were hailed by the critics, making her the darling of what was then the literary set. Early success went to her head and, like a bad cold, blocked it. What she called her "real writing" came harder and harder. She had frantic periods, and has them still, of wanting to make money at her writing, which even those first novels failed to bring her. She has ghosted a couple of books for celebrities and written some nonfiction with blockbuster titles much more provocative than their text. Still, she never really struck oil.

"Why do you have to make money?" I've asked her. "John makes a good living." John, her husband, is a biologist on the faculties of two universities. They have only one child, Daniel.

"I want to see how it *feels*," she says. "I've never really supported myself. First there was Daddy, and then there was John." I know what she means. For me, too, first there was Daddy, then Peter, and now the trust fund, modest though it is. Earning real money of my own is why this Candleman business tempts me.

The ceiling at which I stare, wondering if Harvey Candleman could possibly be anything but a phony, is as blank as the sheet of paper that has been curled in my typewriter for three days. So smooth, so white, so unblemished. When my father was dying and his mind gone, he spent a lot of time looking at ceilings and cursing, inveighing, bewailing, not going gentle. "Ceilings," he said mysteriously in a milder moment. "Who needs so much of them?"

I grope a little frantically for my bedside *Zodiac International*, and open it to today's cautionary tale. *"A slow and uneventful day, although the moods of Leos are likely to undergo some distinct changes. Club activities may be expensive. Not a day for lending large sums of money to friends."*

The worst that could happen, I think with dead certainty, is that Amos would not know who I am.

"He who falls in love has come to the end of happiness."

—Japanese proverb

One of the problems with Lisa is that she wants to have those conversations with me that I no longer have. Serious conversations about One's Self, about Who Am I Really, about What's It All About. It isn't that I have a closed mind or that I have found final answers. What I have learned after the years of analysis, both professional and amateur, is that introspection is best done in absolute privacy. The probing is like peeling away the layers of an onion in search of the onion's heart; it makes you cry, and then you find that the onion has no heart, it *is* those layers. I am endlessly interested in layers still, but when I talk about them, Lisa will look at me as if "so what?" She is still after the heart.

It is Sunday morning, and Lisa is snuggled into a corner of the sofa, her feet tucked under her, nursing her second cup of coffee, still wearing the Mickey Mouse T-shirt she slept in, her breasts distending the ears. I am leafing through the *Times Book Review* section, counting the men against the women, fiction and poetry against nonfiction. So far, seventeen men have written books worthy of review as against two women. Seventeen men have reviewed the men's books. The two books written by women have been reviewed by women, on the same page. And the ratio of fiction to nonfiction is diminishing weekly, to the point where fiction has all but vanished. This has put me in a foul mood.

"Let's talk," Lisa says, putting down the coupon section she has been poring over. The morning sun streams into the room, backlighting her, and she sounds and looks comfortable and cozy.

"What shall we talk about?" I ask.

"Something *interesting*," Lisa says.

"The Supreme Court? Your parents?"

"Isn't there anything that interests *you*? Do I have to initiate everything?"

"Baseball. Let's talk about why some people become Met fans and others Yankee fans."

"You're really not interested in anything I think, are you? When I'm with Peggy or Marlene, we never stop talking. You don't take me seriously."

"What do you talk about with them?"

"Everything. Anything. The world. Men. Our psyches."

"Has Marlene got a psyche?"

"You don't like any of my friends."

"It's not a question of like or dislike. They just don't interest me much."

"Nothing about me interests you. I don't know why we go on."

"Sex."

"Thanks a lot."

"You interest me when you're angry. You're mature and intelligent when you're angry."

"You really stink, you know that? You're a mean fuck when you're not working. I wish to Christ you'd stop spraying your fucking writer's block frustration all over me."

"Watch your language, kiddo." But it's true, I'm feeling mean. I'm afraid that Lisa, with the least bit of encouragement, may begin to babble. One of her sisters, the one she is closest to, is a babbler, and while it annoys Lisa, she is sometimes capable of doing it herself, of going on and on pointlessly. Babbling embarrasses me, and it makes me furious. Silence is not the equivalent of darkness and any word thrown into it a ray of light. There is something hysterical about this need to dispel quiet as though it is a threat. Lisa's sister is a compulsive talker. She will say anything, no matter how meaningless and boring, in the hope that in all that jumble of words, somewhere there may be one that is golden. I can just tolerate it in her sister, but I am impatient when Lisa does it. I am afraid that I will have to come to terms with her occasional childishness, even though I know that she is quick and intelligent and her frame of reference surprisingly broad for one her age, especially since she really doesn't read. For three years she tried and failed to read *To the Lighthouse*, such a thin book, so delicate, so luminous, so perfect.

"There's nothing I like better than a nice companionable silence," I say. "I often feel closer to you when there aren't any words in the way." Words, I mean, that Lisa and I so frequently mis-take, mis-hear.

"Well, not me!" Lisa says, angrily.

"I like to feel what you're feeling without being told."

"How do you know what I'm feeling? Or who I am? You want to preserve your illusions, and you'd rather not hear anything that contradicts them. You don't begin to know who I am."

Since this is a charge that has been leveled at me previously by two of my three serious postmarital lovers, I am nonplussed. Is it true? Is this the tragic flaw that drives my lovers away, that has kept me from settling into a blissfully permanent liaison?

"Touched a raw nerve, right?" Lisa says smugly, seeing it on my face, which is often more eloquent than my mouth.

"Right."

"It's come up before?"

"Yes."

"Naturally. You're so negative and critical and unaccepting. You don't love me. You probably never really loved anyone. How could you? You love what *you* are feeling, and what is that but self-love?"

Lisa, who rarely says anything to surprise me, has now surprised me. In my arrogance, I beam at her as if she is my own creation. I want to give her an A-plus, but if I grade her, it will make her even angrier.

"You're probably right," I say humbly. "Though I'm not sure it's self-*love* so much as self-*ish*."

In the final ghastly years with Jane, my first woman lover, the one I used as the rock on which to dash the frail craft of my marriage, we fought constantly, and while I felt that I was fighting for my survival, Jane began more and more to claim that I did not *see* her, that I did not see *her*. I was positive that what had happened was that I no longer saw her with the blinding adoration of that first in-loveness, but had come to see and love the real Jane, the frail, vulnerable one with the ego so shaky it made her arrogant and unable to accept any difference of opinion as less than a personal judgment. She wanted only my blind, unquestioning adoration, and I found myself more and more examining everything I was on the point of saying, and then not saying it. In the end, though her departure devastated me, it was also a relief.

Later, after Dibbs, there was Ani, the most vociferous about her love, the most demonstrative. She could not speak of her love for me often enough, the range and poetry and precision of its expression was sheer technical brilliance, she trembled with it, it washed over me like a warm, perfumed bath; I luxuriated in it and turned pink and swollen with the comfort and artistry of it. But it was all style, for I soon learned that there were serious plans afoot that did not include me, and that there were other lovers, too, of both sexes. When I charged her with deviousness, and even dishonesty, she cried out in pain that I failed to understand her, that she was not that person at all, and, finally, after a long period of mutual torture, she said, "I cannot be the person you want me to be." I knew it was true and accepted it, and went away.

It was not, I truly believed, that I failed to see them, but that I had ceased to see the them my lovers wished to believe they were and, for a while, had fobbed off on me. I was never accused of not seeing them when, in fact, I was not seeing them; only when I was.

"With whom?" Lisa says. "With whom has it come up before?" I tell her.

"And Dibbs?"

"No, not with Dibbs."

"Because she was the worst. Real food for your masochism. You accepted her totally because she *really* abused you."

"She never abused me unless she was drunk, and then she abused everyone. It was nothing personal."

"But she was always drunk."

"Not always. Sometimes she was recovering from being drunk, or not yet quite drunk, or just beginning to be drunk. But she always let me *be*, and I guess I loved her totally."

This is hardly the right thing to say to Lisa, who has always been jealous of Dibbs, although she happened so long ago.

"How could you have loved her totally, you jerk? Deep down, she was anti-Semitic. She called you a Jew who was only interested in 'a buck and a fuck.' How many times did she say that to you? She blew her nose in her hand and wiped it on you and spat in your face and broke your nose and set fire to your apartment and tried to run you over in the snow with her dirty little Datsun. How many times did you have to clean up her vomit or go sleep in a hotel or in your car because you were afraid of her violence? You dumb shit, how can you say that she was the love of your life?"

She was. I have said it. I gird myself, sighing. Love is such idiocy. "Whatever it was," I say, groping, "that made life so unbearable for her that she had to drink may well have been the same thing that made her so charming and unique. There wasn't a cliché in her, body or soul. She believed in magic and mystery and enchantment, and she *was* magical and mysterious and funny and enchanting."

"Balls!"

"She never spoke a trite word, or a homily, in that wonderful voice of hers. If you asked her how she was, she never said 'fine' or 'lousy'; she said, 'splendid' or 'dismal,' and she somehow contrived to make those words onomatopoeic. 'Splendid' shone, and 'dismal' was a gray, ratty thing. Love was a miracle, and weren't we blessed. And she never said, 'I love you.' She said, her voice filled with awe, 'I've never been in love before.' "

"So what? So what's so wonderful about that?"

"She rarely cooked, but when she did, it would be something delicious she'd invented and then named, like 'Little Bits,' or 'the Speckled Threat,' or 'Stonehenge.' "

"That's *so* cute!"

"When we drove cross-country, she didn't bring a camera, she brought a tape recorder, and whichever of us wasn't driving had to tell what we were seeing into the recorder. I have hours of tape that are infinitely better than pictures."

"So you've told me."

"Once, when she went away for two days to visit an old friend, she came back like Santa Claus, laden with extravagant gifts she must have spent the whole time buying, so that I knew she'd been thinking of me all the time she was away. And even though the things she bought were in that awful taste she had in clothing or furniture, even though I never wore any of those clothes, I loved them. And I loved how delighted she was in bringing them to me. It was years before I could throw any of it out."

Talking about it has made me teary.

"When Louise Bogan died," I say, unable now to stop, "she got *Blue Estuaries* from the bookshelf and went to bed with it clutched between her thighs, against her crotch, as though she wanted it inside her womb, and she wept all night and mur-

mured, 'goodbye, goodbye/ there was so much to love, I could not love it all;/ I could not love it enough.' When her friend Molly Partridge, whom she adored, was murdered at the age of eighty-four, she bought a bottle of Johnny Walker Red and drove to Amherst to lay it on her grave."

"Why Johnny Walker *Red*?"

"Because that's what Molly Partridge drank, you fool."

"She was crazy," Lisa says. "You have been describing a person who was obviously insane."

"She wasn't insane. She was different. She might have been insane. What difference does it make? She would come into the bathroom when I was on the toilet and sit on my lap, facing me, and make me laugh. When I was taking a bath, she would suddenly appear, naked, and slide into the tub with me. Then she would cross her eyes and tell me she was pee-ing."

"How delightful! *Was* she pee-ing?"

"Probably. Once when I was away, she wrote to tell me that I had been gone two rolls of toilet paper, and it was time for me to come home."

"What a lot of disgusting bathroom stuff there is in your memories of her! You must have made quite a pair. How come you ever let her get away?"

"She fell in love with another," I say woefully, dramatically.

"Only after you had left her."

"I hadn't absolutely left her. I was only trying to leave her."

"Tough luck, kiddo."

"I know."

Lisa has gotten up off the sofa and is stretching her arms, looking at me with disgust. She is wearing only the gray Mickey Mouse T-shirt, nothing on her bottom. She looks charming.

"There you are, Lisa," I say. "There's your conversation. We have just talked about something that interests me."

"I have never been more bored," she says.

Rebecca looks charming, too, but in a very different way from Lisa, and it takes me a while to figure out why. We have been friends for so long, more than forty years, and I see her so often that, as with family, I see her and I don't see her. Is it that familiarity breeds a kind of blindness?

"You're letting your hair grow," I say at last, realizing that this has been going on for a while. "How come?"

Disgust wreathes her face. "Because *everybody* is wearing it this way now." For years, Becky has looked like Gertrude Stein and Alice Toklas—Gertrude's head, Alice's body. She looks softer, younger now. I am jarred into memory of how she looked when I first knew her in adolescence, when I was struck by the combination of beauty and intelligence in her face.

"It's so much more becoming," I say. "I don't know why you ever wore it the other way. As though you'd been shaved for consorting with the enemy."

She makes a gesture of impatience, though she is pleased.

"Because it was chic?" I ask. "You prefer stylish to becoming?"

"Of course!" She says it as though who in her right mind wouldn't? I wouldn't.

I have persuaded her to come shopping with me, as I always

do, because I have so little confidence in my own taste. Dressing for anything but work or hanging around the house has always been painful for me. I trace this back to my tomboy childhood when my mother was forever trying to make "a little lady" out of me, and my father, who went to Paris every year to check on what was currently stylish, never cast an approving eye on me.

But I must be on my guard with Becky or she will talk me into buying something I will never wear, and it's always something expensive. I say she sees the garment out of context, the context being me. She says, scornfully, "Customer!" Our parents were in the same line. My father manufactured women's dresses, and her mother sold them. She will take something off the rack, feel it, hold it at arm's length, peer at it back and front, then nod vigorously.

"Yeees. Yes. Not baaaad."

But on me it's bad.

"No," I say, standing in front of a mirror, wearing it. "It's not right."

She will grimace and roll her eyes with impatience. She sees the beautiful blouse/skirt/sweater/dress, and she sees me as merely the device, the fixture on which to hang it, to body it forth into the world.

"I don't know why you insist on my coming with you," she snaps. "You don't want my advice."

What I need her for is to keep me from making hideous mistakes *of my own choosing.*

"You can bring me the stuff," I say, "but I have to make the decisions. Then you have the power of veto."

"What you need me for is to hang up these discards," she

says, taking the latest from my hands and returning it to its intricate hanger. We're in a discount place with an army of saleswomen who capture you by telling you their names, and then sit down and watch you. No service—and who needs it with Becky in attendance. I am perfectly capable of hanging these things up myself, but Becky does it faster and better. She is effortlessly, automatically efficient. She seems to have a system for everything: for keeping the car uncluttered on long auto trips, for having thirty people to sit-down Passover Seders every year, for traveling abroad with a minimum of luggage. I envy her quick powers of organization. If she weren't my best friend, I'd hate her.

And then there is this matter of taste, which is so arbitrary to me, and such a tyranny. I don't know how people like Becky are so sure of themselves, but Becky *knows*. She knows what is garbage, what is good—in dance, theater, architecture, clothes, literature, interior design, movies. Often, she knows it long before anyone else does.

"You ought to be a critic-at-large," I have told her.

"I am."

"I mean professionally. Write a column."

"If I wrote what I really thought, I wouldn't be at large for long."

I'm forever urging her to put it in writing, to grave it in stone, to give herself to the world instead of only to Paul and a few friends. I am forever deploring the waste of her extraordinary perceptions and keen, informed intelligence.

"Why is it a waste?" she asks. "I *am* a creator. I've created myself, my life. I'm a creative *appreciator*. Where would you writers be without me?"

"It's a cop-out," I say. "You don't have the nerve to venture outside your safe circle."

"Baloney. We're different people with different needs, different egos. I understand myself."

Now, standing in this vast dressing room, its walls lined with benches and mirrors in front of which women are pulling garments on and off, standing in our pantyhose and bras and aging bodies, remembering ourselves svelte and perfect—it was only a few days ago—Rebecca says to me through the mirror, "Anyway, I don't know what I think until I say it. I am 'a servant and addict of the word.' "

"Who said that?"

"I don't remember. And then I don't think it or say it until someone else has said something I can *react* to."

"Nonsense. You always have an opinion."

"Of course I have opinions," she says, adjusting a shoulder pad. "Anyhow, you think because *you* write, everyone else should, too."

"Oh no, God forbid, not everyone!"

"I don't see the point of doing something unless I can do it better than it's been done."

"How do you know you can't until you've done it?"

"*I* know."

"If everyone felt the way you do, we'd *all* be paralyzed."

"And what a lot of garbage the world would be spared!"

On the subway, earlier, we both studied an advertising placard directly across from where we were sitting. It showed a pleasant, smiling young woman in a mauve dress, very neat and clean, wearing a single-strand pearl necklace. This is what she was saying: "A cockroach ran over the roast chicken RIGHT

IN FRONT OF MY GUESTS!" We looked at each other and shuddered.

"That's the sort of thing I wish people would keep to themselves," I said.

Even though the woman goes on to say that, thanks to the Product, it would never happen again, it made me sick to hear about it.

"What worries me," Rebecca said, "is the implication of 'RIGHT IN FRONT OF MY GUESTS.' As though that's the worst part of it, the embarrassment. Suppose it happened in the kitchen before she brought the chicken out. It would have been all right, right? Nobody would have been the wiser, and she'd have come out wearing that same smile, carrying the chicken."

Leave it to Becky to find the morally reprehensible subtleties hidden everywhere.

"You think so?" I asked.

"Certainly."

"Maybe she'd have come out emptyhanded and said, 'Sorry folks, I've changed my mind. Let's go out to dinner.' "

"Oh, fat chance! She's just the type!"

But now, deciding against the dress she had on and pulling it over her head, she says, "I thought of a new business." She is always thinking of businesses for us to go into, usually retail, of course, and mostly so that we can think up names for them. Years ago, she wanted a Chinese cafeteria called Suey Generous. Today, she has come up with an Italian dim-sum restaurant to be called Summa Dem.

"Good idea," I say. "Better still, let's go have lunch."

And we get dressed and leave in search of the nearest Chinese restaurant, though it is getting harder and harder to find one that serves chow mein with chicken rubber bands on top, our *déjeuner nostalgique.*

The ambitious urges of Leos can be overstimulated today. Cooperative efforts with family members can increase the values of homes.

I haven't had a food dream lately, glutted perhaps by Peter's 250 hungry guests, or maybe because I'm trying to lose weight. But of course I dream in color; why would one not? One dreams as one sees. Why the assumption that dreams are movies and Technicolor is still in the future? Last night one of the players had eyes the color of lilacs. I wouldn't have missed it for anything.

Deirdre, whose eyes are Irish green, has moved into the new apartment at last vacated by Marcus. She has no furniture. All her "bits and t'ings" were put in storage years ago, and she has long since stopped paying the bills. I've given her a box of kitchen supplies, a few dishes, pots, pans, cutlery, odds and ends, just to start her off, an old army cot, a blanket, a pillow, and now, ringing her doorbell on this winter twilight, I'm laden with additional supplies: sheets, a few towels, an old bath mat, nothing in matching colors. Having once been a woman of family, a woman who has pared down from an eleven-room house, I still have residue to spare. But when I'm inside Deirdre's

apartment, our voices ring hollow in its emptiness, and I wish
I had more. I wish I had rugs and armchairs and tables, dressers
and vanities and huge beds, books and paintings and draperies.
I've brought a bunch of daisies, but there's nothing to put them
in.

"Wait!" Deirdre says. "There *is* something." And from a
brown paper bag of garbage in the kitchen, she pulls a Styro-
foam coffee cup, which she rinses and fills with water. "There!"
she says triumphantly. "Aren't they lovely? Now I have everything!"

"You need a lamp," I say. "How could I not have thought
of that? What do you read by at night?" There aren't even
ceiling lights. It's one of those modern apartments, all graying
white walls and uninterrupted ceilings, with wall switches that
activate baseboard outlets. But then I remember that it is a long
time since I have seen Deirdre read anything but the *Daily News*
or the *National Enquirer*.

"It's never dark in here," she says, walking me over to the
living-room windows. She is on the twelfth floor, and her windows overlook Eighth Avenue and whatever of theater-district
Broadway is not yet blocked by new construction. Lights in
garish colors move about, telling Deirdre what cigarettes to
smoke, what beer to drink, the signs actually smoking and drinking, and there is a waterfall and a huge digital clock that gives,
in blood-red numbers, every passing second, like a heart beating
out its life.

"Never a dark moment," Deirdre says, "never a dull one."
She loves this seamy hub of the city, God knows why, and has
never lived or worked far from it, except for the years of her
marriage, the time of her "t'ings," when she and Cromwell lived
somewhere fashionable up the Hudson River, from whence they

occasionally commuted to their separate offices. Cromwell was his surname. His given name was Compton. It was a name that could have gone either way, but Cromwell was what she always called him, somehow contriving, against all the odds of its mellifluous components, to say it crisply.

"How long were you and Cromwell married?" I asked her when she first talked about him.

"Door to door," she said, "seven years. Poor man, how he hated me in the end." I didn't feel I knew her well enough to ask her why.

"Did you like it, living there, wherever it was, in suburbia?"

"Parker's Landing? Oh, it was very grand, terribly snooty. No blacks, no Jews. You would not have been allowed there, Rachel."

I always love it when my Gentile friends make their little anti-Semitic comments, as they invariably sooner or later do, no matter how much they insist on their freedom from prejudice. "You could have come at night, though, Rachel. After dark." I thank her. "We had a garden. In Dublin, we always had a garden. A small one. My mother was very good with roses. It was lovely having a garden again, but neither Cromwell nor I had the touch. What a mess we made of it. After the first year, it was a jungle. Even so, it always smelled wonderful. Honeysuckle, I think, and other tangled things."

Now, here she is, overlooking the Great White Way, which is everything but white, living in this other jungle among pimps and whores and junkies and killers, the marquees of porno movies spread beneath her, the storefronts of sex parlors and head shops and fortune tellers.

"The gypsies," she says. "Do you know, a few days ago they all vanished, the ones on Forty-ninth Street. I would see them every day, but for some reason they never spoke to me. They looked at me as though they hated me, or as if I wasn't there at all. They looked *through* me. Then, just the day before they all went away, one of them looked at me as though I *was* there, and she told me that my hair was beautiful." A look of pure bliss crosses her face. "It made me so happy, Rachel, I cannot tell you how happy. I floated all the rest of that day." She frowns. "I wonder where they all went."

We are still at the living-room window, looking out at the panorama. The room is as empty as its view is cluttered.

"You don't even have a chair," I say mournfully.

"Look what I bought today," Deirdre says, her little eyes lighting. She trots from the room and returns, a moment later, bearing a toy locomotive, black and heavy, a foot long and half again as high. She places it on the floor and presses a switch, and it begins to circle the room, its lamp flashing, its train-call a sad and lonely owl hoot, repeating and repeating.

"You bought a train," I say, watching it, mesmerized. This woman who has nothing, who needs everything.

"Yes. And a Mickey Mouse watch." She shows it to me. It is on her child's wrist, the strap too large, too loose. "I don't know why I bought it with that big clock out there." She contemplates it fondly. "A man was selling it on the street. He had the look of someone from whom no one has bought anything all day. It doesn't even keep time."

Tempus has a pension plan for its longtime staff, its regular contributors, that Marcus told me is very generous, but whatever it is, for Deirdre it can never be enough. How she despises money, and loves it. For her, it is some kind of excreta to be disposed of as quickly as possible. She loves expensive clothes, smoked Scotch salmon, only the best imported gin. When her money comes, there is a desperate race to spend it or to give it away, whichever comes first. I have pleaded with her to let me manage her money, so that I'll know that the rent will be paid. "I'll put it in a bank account for you," I've told her. "I'll pay your bills. I'll give you an allowance." For a little while, she actually allowed me to do it, but of course it was hopeless. She became sly and devious, cashing the check, turning over less and less of it, treating me like an enemy she has outsmarted.

"Does *Tempus* know you're here? Do they have the address?"

"If it's my money you're worried about, Rachel, I always pick up my checks, such as they are, at the office. You're not to give another thought to my finances." Then her face hardens. "Though I do wish they'd stop doling that money out to me in bits and pieces. After all, it's *my* money."

"If they gave it to you all at once, Deirdre, it would disappear and you'd have nothing. They're doing it for your own good."

"They have no right. I'm not a child."

"What would you do with it if you had it all?"

"I'd go back to Dublin and buy a little shop at the edge of the sea. With a bell on the door, so that when anyone came in, it would tinkle." She is smiling, dreaming. "And a room at the back where I could live. I would only need one tiny room to live in, and the other room would be the shop."

"What would you sell in the shop?" I ask.

"Oh, little t'ings. Useful t'ings. Matches. Candles. Sewing thread."

"That's very romantic," I say. "But meanwhile, I'm glad you finally have a place of your own here." In all the time I've known her, she has been living like a gypsy herself, in borrowed apartments, seedy hotel rooms, artist colonies, for six months in a rented attic room in Vermont. "I don't understand how you could have lived so long without a place of your own."

"My own?" she says. "This is not mine. I've *never* had a place that was mine."

Still, I know so well the Dublin house she lived in when she was a child, the house of her parents. I know it almost as vividly as if its memory were my own, the small, shadowed rooms, the oily smell of the brown linoleum with its pale flowered figures, the lace curtains, the silences, the front parlor, the small back bedroom, the narrow dark stairs. So many of her stories, her wonderful sad stories, happen in that house. The house holds her parents, her sister, her childhood, perhaps the only true center she ever had. In her best writing she mined it obsessively as, later, hidden inside her colorless raincoat and behind the huge black sunglasses, smoking Pall Malls and hoping that she was invisible, she would observe the life around her in this city and, in particular, this squalid corner of it, this cesspool, and write prose poems to it with those leaps into the unexpected, seeing through her own eccentric vision what no one else could ever have seen.

"That stuff in the corner," I ask. "What is it?"

"What *stuff*?"

"There, that green . . ." I had noticed it in the hall, too, on my way in, strewn about along the baseboards, lettuce, celery leaves. My first wild thought was that perhaps rats had gotten into her garbage and scattered it, but surely Deirdre would have noticed, and surely there could not be rats.

"It's just some veggies . . . some greens," she says, as though it is entirely natural for it to be there. "I get it for nothing on Ninth Avenue."

"But why is it . . . how did it . . . shall I sweep it up for you?"

"No, no, I want it there. I put it there."

"You put it there? Why not in the refrigerator? It will spoil. It will bring roaches."

"And what is so dreadful about roaches?"

I am taken aback. I think of the woman in the mauve dress with the roast chicken, the woman with guests. Surely everyone despises roaches. I myself recoil from them in sickened, disgusted horror. Now I am forced to think why, apart from their bad press. I recall a night soon after Peter and I moved into our first apartment, which I loved, where I felt so lucky to be. There was a strange insect, motionless in the bathtub. "Yes," I say to Deirdre. "When I saw my first roach, before I knew what it was, I thought what an attractive, streamlined amber insect."

"Amber? Then it was starving! When they are well fed, they darken."

"Oh, God, Deirdre! You're *feeding* the roaches. You want them to come. You've spread this banquet for them!"

She looks at me with a mixture of hatred and wicked amusement and begins to lie. "No," she says. "Well, yes, I want them to come."

"Why?"

"Well. When they come . . ."

"Yes? When they come?"

"I gather them up."

"Deirdre!"

"In a little box."

"Oh, Deirdre! You don't."

"Yes, yes, I do. Lined with cotton."

"And then? What do you do with them?"

"Then I send them off," she says very quickly.

"You mean you kill them?" I remember the cats. Soon I will tell about the cats.

"I don't kill them, Rachel. I send them . . . I send them off to someone I know who collects them. And that's the end of that!" Her mouth shuts tight on the subject forever.

I stare out the window. Krazy Kat is fooling around with three smaller versions of himself. They jump on a unicycle and ride off. I think not about Deirdre's life but about my own, wondering how I have arrived at this moment. I grew up in Brooklyn, the daughter of a dress manufacturer and his wife, a graduate of Eastern District High School, where she had majored in secretarial skills that she never had to put to use, thanks to her successful early marriage. Except for being Jewish, we were the most ordinary of families, and even being Jewish was, in our neighborhood, ordinary. I was trained to think of myself as a future bride and mother. Any other plans I dreamed of for myself, if I was fool enough to voice them, were ridiculed, dismissed as childish nonsense. What I was supposed to hope for was that a man as successful as my father would marry me, and maybe we would move to an even better neighborhood. There was nothing, nothing at all, in that scenario to presage this late-afternoon hour in my life. I glimpse the reflection of a bloody sunset in a grimy window across the street, and I am suddenly unaccountably happy. Life is terrible. Life is wonderful.

"Let's go out and have a drink," I say.

Like the setting sun that, until this moment, has been partially covered by a cloud, Deirdre brightens. Like Krazy Kat, she grows animated.

· 85 ·

"Oh, a dee-licious martini, yes, very cold. I know just the place. I'll put on a bit of lipstick."

Leos have just begun an important period in which they will be able to improve themselves academically and knowledgeably. Business and public affairs can be helped by the support of public officials. Travel can be helpful to romance.

For ten minutes, from my table near the entrance, I have been watching everyone who comes into Wolfie's. Because it is early, this is not too taxing. I have already eaten three pickles, which are part of the table setting, and informed the waiter twice that I am waiting for someone and am not yet ready to order. When I was a smoker, this sort of thing was easier. I have no idea why I am here, waiting to meet Harvey Candleman, a stranger who is in a business I deplore, a packager of television properties, who wants me to be part of a package, which I am almost positive I don't want to be and probably never could be. It's almost two years since I've made any money from my writing. Samuel Johnson said that no man but a blockhead ever wrote except for money.

Margo's treatment, written for Harvey Candleman, is still not past the "lots of interest" stage, but she has just signed the contract with the book packager to whom she was brought by her agent. Margo describes him as loathsome, toadlike, completely illiterate, but not lazy. He has written a 200-page outline, the Property, and sold it as the work of Jessica Kenilworth, a fictional name owned by him, to one of the big paperback houses for $150,000. After the agent's 10 percent, Margo, if she writes an acceptable book, will get half the balance. I've asked Margo what the book is about, but she tells me it's supposed to be a secret.

"There's a formula," she told me. "You choose an industry or a profession that's of some general interest, like fashion, or cosmetics, and then you build a dynasty around it, several generations, with the heroine a grandchild, or even a great-grandchild. Yes, it must be a heroine, these books are read by women. Preferably, they originate somewhere outside the United States, some place in picturesque upheaval, and eventually they make their way to our shores, destitute. As they slowly build toward the great orgasm of success, there must be all sorts of barriers and impediments: war, famine, disease, weather, geography, competitors, dishonesty, betrayal, greed, black sheep, love gone wrong, love gone too right. Mountains of plot, tons of sex. And the sex must be graphic and of infinite variety."

"Is that what's called a romance novel?"

"Oh, no. The romance novel is to this as *The Bobbsey Twins* is to *War and Peace.*"

"Margo!"

"I mean in terms of complexity. And length. Not artistry. This is going to be six hundred pages long. God knows it isn't literature, but it will be better written than any romance novel. This kind of book must make the best-seller list to justify itself, and it should eventually sell to the movies."

Literature. Entertainment. "Write what will sell!"—E. Copleston (Bishop of Llandoff), 1807. "I am now trying an experiment, very frequent among modern authors; which is to write upon nothing."—Jonathan Swift, 1704. "Every kind of writing is good save that which bores."—Voltaire, 1736.

On the other hand: "The aim of the superior man is truth."—Confucius, 500 B.C. "Rather than love, than money, than fame, give me truth."—Thoreau, 1854. "This above all, to thine own self be true."—Shakespeare, 1600 (?). "Truth is tough."—O. W. Holmes, 1859.

"There is something to be said for everything, and it has all been said."—Rachel Levin, 1988.

"Do you think I can do it?" Margo asked. She was obviously excited by the prospect, and nervous, probably because of all that money. Doctors and lawyers and people in business and advertising, on Wall Street, expect that kind of money for a year of their time. But where we are concerned, there is a different standard; most writers have no experience of that kind of money.

"I'm going to have to do a lot of research into . . . well, I can't tell you. I'll love that part, but do you think I'll be able to write it? Actually write it?"

"Of course."

"What if I'm good at it?"

"You will be good at it. Quick, too."

"What if I am? What if it's a huge success? Will I be forever lost?"

"To what?"

A murderous expression crossed her face. "Rachel, you know very well what I mean. You don't think I confuse this trash with what I really do, do you? John does. He thinks everything I write is trash."

"As long as *you* don't confuse the two," I said in my customary platitudinous way, leaving aside the deeper issue of her husband, John. "And if it's honest trash."

"Oh, God, Rachel, honest trash!"

"Why not?"

"You're writing something by formula, for a market, for someone who's *ordered* this particular book, as though it were something on a menu. That's not honest. It's cynical and manipulative."

"But if you know what you're writing is entertainment, and you make no pretensions to art, why is it dishonest? It's like making anything, a chair."

"A chair is useful. It's not a waste of time. It can also be beautiful."

"Then a crossword puzzle, or a board game."

"It's different."

"Only because you don't think of reading as recreation. You think of it as somehow virtuous."

"Yes. I venerate it. Usually."

"So do I. But this kind of reading is what some people do when there's nothing on television. It's another distraction from their own drab and lonely lives. It gives them a little vacation from themselves."

"*Good* books do that, too."

"But with a good book, you run the risk of occasionally being made to think. With this kind of book, you know you're safe."

"I could sneak some good stuff into it," Margo mused, "but what would be the point? They'd only take it out."

She lit a cigarette and thoughtfully blew a smoke ring. It didn't really matter what she said. Her declaration of ambivalence was merely a formality, a bow to some sterner self of whom I have rarely seen a sign.

"Oh, hell," she said, "of course I'm going to do it. How could I not? We can certainly use the money, and anyhow I don't seem to be doing anything else."

"What about the TV treatment you did for Candleman?"

"I haven't heard a word."

"We're having lunch tomorrow. I'll ask him about it."

Harvey Candleman comes through the door and stands for a moment looking at me. I know it is Candleman. In addition to the promised sunglasses, he is wearing faded jeans and a bomber jacket and he is holding a small canvas athletic bag. In this outfit, he is all business. I wave to him.

"Hi," he says, sitting opposite me and dropping the bag at his feet. "Am I late?"

"No. I just got here," I lie, knowing that my promptness could be construed by him as eagerness for this meeting. "On your way to the gym?"

"I've just been," he says. He's a pleasant-looking man, somewhere in his forties, strong and purposeful, graying hair, a nice mouth, and a neatly trimmed beard. "I play squash. Have to keep in shape. A year ago, I weighed three hundred pounds."

I tell him that this is hard to believe, which it is. Considering the determination and discipline he must have, I feel more inclined to trust him.

"Took off a hundred and twenty-five pounds," he says proudly. "I've got a bag of sand home that weighs a hundred and twenty-five pounds, and whenever I'm tempted to send out for pizza, I pick up that bag of sand and carry it around for a while. I remind myself that that's what I was carrying all those years, everywhere, up and down stairs, stressing out my heart."

I express unfeigned admiration. It wouldn't hurt me to take off twenty-five pounds, even fifteen, and I often think about it, the way I used to think about quitting smoking until I finally did it. But quitting smoking exhausted my supply of self-denial. I tell this to Candleman, who is lighting a cigarette.

"Oh?" he says, looking up from his discardable lighter, concerned. "Do you mind if I smoke?"

"No. Do you mind if I eat?"

He hails our waiter and I order a corned beef on rye and a Cel-Ray. Candleman orders two poached eggs in a cup.

"Not on toast," he says clearly, as though he has told this story before to any number of idiots. "In a cup."

"So why not boiled?" the waiter says.

"Not boiled. Poached."

"You're the boss," the waiter says, writing it down.

"And tea."

"Lemon or cream?" Waiters are always forced to request this information, since tea drinkers rarely volunteer it.

"Milk," he says.

"Tell me what it is that you really do," I say, when the waiter has shuffled off.

"I'm a writer," he says, "but I also have a stable of writers. I supply the ideas, usually, and we do a treatment, and then I see if I can sell it. I have a lot of contacts in the business. When I sell it, you write it."

"You" refers to those plugs in the stable. What about the hay?

"What about money?" I ask.

"We split it. Fifty-fifty."

"So anything I do is purely on speculation?"

"Until it's sold, sure."

I sigh. Was I expecting a salary? "I don't know if it's something I could do," I say, dispiritedly.

"Margo gave me your last book. I loved it," he says. "Your dialogue is terrific. You have a good ear. And your characters are real. I *know* you could do it."

At this point in my life and career, flattery from anywhere is welcome. I warm to Harvey Candleman. Why was I feeling so patronizing? Why shouldn't he do what he does? He doesn't set the standards or create the demand. "Give 'em, let 'em eat."—Nathan Handwerker, of Nathan's hot dogs, Coney Island. And what else has lured me here except the desire to see if I, like Margo, could actually make money at writing? There is also that chronic ambivalence that forever fuzzes the contours of my self-perception. Not my values, my recurring identity crises. "Oh, if only one living creature had definite shape."—Camus.

"Tell me what you have in mind," I say, as he peppers his poached eggs in their cup. He shakes vigorously, and the top of the shaker flies off and drops into the cup along with all the pepper.

"Oh, shit," he says. *"Waiter!"*

The waiter looks with disgust at the ruined eggs, and clears away the mess. Candleman, embarrassed, urges me not to wait, to go ahead and eat, which I do.

"This is a true story I came across in the *Post*, Rachel," he says, establishing our first-name basis. "I think it would make a terrific one-hour Christmas special. This guy, because of drink, loses his little business, becomes depressed. He leaves his wife and two young children, just vanishes. The wife doesn't hear from him whatsoever. Of course, this is just the bare bones of the idea for the story. The rest has to be fleshed out. So two years go by, and the guy gets on top of his drinking problem. He joins AA. Then he gets this temporary job as a department-store Santa Claus. You know, where the kids come in and sit on his lap and have their picture taken and get a lollipop and tell him what they want for Christmas. One day the wife comes in and his own kids sit on his lap, and when he asks them what they want most, the boy says his daddy. They don't recognize him, but you can see that he recognizes them. Then the wife sits on Santa Claus's lap and—"

"The wife sits on his lap?"

"Yeah, and the guy realizes how much he has given up, you know, and how much he misses them, and he begins to cry."

"Why does the wife sit on Santa Claus's lap?"

He has paused to acknowledge the arrival of his eggs, and he hasn't heard me. While he peppers the eggs, I chew my corned-beef sandwich, trying to digest the story he's been telling me, this perfectly serious, full-grown man who has lost all that weight.

"Does he say anything to his wife?" I ask, nonetheless encouraging him. "Does she recognize him?"

"To tell the truth, I can't remember the end of the story, except that she didn't go back to him."

"Good for her."

"But in the script, you know, they should be reunited. Christmas. It has to be upbeat."

"Then the whole idea for this script, really, turns on the coincidence of his being Santa Claus and his abandoned family happening to sit on his lap?"

"It sounds gimmicky, but it's a true story."

"It would have to be true," I say. "You could never get away with it in fiction." I take another pickle. "There's no way," I say, finally, "that I could get a believable adult woman to sit on Santa Claus's lap."

This seems to stun him. "Why not?"

"What kind of woman would do that?"

"In the right circumstances, any woman."

"What are the right circumstances?"

"You're the writer. Listen, if you don't like this idea, I have another one that might suit you more. I can understand that not every story is right for every writer."

"What's the other idea?" I tremble to ask.

"It's not an *idea* exactly. What it is, I have like ten hours of taped conversations with a woman dying of cancer, a wonderful woman. The tapes are terrific. I know there's a script there for a sensitive, imaginative writer. Would you like to listen to the tapes? The last one was made just a few hours before she died."

The place has filled up and grown noisy, but not noisy enough to drown my dismay.

"What made you do that?" I ask. "Tape her?"

"Well, yeah, I guess it sounds weird, taping a dying lady, but it wasn't like that," he says. "It's a long story, but when I was around seventeen, my mother died of liver cancer. I was an only child, close to her, and it was so painful to me that I guess I denied it to myself, you know, what was happening. I've always been sorry, not being there for her, not being able to talk to her or let her tell me what she was going through."

"She probably wouldn't have told you," I say. "You were only seventeen." I can see that this hasn't occurred to him. He looks surprised, then grateful.

"You may be right," he says. "But I felt I owed her something. Owed it to myself, too. And I guess listening to this woman, she was a wonderful woman, you'll see when you hear

· 94 ·

the tapes, helped me in some way to understand what my mother went through, to share it with her, in a way, and to make it up to her."

It's always happening to me. As soon as I write someone off as shallow and stupid, he turns sensitive and sweet. Even if he reverts in the next breath, as he will, he can never again be a cartoon figure to me, or less than human. I reach across the table and touch his hand.

"That's the story," I say. "It's the young man's story."

"What do you mean?"

Instantly, it takes shape in my head, though I don't tell it to him. The young man is a TV scriptwriter with a troubled marriage to a nice woman, whom he doesn't trust not to leave him, as his mother did. He's cold, withdrawn from his wife, who wants more from him, wants to *get through* to him, as they say on the Upper West Side, where they live. There is an older woman with whom he works. They're good friends, not lovers. Lunch together, et cetera. Perhaps a party scene with wife, who is jealous of older woman because they're so close. Then older woman quits job. He, devastated, learns she has cancer, terminal. He goes to see her nightly, straight from work, bringing tempting food, flowers, wine, books. Making her talk to him about it. Tell me, tell me, tell me. She does. Occasional fast, almost subliminal flashbacks to man as boy with mother, different: stiff, mute, frightened. Older woman helped by being allowed to talk and not have to pretend, as she must with others, who behave with her as if nothing is happening. Dies. Funeral. Then moving scene with wife where, understanding, he sobs in wife's arms, tells her all. Wife assures him that dying is only way she would ever leave him, and that dying is not a choice.

"Will you do it?" he asks, seeing that I am thinking.

I doubt that I will do it. I am already so depressed by the thought of it. "I'll think about it," I tell him. "I'll think about both ideas."

He pays the bill, then says, "Oh, by the way, I have to leave for the Coast in a few days. This dame is bringing a palimony suit against me. I don't know how long it will take."

"Thanks for lunch," I say when we are out on Sixth Avenue. He is going west and uptown. I am going the other way, diametrically. It seems symbolic.

"I'll call you when I get back," he says. "I really enjoyed meeting you. I hope we can work together."

On the bus, I find myself thinking about the Christmas story. I'll call Margo when I get home and tell her about Candleman and his dying woman. And Santa Claus. Maybe she'll have some ideas. Is there really no way to get a sympathetic woman character onto Santa Claus's lap? For starters, let's cast her. Meryl Streep? Harried mother, high-pressure job. Interior designer in the store's furniture department. Takes kids with her for emergency appointment on her day off. They wheedle her toward the toy department and Santa Claus. The kids get in line, and when their turn comes, Meryl hovering over them, a battery of public-relations people, TV camera, et cetera, approach with big smiles. "Congratulations, you are our fifty-thousandth mother of the season. Tell us your name, please?" She does. "You are the winner of our ten-thousand-dollar prize. Plus your children will receive five thousand dollars' worth of toys of their choice." The cameras are on her, on the stunned children. "Mrs. Streep, would you please sit on Santa's lap for the cameras while Santa presents you with the check?" "Sit on his lap?" she says. She ducks head, embarrassed, brushes hair off cheek. "Oh, I couldn't do that," she says with real distaste. *Please,* madam!" Firmly, as if she is an ingrate. Extremely gingerly, she sits on Santa's knee. He puts an arm around her waist, hands check to her, peculiar expression on his face. James Garner? But I cannot get tears into his eyes; he is not the crying type. I try and try, but he will not do it. What he does, despite all my efforts, is lean forward and whisper in her ear, "Wanna fuck, Meryl?"

Margo's husband, John, who is Welsh and a behavioral psychologist, is the most romantic of men. He has been working with primates, and a chimpanzee named Ethel has fallen in love with him.

"The manifestations differ only slightly from those of my graduate students who fall in love with me." John is also one of the more attractive men I know, perhaps because of the way he speaks. He is Oxford, but it isn't only the accent. His vocal mechanism is a quality instrument, a Guarnerius, so that every word, and they are invariably well chosen, receives its due in resonance, inflection, and shapeliness, without in any way sounding theatrical or pompous. I have always been attracted to people who speak beautifully if they speak intelligently as well, and they frequently do.

"Of course, she can't send little billets-doux or poems (po-wems), and she can't declare herself verbally, as some of my bolder students have done, but she does everything else. She preens, she mopes, she weeps, her eyes yearn, sometimes glassily, her gestures are eloquent and moving. If she could, she would follow me everywhere, with her body as well as with her eyes."

"You must have done something to deserve this," I say.

"What are you suggesting?" John asks.

Margo and I have spent the day playing in the Long Island suburb where she and John live, talking hardly at all about TV treatments. We've been to a gallery to see a collection of French impressionists, then to see a delightful Fellini film, and afterward we dined in an Italian restaurant in the village near the train station where, among other things, I had exquisite fiddle-head ferns. It's been a day filled with sensory pleasures, and now we're having a nightcap with John, who rarely joins us on these outings, though we sometimes invite him. He likes to be alone in the house, working.

Margo and John have been married for seventeen years, and I can't imagine how. I have known many marriages that have ended in divorce, but even the worst of them have seemed more stable than this one, which has always had an air of improvisation, as though neither participant has the least idea of what marriage means and must each day invent and reinvent his or her part, Margo whimsically, stagily, and John with a kind of reactive coldness, interrupted, she tells me, by frequent outbursts of quiet brutality or stentorian temper. One imagines him working hard to keep this marriage from failing, because he has already had a failed marriage. Still, he often looks at Margo with the unmistakable glow of love in his eyes. It has never occurred to either Margo or John to deny themselves anything; they are both self-indulgent, and they both drink too much. She has told me that, in the wee hours of their cups, when the guests have gone and they sit amid the wreckage, examining through their blurred vision the damage each has done the other, hurling charges and countercharges, they are apt to grow increasingly venomous. They are literally intoxicated, smeared with poison. This may happen tonight, but it will be hours later, long after I've gone and am peacefully asleep in my own bed.

Lisa no longer comes with me on these outings with Margo, as she used to do. We have finally recognized that our discomfort with each other's friends is unavoidable, arising from immutable differences. There is absolutely no point struggling to share our social lives.

"It's all right when Lisa is with us," Margo said earlier, "but it's different. I like her all right, but I like it better when it's just the two of us."

"You like having me to yourself. You're that way with all your friends. You want their total attention. You want to be the star."

"I know. But let's face it, bright as Lisa is, she's not the world's most original thinker."

"She's young."

"So is Daniel." Daniel is Margo's seventeen-year-old son. "We rarely take him along."

So Margo and I have spent this lovely Sunday alone, enjoying each other and being whoever it is we are only with each other. And now we're back at her house, sharing our happiness with John. I am sipping scotch, waiting for it to be late enough to avoid the Sunday-night traffic on the drive back into the city.

"Are you flattered?" I ask John.

"Yes, oddly enough. In the way I'm flattered if someone else's cat likes me."

"It's probably only the way you smell," Margo says.

"Even that. But now, of course, I'm interested in a scientific way in Ethel's being in love with me. I'm trying to devise a series of steps I can take to cause her to fall out of love with me."

"Are you hoping your findings may be applicable to humans?"

"I don't know. Naturally, I'll tailor my behavior to the primate personality . . . what we know of it."

"Will you be cruel?"

"Possibly." He grins. "Though cruelty may only inflame her further."

"Then what you're looking for is a cure for love? As if it were some kind of disease?"

"Not love. *Being* in love. Unhappily, inappropriately, unsuitably in love."

I find most conversations with John interesting, perhaps because I have such an unscientific mind. I want to pursue it, to ask him what specific steps he plans to take. Will he feed Ethel disgusting food, withhold meals altogether, change his scent, introduce her to some attractive, virile young male chimp, give her cold showers and hot bananas? But I suddenly feel very tired, and a little sick to my stomach.

"I have to go," I say.

"So abruptly?" Margo asks. "Finish your drink."

"It's late. I'm really tired."

"Then spend the night. You look pale."

This is the sort of observation that is likely to trigger the hypochondria, rampant in my family, that I have frequently succumbed to. Perhaps this is the onset of something really serious, not merely too much wine and rich food. My imagination rapidly riffles through all the possibilities, a habit, while my adult, sensible self tries to keep me calm. It's so hard being the boy who cries wolf as well as the one who hears him.

I get up to go. "I'm all right," I say. "There won't be traffic this late. I'll be home in half an hour."

"Call when you get home," Margo says. I promise to do this. I drive at close to seventy miles an hour, not caring if I'm stopped. The nausea continues. Maybe I can break all records and make it home in twenty minutes, and if I'm going to be sick, it will wait that long, and if not, not. I'm proud of myself for not panicking, for being so accepting. What a long way I've come.

Too good to be true. Within a half-mile of the Midtown Tunnel, I'm forced to a standstill by backed-up traffic, cars that have sprung from nowhere. Have I ever made this drive to or from the Five Towns in what ought to be normal time? Has anyone? We stand absolutely motionless for ten minutes, fifteen, half an hour. I turn on the radio, I turn off the engine, I turn off the radio, I take deep breaths. This might not be a bad place to die, so close to all these cemeteries that sprawl on either side of the Expressway. As far as holding up traffic is concerned, it will make absolutely no difference if I'm dead or alive, though it may take days before anyone discovers my body. The prospect is not so terrible. Besides, if I die I won't ever have to start another book. And it would be a graceful ending for Lisa and me. I recall a writer I once knew who told me about a troubled affair with a man she was crazy about. "And then, thank God, one day he dropped dead," she told me. "It was such a relief." "But you loved him," I said, shocked. "I was mad about him. If he hadn't died, I would never have been able to end it."

Stalled in this dead sea of the nocturnal Long Island Expressway, I try to stay relaxed with simple thoughts of death and love. I remember early in my marriage when I was having my breakdown, how endless were the nights, how filled with terror, with waiting in panic for my imminent death. They told me my fear of death was excessive, but I couldn't imagine what they were talking about. Death was so real and inevitable and final; how could you ever fear it *enough*?

Peter was always patiently there then, and he knew that when the fear was upon me it was necessary for me to be touched. He would hold me or put a gentle hand on my neck, my brow, a shoulder, and while the terror didn't go away, it was somehow more bearable. His hand connected me to something outside my imaginings. It grounded me. When I divorced him, I thought, But who will touch me?, and then dismissed the thought; I was no longer that person so afraid of life that I saw my death everywhere.

I was young then, and in perfect health, and sudden death was most unlikely, though I didn't believe it. Now I am at an age when people do more and more die. At any moment some vital part could falter. Yet whatever fear I feel is a manageable one, nothing like those early terrors. It took me years to understand that I was giving myself physical symptoms to focus on so that I could avoid the real problems, the ones I felt just as helpless to deal with.

I turn my thoughts back to poor Ethel, John's chimp, wondering about her suffering and the nature of the thought that informs it. Love-suffering requires memory and fantasy, imagination. Perhaps there is a drug, not yet discovered, that would zero in on that particular neural bridge and temporarily disconnect it. What a blessing, what an energy-saver that would be.

At last we begin to inch forward. The nausea is beginning to subside. I'm probably not going to die. I remain calm and philosophical, willing myself not to respond with Type-A behavior to this jam. It's beyond understanding where all these cars could have come from, and what could have caused this standstill at such a late hour. Perhaps the tunnel has caved in, or flooded, or there has been a ghastly accident, maybe a fire. I try to imagine it, the disaster that I am so lucky to have escaped: mangled bodies, burned flesh, drowned or suffocated humans, all of it so close by.

An hour has passed when I finally arrive at the toll plaza, almost at the booth, thinking that at times like these, *they* ought to pay *us*. Two policemen are standing on the concrete island, chatting calmly. The outbound tunnel has been closed off, and we're being funneled, one at a time, into one lane of the inbound tunnel.

"So what is it this time?" I ask the policemen.

"The circus. Ringling Brothers, Barnum and Bailey."

"They're going through the tunnel?"

"They've already gone through."

"So?"

"They forgot to make provision for a sweeper to follow the elephants. We're waiting for it. Here it comes now." A white Sanitation Department truck, with big twin round brooms, is just entering the mouth of the blocked-off tunnel.

"Tell me something," I say, annoyed. "Why can't we drive through that the way we drive through the rest of the shit?"

"You wouldn't want to do that, lady, believe me," one of the cops says daintily. "You ever seen an elephant's dump?"

Two hours after leaving Margo and John, I telephone them.

"We were just going to call the police," Margo says. "Are you all right?"

"Yes, it was nothing. You'll never guess what held me up this time."

Thursday the 30th is another one of those days when Leos may have to contend with pushy or domineering people. Fireworks are likely, as Leos seldom accept being bossed. It is a good day to improve qualifications.

I have just finished telling Deirdre about the elephants. She smiles faintly, but her eyes are far away and her knuckles are white. I have taken her to a good restaurant, where I watch her pick at her smoked Scotch salmon between sips of her third martini. She is growing thinner. I suspect that she forgets to eat.

"Dee-licious," she says. Her hands, like failed promises, are surprisingly large for the rest of her. I have been trying to amuse her, to make her laugh, but she obviously has more important things on her mind, and my story is an unwelcome distraction. She forgets that she is eating, and slides a cigarette from the pack lying at her elbow. A waiter appears instantly to light it. He does it with such a graceful flourish that I laugh. Deirdre stares straight ahead.

"Why are you suffering, Deirdre?" I ask. "What's happening to you?"

"Despair, Rachel," she says softly. "I hope you never learn the true meaning of the word."

"*Why* despair?"

"I cannot tell you. You wouldn't understand."

"Try me."

She looks at me with pure hatred. "You have a Jewish soul," she says mysteriously. "I am beginning to think you must be one of them."

"One of whom?"

She doesn't answer.

"I'm not," I say. "Whoever they are." Then I am angry for the reference to my Jewish soul. "Have you ever considered, Deirdre," I ask, "the egocentricity and arrogance of your paranoia? To imagine that all those folks have nothing better to do than to persecute you?"

"To *destroy* me," she says.

"Just who the hell do you think you are to deserve to be singled out like that?"

But maybe that's it. Maybe she needs that attention. Is this what happens when love goes? When she was younger, she had so many lovers. I heard it from Marcus, and Deirdre herself has alluded to it. "Rarely out of any compelling desire," she once told me. "It seemed to mean so much to them, d'you know what I mean? It seemed little enough to do for them, for their suffering, but I regret it now. Oh, how I regret it." It was almost amusing then, spoken in that crisp, witty voice, but later I was struck by the coldness of it, of Deirdre giving love because it seemed the decent thing to do, a gracious, cerebral act, devoid of feeling. When I considered my own intense *interest* in my lovers, all the agonies I'd suffered and the delights, my obsessive attention to the details and innuendos, my profound involvement, it was impossible to know which of us was in more danger.

"You cannot save me, Rachel," Deirdre says, "no matter

how much selfish pleasure it gives you to think you can. You are not nearly powerful enough. Don't meddle; it's too tiresome. And for God's sake, don't *spec*ulate."

"I care about you, Deirdre."

She snorts. "You don't even know me! If I hadn't written those stories and books, you would never have concerned yourself with me at all."

Her saying this appalls me, because I know at once that it's true. But so what? What's wrong with loving people for what they've done; isn't that an integral part of them? I love other people for other things, although it's true that they're less trouble.

"I am not those books," Deirdre says. "I feel no connection at all to what I have written."

"You don't? Who wrote those books, then?"

"I don't know. Some fey creature who once took up residence in me, who no longer exists, who is not me, who never could have been me, since I scarcely exist except to my enemies who are destroying me."

"Good God, Deirdre. What enemies? You don't have enemies."

But she shakes her head impatiently, telling me I am wrong. There are fresh rosebuds on the table. She leans to smell them, then looks off.

"I was seventeen when I first came from Ireland," she says. "Since then, my life has had no reality for me. I used always to stand in shadows, hoping no one would see me. In every weather, I hid inside raincoats a size too large for me. Do you know, just having to wait at a bus stop was the worst torture imaginable, especially in bright sunlight."

Some months earlier, she had invited me to be her guest at

the annual National Institute of Arts and Letters awards, at which she was among those honored. She was not being nominated for membership in the Institute; she had published only two volumes of stories and a slim collection of "pieces" written anonymously for *Tempus*, her best work, I think, the observations and small adventures of a peripatetic, anonymous woman that read like some startling new form of poetry. She was given one of the special awards, a citation and a check, for her distinguished contribution to American literature.

Although it was a beautiful May day, she was wrapped in a raincoat during the cocktail party that began the festivities. I, who was thrilled just to be there as her guest, and to be seeing and meeting writers who had been my idols for years and years, had trouble understanding her discomfort and self-consciousness. With difficulty, I prevailed upon her to remove her raincoat for the luncheon. She draped it over the back of her chair, but throughout the long afternoon's ceremonies, she was wrapped in it again, small and anonymous among all the luminaries on the platform. She wore the coat still when she came forward to receive her award. She made no acceptance speech. If it had been expected of her, she would probably have refused the honor. Her "thank you" was barely audible. Pleased that she was receiving this recognition of her genius, I hoped it would help her out of her despair and back to work.

And yet here she sits, only a short time later, denying all connection with her work, her writing self.

"Marcus says that when you first came to *Tempus* everyone stopped work to stare at you because you were so stunning," I say. "Then, when you opened your mouth to speak, everyone stopped talking and listened with disbelief because you were also so brilliant, so witty. They knew you couldn't be all that and write, too, he told me, but then of course, it turned out that you could write rings around all of them. Deirdre, that person Marcus describes didn't hide behind shadows. Who was she?"

"I don't know."

She doesn't seem to be crying, because her face is uncontorted, but tears have begun to slide down her cheeks, first in a trickle, and soon in a great wash. A busboy comes to exchange the dirty ashtray in which her cigarette has burned to the quick.

"Ah, Deirdre, don't," I say, moved and frightened by her tears. She is helpless, a child. I reach for her hand. She snatches it away and begins to keen loudly, and then more loudly. Like an animal, she is entirely unselfconscious, and the sound she makes is as piercing as a siren and scarcely more human. Although it is late, there are other diners in the restaurant. They are all turned toward us, staring. Soon a waiter comes to the table, his face troubled.

"Is there something wrong with the dinner?" he asks. Although this could be the funniest line ever spoken, I cannot laugh.

"Let me have the check, please," I say over the din of Deirdre's keening. Just as I may not know the true meaning of despair, so have I never heard anything like the huge, rhythmic, heartbroken wailing coming from the small person at my table. The sound is something ancient, primeval; it belongs in a jungle or on a barren moor. It does not belong in La Perla, with its pink-and-gray décor and pink-cheeked smiling young waiters in their pink shirts and gray trousers. I can't get her and her wailing out of there fast enough, and once outside, I feel helpless. I hand her tissues and plead with her to go back to the psychiatrist, to give it a chance, to try, to try. I doubt that she hears me, but then suddenly she stops and says, "He gives me pills that make me feel like a zombie. I would rather feel *any*thing but that."

"Then he's giving you the wrong dosage. He can adjust it. It takes time to get it right."

"No, no, Rachel. It doesn't do any good. They are everywhere. Sometimes, when I am walking in the street, I fall down. People think I am drunk, but I am not drunk. I shouldn't be telling you this."

"Go on."

"They have electronic rays," she whispers. "And they come straight at my head with them."

"Oh, Deirdre," I say. "Oh, poor Deirdre."

"You think I'm merely insane."

"Yes."

"Well, there you are, Rachel," she says, cold and crisp, turning away.

Except for me, the women in my writing group, Margo, Anna, and Karla, are approximately the same age, late thirties to mid-forties. We were once part of a larger group, but we splintered off to become a cozier support group. We are so supportive of one another's work that I wonder if we haven't rendered ourselves totally useless as critics, like mothers who can see no wrong in their children because they love them so utterly. Not that my mother was ever like that, or any of our mothers. Karla's mother died when she was a baby, and part of her has always been bereft. Margo's mother was jealous, alternately loving and cold, leaving Margo feeling unbeautiful, arrogant, guilty, and smug. And Anna's mother disapproved of her totally, constantly exhorting her to get her hair cut. I know about all these mothers because they keep appearing in our work. My own mother, too, never had any idea who I was, even though she was occasionally proud of me. She kept trying to fit me into some more recognizable mold, the daughter most of her friends thought *they* had, the stylish, good, respectable wife and mother in the eleven-room house in Scarsdale. To be fair, I can't get her right either, at least in my work. I can't get her voice; I keep making her sound Jewish, which she doesn't, making a mix of her and my grandmother.

When I was in analysis during most of my twenties and all of my thirties, I rarely mentioned my mother. It drove Dr. Dresher crazy. Not mentioning her was a clear indication that she was the meaningful parent and not my father, about whom I complained constantly. Perhaps she was, but the truth was that I could rarely think of anything to say about her. If we had not been so closely related, we would have had very little in common. I'm sure she feels the same way about me. More and more I feel that with Henry. My mother's life is so different from mine. She lives in Florida. She spends a lot of time and money on her appearance, as do her friends. At eighty-four, she still looks girlish if you don't get too close, and she plays nine holes of golf three times a week. She rarely worries about anything, and never feels sorry for herself. She is a prima donna, imperious with shopkeepers and waiters and room stewards and houseworkers, demanding and getting from them impeccable service. She will accept nothing less than she has contracted for. She has always known her rights in the outside world, perhaps because she never got them from my father.

In my own life, my father was so unequivocally the villain, and later on Peter in his own way was such a problem, that in my analysis I had all I could do to cover that ground. It was almost a year before I got around to talking about *myself* in any proper way. While I was growing up, I loved my mother (as I still do) and looked to her for whatever love I could get, since none was forthcoming from my father. I was angry at her, too, for not standing up to that bully with his brutal temper. My brother, David, and I, small and frightened, would look to my mother, that other adult, the reasonable and loving one, to stop him somehow when we were swept into the storm of his wild rage, but she couldn't do it. I suppose she was afraid of him, too. She was always trying to keep peace, as though peace at any price were an acceptable objective. Still, it was the policy that worked best for her. They stayed married for sixty years, and when he died, three years ago, she instantly forgot his true character, transforming him into a paragon, mythicizing and missing him with a loving loyalty that she never demonstrated and probably never felt while he was alive.

Anyhow, none of us in the writing group has had the kind of mother about whom it could be said, "in a mother's eyes," et cetera. In our writing group we try, at least a little, to be that for each other. We do criticize the work, and suggest ways to improve it, but only after we have praised what is good in it, usually gently, and with the firm assurance that our love, respect, and admiration are never in question.

We are in Anna's sprawling apartment in Soho, an erstwhile office building with endless corridors, now a hive of low-rent residential loftlike "spaces" for artists who have arranged the interiors according to their needs. Because she has three children, Anna has one of the larger spaces, a duplex with steep, perilous concrete steps connecting the floors. She has nonetheless made it attractive and functional, with warm colors and her own vivid, splashy paintings covering the walls. As long as I have known her, Anna has lived on the edge of real poverty. For some of those years she has been on welfare. The children are all by the same father, but Anna has been married and divorced three times. I can't imagine how she has managed, since none of her husbands was of any help, financially or in any other way. Anna writes wonderful, funny, terrifying stories about those husbands and about her children and about her extreme fatigue. What makes the stories funny and frightening is her innocence, the childlike matter-of-factness with which Anna's heroine views and accepts the absurdities of her life.

Anna, in her small, high voice, is reading aloud a long chapter from her novel. Every few minutes, one of her sons, growing boys with appetites, comes down from his room upstairs, weaving past us into the kitchen. They are cheerful, half-naked, gangling youths. In an elaborate charade of not wishing to disturb us, they move like Indians, leering, in such an exaggeration of stealth that their caricature makes them doubly conspicuous. Anna, unperturbed, oblivious to them, goes on reading an extremely graphic sex scene. Her lovers lie recovering from their passion, awash in the mixed bath of their exertions. In their zeal to declare their equal right to lust and sexuality, and the important part these play in women's lives, Anna and Karla write scenes like this regularly. It sometimes embarrassed me in the beginning to listen to them, and it embarrassed me to

feel embarrassed, but no more. The scenes are no longer painful. I have become inured, but I sometimes find them tiresome.
There is just so much you can do with the various parts of the
body. Detailed descriptions of sex are fine if they tell us something—the nature of the seduction, a sexual awakening, a sexual
death, some sort of lopsidedness, or perhaps a coming-to-terms,
or something really unusual and maybe shockingly kinky—anything that is fresh or revealing about the characters or the story,
not just another account of the Act because that is what the
writer feels like writing.

Anna and Karla write about sex for their own reasons, some
of them political. Margo, however, in her blockbuster trash-
book, must devote a large percentage of pages to steamy sex
scenes, because this is what sells these books. She has recently
been ordered to go back and put in even more sex. She is heartily
sick of it. Devising ways to make each scene a little different
from the others is taxing not only her ingenuity but her sanity.
She must do that with the deaths of her characters, too. "Well,
good-bye. I have to go kill someone off now," she told me on
the phone yesterday. "Should I have her dragged by a horse,
or should I drown her in a frozen pond?"

Margo has been chain-smoking even more rapidly than usual
throughout Anna's reading, causing Karla, who can't stand cigarette smoke, to shrink further and further away from her, and,
finally, to get up and move to a chair at the other end of the
room. Margo seems nervous, and I wonder if it's because of
Anna's reading or her own, which is to come next. Margo is
more worldly than the rest of us, probably better educated, and
more sophisticated, too, but her cleverness can sometimes make
her glib. She doesn't take things as seriously as Karla, who is
intense and intellectual and often profound. But Anna is in some

ways the most original, perhaps because she is the least re-
strained, the least self-censoring. Or the most naive. At forty-
three, with teenage children, she has the high, thin voice of a
young child, and sometimes her speech is almost illiterate, her
penchant for jargon shameless.

Her heroine's lover lies now with his limp cock curled like a
worm on his pale thigh, and we can get on with the story, which
is bizarre and funny and extreme. When Anna comes to the
end of her reading, Karla, uncrossing her long, shapely legs and
brushing aside a lock of black hair, leans forward.

"I love it, Anna," she says. "Oh, you're *so* good! The scene
in the bathroom is inspired."

Anna's heroine, in addition to the lover who is her paranoid
schizophrenic husband, has a fantasy lover, Captain Ahab, who
appears not at her will but at his, usually when it is most inconvenient, imploring her to leave Irwin and run off to sea with
him. He must get back to his ship, but cannot bear to part from
her. He is obsessed with her, obsession being his forte. Her
name is Rhoda, but sometimes he slips and calls her Moby
darling. He has just done this during her postcoital shower.
"Please, Ahab," she tells him while he soaps her back, "I am
not Moby darling, and I can't leave now. I have to take Irwin
to the hospital in the morning and have him committed, and
then I have to go to the welfare office. Besides, you know I get
seasick, and what about the kids?"

Ahab is Anna/Rhoda's fantasy of the ultimate commitment
(one of her pet words), the man who will not rest until she is
completely his. He is a pest. Anna/Rhoda may be trying to tell
herself that "commitment" may not be so hot after all. She
should know this, after three failed marriages. She and I oc-

casionally discuss her adventures with men, and I am always trying to persuade her never to let the word "commitment" cross her lips the minute she sleeps with someone. "You've had three men marry you already, and what did it mean?" "It meant," she explained, "that we would live together, you know, in the same apartment, with some like intention that it would be, you know, like permanent."

Anna's thin, pale, vulnerable face is set in a tangle, a thicket of curly brown hair double the width of her face on either side so that she appears to be peering timidly through a parting in the jungle. She is earnest and brave and lovable and funny, and she makes me feel tender and protective.

"There's some confusion in the fucking scene," Margo, now our resident specialist in sex scenes, tells Anna. "First I thought they had their orgasm, then it seemed that they didn't."

"*She* came. He couldn't."

"Oh, that was her orgasm. You could make that clearer."

"I didn't have any problem with it," Karla says.

"Maybe I misheard," Margo says. "May I look at it?" She takes the page from Anna. "Yes, here. This dangling, you should pardon the expression, modifier grammatically refers to him when you mean it to refer to her. The 'blurry eyes' part."

"I'll think about it," Anna says, her mouth stubborn.

It's my turn to say something. "It's a wildly funny chapter," I say. "It's you at your best, your true voice. I don't think you should worry about your agent not being willing to try to get you an advance with Part One. Push on and finish the book."

"I need the money."

"And I wish that instead of Irwin saying that about exploring new relationships," I say, "he'd say 'seeing other people.' "

"What's wrong with exploring new relationships? That's what people say."

"It's jargon. It's bad enough when social workers talk that way, but Irwin isn't even a social worker."

"When jargon gets into the language," Anna says, "it's because it says something clearly."

"No, it doesn't," I say. "It gets further away from what it's saying. It puts it at one remove. Instead of being a person's life, it becomes a case history. What is Irwin really saying when he tells Rhoda he wants to explore new relationships?"

"That he doesn't have a real commitment to the marriage," Anna says, and I want to kill her.

"He's saying, I'm bored with this," Margo says, "I don't want to be tied down to you anymore, I need other women, I'm sick of this fucking marriage. But when he says he thinks they should feel free to explore other relationships, he's not talking about his feelings. He's giving the situation a cold, scientific reasonableness that *evades* the truth. Rhoda knows what he's talking about, all right. She's wounded. But how do you argue with a dumb textbook phrase like that?"

How clear Margo is about marriage in her didactic role, I think, while in her own life she is so muddled. Anna, surrounded, seems to be considering what we have said, but she is dubious.

"Are you going to read, Rachel?" she asks, politely changing the subject.

They all know I have nothing to read. They know I am still between books, that I haven't written a word in two months.

What am I doing here, anyway? There will never again be anything in my head bursting to get out. Maybe, like Deirdre, I have written all I was meant to write. I will end up like Deirdre, clutching a pencil with fingers that never move, with a dying brain and a heart filled with despair.

Margo, on the other hand, in the few short weeks since signing the contract with her book packager, has written over two hundred pages, almost a third of *Thirst*. In the beginning, when she read to us, she was apologetic, protesting that she knew it was trash but that, since she was, like us, a serious writer and had never done this sort of thing, she needed our reactions to it. I don't know how many times one or the other of us has used the words *craftsmanship* and *inventiveness* in response to her reading. What else can we say? The stuff *is* trash; there's not a word of truth in it; it's a complete waste of time; it will be a best-seller; she will make her fortune.

Lately, however, Margo has begun to read with less apology, with more pleasure and gusto. She reads now, dozens of pages, in her lilting, happy, pleased-with-herself voice. Plot, plot, plot, the book plots on and on. My mind wanders, and I keep having to force it back. I try not to look at anyone, but Anna succeeds in catching my eye, and the look she sends me is full of fury. Margo rattles on. The words fly off the page as they flew off her fingers onto the page, great flocks of them, tumbling one after the other, deterred by nothing. The words are dollar signs, the music of cash registers. How Anna could use that kind of money! Who couldn't? But Anna most desperately. Karla is chewing her lip, studying her fingernails. When Margo is at last finished, Karla, who is always honest, says, "I don't know how you do it, Margo," and Margo smiles radiantly.

"It's certainly galloping along," I offer. "Was all that stuff in the outline?" Margo is supposed to be following her book pack-ager's outline, on the basis of which he sold the book to the publisher for all that money even before Margo was signed to write it.

"Maybe four percent," Margo says. "I'll probably have to redo it all. I can't follow his outline. It's too illiterate and dis-gusting. As soon as these characters came to life, I knew they were going to have minds of their own."

"You're excited about this, aren't you?" Anna asks.

"It's fun. Like a puzzle. I like solving all the little problems along the way."

"You're so good at it," Karla says. "You sound as if you really believe it. I mean, you make it all *sound* so believable."

"I do believe it," Margo says defensively. "I couldn't write it otherwise. I'm entirely inside Molly, thinking her thoughts, feeling her feelings, living her life." Her face darkens. "And a good thing, too, since my own is becoming less and less livable."

"What's wrong?" Karla asks. Margo shakes her head; she doesn't want to talk about it. But a little later when she is driving me home, she tells me.

"John says he's leaving me."

It takes me a beat to find my tongue. "That's ridiculous," I say. "Why should he leave you? He loves you."

"He's not committed to the relationship," Margo says, and we both laugh. "He *does* love me, but he hates me, too. He's constantly reciting the endless list of my sins and his grievances." She pauses. "And . . . there's someone else."

"So what?" I say.

"John isn't normal. He's romantic. He couldn't possibly have an affair without being in love."

"Who is it? Do you know?"

"Some Swede. A biologist. His line of goods."

"The Younger Woman?"

"He says she's older than me, and also boring and flat-chested and that he's never had a conversation with her, except about biology, and that she's not nearly as intelligent, witty, interesting, sexy, or exciting as I am, but that she's infinitely more restful."

"Why should he want rest?"

"Christ, we've been married eighteen years. I can't play the part of the discarded woman. It will kill me."

"He'll never leave," I say.

"He insists he's not really leaving me for her. She's in Sweden, after all, and she can't come here, but he'll see her Christmas, next summer, you know all those academic between-times, those conferences he's forever hanging out at or writing papers for. He says he's really leaving because he needs to be alone, that he'd have left long ago, but he wanted to wait till Danny goes off to college. I don't know what the truth is, and I doubt if he does, either."

We pull up in front of the brick container with its shelves and slots, where in a corner of the ninth shelf is the slot through which I pass into what I call my home, the boxes where I feed and clothe and cleanse and restore myself, where I hang my garments and pictures and store my effects. Margo switches off the ignition and the lights, and we sit a while longer, talking.

"How am I going to stand it, Danny going off, John leaving me? Thank God for you, Rachel. You won't die for a while, will you?"

I am fifteen years older than Margo. To her, my death seems imminent.

"I'll try not to," I say. "For your sake."

*Today is likely to bring welcome opportunities for Leos to display
their organizing and leadership capabilities. It is especially good
for joining clubs and societies. Hobbies and all forms of self-
expression are favored.*

"Amos is upstairs with Paul," Rebecca says.

"I need a drink before I go up," I say.

"Don't be silly." She's being either encouraging or opaque.
I doubt if she has ever known the occasional comfort of a drink.

I can barely see Becky. She is doing some last-minute fussing
over dinner, moving briskly and efficiently, as is her way. And
as though she can see what she is doing. It is dusk, and for some
reason she is working without putting on the lights. Her kitchen,
a huge area, white and functional, is a city brownstone version
of a country kitchen, the heart of the house. The rest of the
house is cluttered with all the colorful stuff of Becky's years of
insatiable foraging in flea markets, junk stores, and dim, dusty
antiques stores. Becky the huntress, her home filled with her
trophies, her spoils, only some of them functional, each treasure
there entirely for its own sake, proclaiming the success of her
safaris, those daring trips to the interior armed only with loaded
purse. I think of this place as the House of Many Conquests.
She thinks of it as the Victoria and Albert.

Occasionally, I have accompanied Becky on a hunt, trying to
see with her eyes the attraction of these used and useless Things,

these Objects, to see if there might be any category of Thing that would arouse the collector's instinct in me, but I seem to have been stricken with blindness in this area. Except for paintings, an entirely different category, I can appreciate the beauty of a vase or bowl or fine crystal, but I am drawn only to those objects that I can put to use, and even then not with the requisite passion.

Becky collects mercury glass, doorstops, brass shoes, fortune-cookie fortunes. Her favorite is, "Let a smile be your doormat." Although I profess, with honesty, not to understand, it has occurred to me that I do have the collector's instinct, after all. I collect gadgets. A kitchenful. And I, too, collect fortune-cookie fortunes. My favorites are, "Your face of love has changed, oh but you remain ageless," and "You may at one time be impractical, sporty or intensely restless."

And I collect books. My walls are lined with them. Most I will probably never read again, there because I have once read them, so that they are now solid entities with corporeal warmth and color as well as the life of their contents, now part of my own life. Of course, there are also the usable books, reference books, and the dearly beloved books, and even some books I have not yet gotten around to.

I don't collect them, but my life has been cluttered with people taken up and dropped, or not quite dropped, or lost, people who did not turn out to be successful as friends or with whom I did not succeed, after that initial thrill of discovery, who did not quite stand up, or develop, or blossom, or take, or endure; people who have died, or gone away; people with whom I have lost touch, or maintained Christmas-card touch; people who have satisfied my curiosity and with whom there is nothing more to be said; old lovers parted from with bitterness on one side

or the other, or else with killing indifference. I cannot keep
people for auld lang syne, for sentimental reasons; I keep them
only if I love them, and I do not love easily.

Becky I have kept since childhood. She is the only one. Occasionally, we have little to say to each other, but with Becky
this is different from what it would be with most others. We
know each other so well, we are like sisters, but closer because
we chose each other. It has been a long time since there were,
between us, tests to pass. Once when we quarreled, Becky asked
me if I wanted a divorce. I laughed, the word was so appropriate.
I could no more be divorced from Becky than from my own
head.

"Can I help?" I ask now. A stupid question, since Becky can't
bear to be helped in the kitchen.

"Go upstairs!" she says impatiently. "I'll be there in a
minute."

Becky seems not to understand that I am nervous. How could
I be nervous about seeing Amos these hundreds of years and
lovers later? I am more than nervous; I am scared. I turn and
make for the stairs, dragging my feet, conscious of my heartbeat.
The light is dim. When I am halfway up, a man who doesn't
seem to be Paul and must therefore be Amos starts coming
down.

"Hello," I say. We pause on the stairs, he coming down, I
going up. I put out a hand and he shakes it.

"Hello," he says pleasantly. We smile at each other in the
dark. He goes down. I go up.

"Why don't you turn on the fucking lights?" I ask Paul while
we are kissing each other's cheeks by way of greeting. "What's
with all this darkness? And why are the drinks up here?"

"It *has* gotten dark. I hadn't noticed." This surprises me. Paul is a solid man both in spirit and appearance. He always knows where he is and where he is going and the best way to get there. Before he turns on the ignition, he memorizes the map. Before he says the first word, he plans the whole sentence. He is four square, true blue, the Rock of Gibraltar.

I go to the makeshift bar on top of the piano and help myself liberally. "This is a dumb place for a bar," I mutter.

"Did you see Amos?" Paul asks, switching on lamps. Soon the room is ablaze.

"We met on the stairs."

"It's a long time since you've seen him, isn't it?"

"About thirty years," I say. "Is that a long time?"

"Not eonwise or erawise. But lifetimewise, yes."

"That's the wise we're talking about," I say, gulping my drink, hoping to be drunk at once. "Were you and Amos having large talk?"

"Has Amos ever had small talk?"

I try to remember. In all, I knew him for perhaps three months. That would be an almost incalculably small fraction of his entire life. Or mine. But during those three months, if we had small talk it was undoubtedly initiated by me.

I am nearly as comfortable with Paul as I am with Becky. When they married, I was almost sure he wasn't good enough for her, but I was wrong. They complement each other perfectly, and they are such good friends that neither would dream of doing or seeing anything of more than minimal interest without the other. Psychiatrists might frown on that, but theirs is one of the very few happy marriages I know, despite or because of the marked difference in their rhythms and temperaments. Becky is quick and impatient, Paul is thoughtful, steady, ponderous, but he enjoys our silliness as much as we do, and has the same sense of humor. He anchors Becky, she uproots him. She is the roiler of his untroubled sea. He adores her. They both wear special faces when they talk to each other on the telephone. He beams. She twinkles.

"What were you talking about?" I ask.

"Kafka. The Minotaur. How the Minotaur wasn't there; it was himself.

"Shoptalk," I say, beginning to feel better now that I have downed most of my drink. I suppose this makes me a borderline alcoholic. I have never been able to cross that border, try though I sometimes do. My tolerance for alcohol stops with the third drink, more often with the second. I freshen my glass and sit in my dim corner of the love seat, a little sorry now to have been the agent of all this electricity, feeling like Deirdre. I am wearing something stupid and unflattering, chosen in reckless defiance because I was ashamed to be feeling so much trepidation while I was dressing for this evening I swore I would eschew. It doesn't matter *what* you wear, idiot! I screamed at myself, and pulled some velour rag out of the closet. Still, I am not displeased to know about myself that my curiosity is more compelling than my timidity. It's possible that I am getting less neurotic as I age.

When we come down, I observe Amos while trying to steady the hand that is raising the glass it holds to my lips. He is shorter, surely, than he used to be? He never had that beard. He is a bit misshapen, too, as though the weight the years added to him could not be supported by his frame. Not that he is heavy; just that normal weight that fills men out, making them no longer boys. It is the same weight that the years add to women, the natural accretion that makes them womanly, ungirlish. Of men maturing thus, it is often said, "How nicely he has filled out."

This is never said of women. Women never fill out nicely; they thicken.

The mustache and beard conceal Amos's fine, sensitive mouth. They are speaking, all three of them, but a roaring in my ears prevents me from making out what they are saying. I wait for a sentence I can grab hold of. No, it's nothing, they're talking about flying. Amos's trip east. The smallest of small talk.

". . . the little steaks with the stripes painted on," Becky says.

"A backyard barbecue in the ionosphere," I say, hoping to sound clever. "It's all illusion, anyway. Everyone knows planes can't really fly. It's against nature."

"And the earth is really flat," Amos says.

I confess then that I was in my forties before I ever flew, long after everyone I knew had done it.

"I was terrified. Of course, I pretended that it was something else, that flying was undignified, that it was not the proper way to travel, because you weren't honoring distance and time. How could you feel that you had truly crossed an ocean or a continent if it didn't take at least five days? What a coward I was. And still am, though I do it now."

"You were so reckless when you were fourteen," Becky says, smiling fondly. "You were much more physically daring than I was."

"You knew each other as children?" Amos asks. Could he have forgotten that? Surely he knew.

"Oh, yes," Becky says. "We've been friends forever."

Chitchat, chitchat. We are birds hopping about on the branches of trees, keeping an eye out for a snack, for danger, for a better branch. I look at Amos and think, If you only knew, always for me you were the road not taken. How many times, at least during the years of my marriage, did I not speculate in what ways my life might have been different, how *I* might have been different, had I waited for you, had I had then what I thought of as the courage for you, had I not, instead, so blithely and carelessly slipped into marriage with Peter.

Why has he no curiosity about me? He's a literary bloke. He has looked my way politely, but no more often than necessary.

Not many years ago, a poet friend of mine was invited by you to give a three-day seminar at your university, I want to tell him. When she returned, I asked her if she had met you. "Of course," she said. "He met my plane. He drove me everywhere. There was a dinner party at his home for me." His home? "What was that like?" I asked, avid for clues. "Oh, you know. Big house, messy, lots of kids, broken toys on the lawn." "His wife?" "I hardly noticed. Typical academic wife, I suppose. In the kitchen most of the time. Long hair, one of them in my soup." Though brief, it was a satisfying description. It was a picture in which I would never have fit. Lucky Amos, I thought then. You'll never know how lucky. I check an urge to mention my poet friend. What would be the point? She has become so famous he might think I was name-dropping. How could I explain that she was like a letter to me from you, or at least a postscript? "This is the life I said I wanted, and would have and see, I have it, a big, warm, messy, beloved family, friends, talk, safety. You didn't trust me, you thought I was not a solid man, you were afraid I would fail, and that, by extension, you, too, would fail. But I am a solid man, a good man, a loving man, responsible and trustworthy, not like Peter, not like your father, not like any of your choices."

"Do you still write poetry?" I ask Amos. He looks at me sharply, his eyes narrowing, as though he is surprised, as though he is trying to get me into some kind of focus. When I knew him then, he had published half a dozen poems in a university-press quarterly. I loved them. I loved the Amos in them. Timidly, I showed him one of my stories. How solicitous he was, how he encouraged me. In my late thirties, when I finally really got down to writing and my first story was accepted by a magazine with a wide circulation and I sat with the letter of acceptance on the front steps of my Scarsdale house, weeping and trembling, he was the first person I wanted to tell about it. Later, too, when there were stories in the prestigious quarterlies and in anthologies, I wanted him to know, I wanted to say, "See, I said I could do it and I am doing it. And aren't you pleased, you said I could do it, too."

He was the touchstone.

"How . . . ? Do you know my poems? I publish so few. I've had so little time. But how . . . ?"

He is confused. *Oh, my God.*

"You don't know who I am," I say.

And now Becky, unflustered, says, "This is *Rachel.* Rachel Levin."

He colors. His mouth falls open, and it is his turn to say, "Oh, my God. Of course. How stupid of me."

The worst thing that could have happened has happened, and I am devastated. I sit stiffly in my wrong clothes, furious with Becky for not having made clear to him who was coming, for not telling him who I was, for subjecting me to this. As for Amos, I have nothing more to say to him. I look at him with a cold, objective eye, and I fail to see anything the least bit attractive about him. Later, during dinner, he will look at me again, again with a small amazement, and say, "Well, time has been kind to us in one way, at least. We're still alive."

Illusions, illusions. What we do with our memories, how we keep them, like photographs in albums, to warm us, to tell us who we are, what our life has been. What a collection I have, Becky. It would put yours to shame, my collection of illusions. Again I am reminded of my separateness, as I so often am, of how my feelings are only my own, my version of the past. My memories are mine, fashioned by me, belonging only to me.

Much later, long after I am home, recovering, I realize that if I had met Amos unwarned, *I* would not have known *him*.

"There is no passion wherein self-love reigns so powerfully as in love, and one is always more ready to sacrifice the peace of the loved one than one's own." —La Rochefoucauld, 1665

With most people I, a true Leo, prefer to do the driving, my confidence in my own capability never wavering. Also, I really enjoy driving. I used to have dreams in which Peter was in the driver's seat and I passive beside him. We always came to grief. Peter was a perfectly good and careful driver in waking life, but the symbolism in my dreams was truer, more real. Peter was not one to be trusted in the driver's seat of life, as I slowly learned in the first years of our marriage, and so, little by little, I edged him out of it, at least to the extent that that is possible with someone like Peter. Trying to shape a life with Peter often seemed to me like building sand castles with nothing but dry sand; they will not hold. The tyranny of the weak is that in the end they prevail; there is nothing you can do with them except love them as they are or leave them.

I trust Lisa to drive the car, the real one, my Volkswagen Dasher. In fact, I like her to do the driving. I can relax and enjoy the scenery and make up songs about it while she rages at all the drivers in her path, and even not in her path, who can all be counted on to do the wrong thing, and who must be taught by Lisa at the top of her lungs even though they cannot hear her. "Dumb shit!" she is screaming at a little old man who is vacuum-packed inside an air-conditioned Oldsmobile. "You're supposed to stay on the right unless you're passing, you fucking moron!" She has been trying to pass him for about three miles, because he is doddering along at a careful fifty-four miles an hour in a fifty-five-mile-per-hour zone. "There ought to be a mandatory retirement age for drivers, like there is for every other important kind of work."

"Like the Supreme Court," I say. "Or the presidency." I return to the song I have been improvising: "Oh, where are the cows, the brown-and-white cows, the lovely old lumbering cows of yesteryear? They ought to be here, they used to be here, the landscape without them is terribly drear." The tune, though I haven't the voice for it, is even better than the lyrics.

"Look at that bastard! *Regardez-lui.* You goddamn prick, GO TO JAIL!"

"*Regardez-la.*" This sudden lapse into French is entirely out of character. This outburst has been addressed to a young woman with three children in the rear seat who has cut in front of Lisa and behind the old man and is now honking at the old man. Lisa never once honked at him. She is a screamer, not a honker.

"The driver is a direct object," I point out.

"She's endangering the lives of those three tots."

"And she cannot be called a prick."

"I say she's a prick."

"You can't call a woman a prick, no matter how equal."

She opens her window. "Asshole!" she screams.

"Becky is right," I say.

"*Now* what is Becky right about?"

"It's terrible to use parts of the body and lovely things like fucking as curse words. Why denigrate our nice bodies?"

"Then what's left? God? Jesus? Mother? Making love? Those are okay things to use?"

"You're so vulgar for a Wellesley woman. When I first met you and learned you were Wellesley, I said to myself, This must be a real class chick, a lady."

"You're a fucking snob."

"How impressed I was by that Wellesley credential. I admit it. In my day, if you were Jewish, you simply couldn't go to Wellesley. They had tiny little quotas, maybe one half of one percent. If I had been in the upper one-percentile bracket, which I wasn't except IQ-wise, half of me could have gone to Wellesley, but the other half would have had to go to NYU."

"That's what attracted you to me? Some dumb prejudice left over from the forties?"

"That was the second thing." I had been taken to a meeting of a feminist writers' group. Lisa was its treasurer, and was called upon to give certain opinions, and she gave these and others for which she was not called upon. Although she was aggressive in her delivery, it wasn't until our third meeting that

I really saw her. I might have noticed her sooner, but she was of that generation to which I rarely pay attention any longer unless the member happens to be my child.

"What was the first thing?"

"Your emphatic bosom." She had been wearing a sweater that was at least a size too small, something she still tends to do. She is a flaunter. On the street in some neighborhoods, men whistle at her, and then she is indignant. When I tell her she has no right to her indignation, she rounds on me and calls me a traitor to feminism. This has led to many long discussions, often heated, during which I try to determine exactly what is in her mind when she gets herself up in ways that call particular attention to her erogenous zones, and whether she can in all honesty insist that her intention is not to evoke a specific response. She claims that she dresses for herself and that I am the kind of person who would blame the woman and not her rapist.

"After your bosom, Wellesley. The third thing, and perhaps the most important, since I'm a Leo with a bottomless vulnerability to flattery, was your obvious interest in me."

"Nothing lasts forever."

"How true."

A few nights ago, I looked back in my journal to see what I had written at the beginning of our affair. After the usual hurdle of hating my journal voice, that self-consciousness that seems to be unavoidable in journals since self-consciousness is precisely what journals are about, I was surprised to find that at the time I considered Lisa to be perfect. *She's always so much herself*, I wrote, *that she's never intrusive, and there's nothing about her, nothing at all, that irritates me.* Ah, there is so much now that irritates me. Two months later, I wrote, *I love being with her. We laugh a lot and touch a lot and are sweet and tender together—but I have a persistent sense of unreality, as though I am not entirely present.* I hadn't realized how early with Lisa I began to feel that odd sense of detachment from my own life and being, from my feelings. A form of deadness. I thought at the time that perhaps it was a way of protecting myself against pain, from becoming too vulnerable. How many deaths of the heart can one sustain? Now, I wonder if that was true.

"There used to be cows here," I say. "This was once a meadow." It is a golf course now. Each year, suburbia's greedy hand reaches further afield, and the cows leave. We are on our way to the cottage I rented for six months but where I have spent so little time. Summer is almost over, but I will have the house through Thanksgiving. When I rented it, I thought I would love it. I thought Lisa would love it, too, but she hasn't wanted to be there at all. Her job is demanding, the hours so long that on the weekends she only wants to sleep late and play and, as she says, hang out. She is a woman who still sits on stoops, weather permitting, gassing with her neighbors. I thought I would be able to work in the house, alone, but mostly I feel my loneliness when I am there, and the long, dark, quiet nights. Even my cat, Colette, who loves the country and is a great hunter, doesn't like this house, charming though it is. There is something in it that frightens her, ghosts, perhaps, or death in the walls. She ignores the mice who freely leave traces of their nightly visits to the kitchen and who cavort in the dresser drawers, shredding my underwear for their nests. That Colette should show no interest in these mice is weird; she has always been so dependable, so effective, so tantalized and challenged by the slightest hint of mouse. No, she does not like this house, her personality changes when I bring her to it, and this has prejudiced me against it, too. She knows something that I don't know.

As if on cue, Colette begins to gag and retch somewhere in the back of the station wagon. I say soothing words to her, but cats are too smart to be soothed by mere people, who are so unaware of what is *really* happening, who can't smell anything, who can barely hear, who stumble about in the dark.

"Phugh!" Lisa says. "She's crapping, too."

"Cats don't crap," I say. "They're too fastidious."

"Then what is that she's doing?"

"She's moving her sweet little bowels, and she's such a private creature that she's hoping you won't notice, because, really, she has very little choice."

"Is she crapping on my suitcase? If she's crapping on my suitcase, you'll have to buy me a new one."

"She seems to be in the vicinity of the groceries."

"What a relief!"

Lisa has a cat, too, a small black cat with malocclusion and disgusting halitosis, but smart. A couple of years ago, we both brought our cats to the Connecticut house we'd rented together for the summer. Lisa had gotten a summer job in a law firm there after her second year of law school. It was the summer she was on the girls' softball team and I was playing suburban mother, or whatever. My cat was spoiled, and too old to adjust to a strange black cat. They both drove me crazy in their insistence on claiming the territory. "Share it!" I kept screaming at them. "Or divide it, for God's sake. There are twelve rooms in this house, and two acres of garden. Leave me alone." Lisa was away all day learning to practice law, or playing ball, and I was at home trying to think while the cats hissed and scratched each other's eyes out. Now that I don't allow Lisa to bring her cat, she is quite naturally resentful. She tries to be fair, though, by not disliking Colette too much.

"What I've noticed about you," I say, "is that when you're angry you're a cool, mature, intelligent, articulate, educated woman. But when you're relaxed and happy, you turn into a truck driver, a hardhat. Or maybe it's a teenage boy from a lousy neighborhood. Why do you think that is? Which is the real you?"

"They're both the real me. I'm a person of parts."

"Most of us are, but the parts usually fit together better."

There is a third Lisa, but I don't mention that one now. The third Lisa is the one who would secretly like to be a streetwalker, the most self-conscious of the Lisas, the one who is being the sexual woman in a heterosexual world, the one who is thinking hard about her body, not as though she is inside it, maneuvering it, but somewhere outside, detached, trying things out like a film director. Her first lover was a boy, a classmate, and, having grown up in a time of far greater sexual freedom (even that's an understatement!), Lisa stopped being a virgin at a much earlier age than I. It was all right for her to experiment with women, too, which may have been worse even than incest in my day, really too shameful to mention, rare even in literature. All I had was *The Well of Loneliness* in those days of sin and guilt. How interesting it was, and yet how disappointing, to learn that my androgynous feelings were not unique. Forced to repress my unacceptable side, I began to fall in and out of love with boys, then men. What a relief! My two selves were really not in conflict, at least not much of the time.

But Lisa seems no more at home in her hooker self, when she is either pouting or frowning, her eyes hooded, trying to look dangerous, fatal, than she is in the hardhat persona when her speech changes so that she drops g's and swears and is incapable of saying an interesting word. The Lisa I love is the grown-up, articulate woman one, which she becomes not only when she is angry with me, but also when she is being a copy editor or a lawyer, or when she is with those elderly people, my friends.

When we make love, she is not a boy or a tramp, either. She is a lovely woman, entirely natural and free and graceful. I sometimes try to imagine how she was, or is, making love with men, and whether bisexuality has anything to do with all that role-playing, and whether she will ever grow entirely into that self that is so natural to her and so much more attractive than those others.

It occurs to me now that her kid-on-the-block self is how she must have been when she was trying to get the boys to let her play ball with them, since the girls weren't good enough athletes for her. Having succeeded, finally, in becoming one of the boys, she would have had to go on being that. She must have loved herself then. She has told me that she was as good an athlete as most of the boys, better than a lot of them. How she must have swaggered, though the tomboy nowhere shows in the photographs I've seen of her as a child. In those photos, she's a pretty girl, wide-eyed and a little plump, with hair even longer than it is now. Though she looks serene in the photos, she did not have an easy childhood. Her family lived in a corner house in a middle-class neighborhood. Her father was an advertising executive making good money, steadily rising, and when they were small, his three daughters, of whom Lisa was the second, adored him, as did all the children in the neighborhood. Lisa's older sister was that cliché of a genius who actually did blow up half the basement with a chemistry set. Her younger sister was feisty and cute. And to Lisa, everything came easily—smartest in her class, popular, an athlete. She sang, she acted, and later there was a scholarship to Wellesley. What could sound more situation-comedy normal?

But Lisa's mother was gradually turning into an alcoholic, and her father into a philanderer. Whether her father philandered because his wife drank, or she drank because he philandered, or whether each used the other as an excuse for his own excesses, Lisa never knew. The suburban house they lived in was neglected, never painted or repaired, and soon deteriorated to a state of near-squalor, echoing the marriage. Lisa was too ashamed to ask friends over. Her older sister, the genius, now the babbler, fell in with a bad crowd heavily into drugs and sex, and dropped out of school when she was fifteen, disappearing for months at a time, in and out of serious trouble. Lisa's younger sister hung herself in the breakfast room when she was seventeen, leaving a twelve-page single-spaced typewritten note, extremely well-written, rolled up tightly in her napkin ring, listing her reasons, none of them having anything to do with the family situation. No one in the family ever fully recovered.

Lisa's father died of a coronary a few months later, and her mother joined Alcoholics Anonymous and slowly and bravely pulled herself together. The older sister came home, married a boy she'd grown up with, and, showing no sign of her earlier genius (perhaps she blew her mind on drugs), took a job clerking in a hardware store. She takes her job very seriously, and tells endless, pointless stories about washing machines and microwave ovens.

And there is Lisa, involved for these past five years with me, a woman and twice her age. Now she is a lawyer, but bright though she is, logical, quick to grasp, and with great powers of retention, she did not make Law Review, failed to graduate with honors, failed to land one of those plummy jobs that were hanging from so many trees, hates the job she finally got, and lately talks more and more about quitting. At crucial moments she is apt to become paralyzed, to sink into a quagmire of apathy. Her eyes glaze, her jaw slackens, time passes. I, who am compulsive about getting things that must be done out of the way before I can proceed, become wildly impatient, telling her not to procrastinate, not to leave everything until the last possible moment. I sigh. My stomach knots. My teeth grind. I feel with her as I felt with Henry during a period in his adolescence when physical and sexual growth drained all his energy and he became sloth incarnate. I couldn't bear the frustration I felt then, and I can't bear its resonance now, in Lisa. That's one of the problems of aging. Early experiences compound present ones and may detonate the charge of feeling evoked then, not appropriate to what's going on now. I am forever having to sift through feeling and memory, and what a nuisance that is.

Lisa is not Henry at fourteen. Lisa, though partially crippled by her childhood, has miraculously survived. She will get things done in time, in her own time, and she will do them, if not always to the reaches of her capacity, not sloppily, either. Her inner clock is different from mine, but it works as well. She has her own self-destruct button, but so do I. Furthermore, and most important, I am not her mother.

As the car turns into our parking spot, an alcove in the trees on a rise above the house, a wide startle of birds sweeps up and away. The house, off a private road, is secluded. The birds that have staked out its two acres have foraged here undisturbed for days, as have the mice inside. The day is beautiful, and the house, in its fairy-tale setting, is charming. Perhaps if I were not a short-term visitor and the house were mine, my pulse would quicken at the sight of it, possession often being the better part of love. Instead, I sit for a moment in the stopped car, wondering what we're doing here, reminding myself that one comes to the country for respite from the city, for that restorative dose of nature and quiet. I get out and breathe deeply, smelling the air, while opening a rear door of the car for Colette, who, now fully alert, stands on the backseat looking out, her tail whipping back and forth, propelled by intimations of danger.

"Take your time, sweetheart," I tell Colette, going around back to help Lisa with the luggage.

"Yuck," she says. "She barely missed my briefcase."

"Try not to think about it. I'll clean it up later." I load up with the bags of groceries and carry them to the kitchen door. Before unlocking the door, I must first unlock the latch to the cellar, descend into its dank, furry interior, and with yet another key turn off the alarm system. This modest cottage came, like a fortress, with a weighty ring of keys. When I am finally inside, with all the doors opened wide to let in the fresh outdoors so that it will displace the stale indoors, I begin to unpack groceries in the kitchen, squeamishly inspecting for signs of mice, which, predictably, are all over the sink and counter.

"Shit," I say. What other creature cannot take a single step without leaving a turd in its wake? What this world would be if we were all engineered that way!

"Mice?" Lisa calls from the screened porch off the kitchen, where, the suitcases dropped at the foot of the stairs, she is arrested before the TV set. Yankees, third inning.

"Or one extraordinarily prolific mouse," I say. "I can't imagine what he uses to manufcture these turds with. I never leave him anything but that little dish of poison."

"I'm gonna get the fucker," Lisa says. "I bought a trap." She screams with joy. "Way to go, Davey! Boy, that one traveled clear out of the ballpark."

Colette, who in her own good time emerged from the car and sat in a patch of sunlight eating grass, now scratches politely at the kitchen screen door. I let her in and put down food for her, while she sniffs the base of the sink.

"Mouse," I say. "M-o-u-s-e." It's one of the seven words I know she knows. "You going to let Lisa catch it with a trap? Shame on you." She looks at me sweetly, then pads over to her bowl and nibbles daintily at the Purina Country Dinner I sometimes feed her here because it is appropriately named. I feel peaceful and content. We are cozy and domestic. I am in the kitchen, the nurturer, sorting boxes, cans, bottles, into cupboards, refrigerator, freezer. The cat is dining. Lisa's team is winning. The sun is shining. All's right with this tiny moment in this small corner of the world. I fold the last of the shopping bags away in the closet, where they are accumulating faster than I can turn them into garbage bags, and go out to the screened porch, where I stand behind Lisa and massage her back, a pleasure she can never get enough of.

"Ooh," she purrs. "Harder. There. Where your right thumb is. Oh, that's it, right there. Harder."

I try to imagine what my life will be like after Lisa. Her absence will certainly create a void, even if it is sometimes welcome. What if no one else comes along to fill that void? Until quite recently, that possibility would never have occurred to me. Now that it does, it is accompanied by a faint intimation of fear. But I know what stupid and ugly lives are often led by people who are afraid to be alone, and I make promises to myself.

"It's too bad we aren't going to make it," I nonetheless say. "I'm probably going to miss you."

"I'm not going anywhere," she says.

"You'll find someone soon enough," I say. "Maybe you'll get married and have that baby."

"I'll still be your friend. I'll always be your friend. I really do love you, you know. God knows why."

But will I want Lisa for a friend? For me, as with the house, possession is a large part of love, alas. I'm also pretty sure I won't want her for a friend along with whoever her new person turns out to be.

"What would we talk about?" I say.

She looks at me warily, trying to figure out what nasty thing I mean by that. "Maybe more than we talk about now," she says.

I doubt it. We don't really have much in common beyond this dying relationship.

"Well, we gave it a good run," I say. "Five years ain't bad."

"Remember in the beginning? It was one day at a time. You gave it two weeks, tops."

"It was you," I say. "You were the one who was so unsure." My hands are tired. I stop rubbing her back, and then I see that she is crying.

"Why are you crying?" I say, putting my arms around her.

"What do you mean, why am I crying?" she sobs, exasperated. "That's the trouble with you. You can't get it through your head that I might have feelings, too."

Tuesday the 13th is deceptive. No changes should be attempted in places or types of work. Leos can unwittingly cause secret enmity. Tact is necessary. Secret affairs can be helpful to real-estate endeavors.

As I come through the doorway into the apartment, I hear the telephone ringing. It sounds tired, as though it has been ringing for a long time.

"Ray-chelle?"

"Deirdre! Where are you?"

"Thank God, Rachel. I've been calling and calling."

"I was in the country."

"You're always running off somewhere. Why are you so restless?"

"Hah! Look who's talking restless. I tried to find you before you left, but you were no longer in the apartment."

"I had to give it up."

"They don't let you keep those apartments unless you pay the rent."

"Don't talk to me that way, Rachel. I am not an idiot, you know."

"Then why didn't you pay the rent?"

"When the time came, there was no money. For very important reasons."

"Why didn't you pay the rent before those very important reasons arose?"

"It was a dreadful apartment. I hated it."

"Deirdre, where are you?"

"I'm in Bellevue Hospital. And, of course, there's no view at all."

"Oh, God, Deirdre!"

"The women's psychiatric wing, fifth floor. Could you bring me some ciggies? Parliaments?"

"I know what you smoke!" I also know what she drinks and what she eats. What I rarely know is what she thinks. "How long have you been there?"

"And bedroom slippers, size four? Nothing too elaborate. Comfort is all."

"When are visiting hours?"

"Oh, dear, let me find out. Nurse!" There is a muffled moment. "Three to five in the afternoon," she says in that cheerful, inappropriate voice, as if she is asking me to tea.

"I'll come this afternoon," I say.

"You're an angel, Rachel."

"No I'm not, Deirdre." I am very close to tears. "You're getting to be a terrible nuisance." But we have been cut off by that series of mechanical gargles pay phones utter in their death throes.

When I finally make my way through the dismal labyrinthine ways between the street and the proper fifth-floor doorway to the psycho ward, it is almost more of an effort than I can make to ring the bell I am instructed to ring in order to gain entry. An eye peers at me through a peephole, and the door is unbarred by a strapping orderly who examines my packages while I absorb the stink of illness and violence and the smell of my own fear. The orderly takes the matches out of the bag with the cigarettes and confiscates them.

"They can't have no matches," she explains.

"How can they smoke?"

"We light 'em."

The room is large and crowded with women in hospital wraps, some of them dancing, floating, pacing, others semicomatose, catatonic, still others proclaiming, orating, screaming, howling. It really *is* a madhouse. It stinks of shit and urine and disinfectant and vomit and sick and unwashed bodies. I've read about places like this and imagined them, but the reality is even worse, the horror of a place so barbaric in this "enlightened" day and age. The despair, the helplessness and hopelessness I felt during my own breakdown all those years ago, come back in a sickening wave of memory. But I never had to be put away. I was never that bad. I had Peter. I had my parents. Deirdre has nobody. Only me.

It takes me a while to locate her. She is sitting at one of the rows of long wooden tables, facing the door. She has already seen me, probably from the moment I walked in, and read all my feelings on my face. She has made no move to help me find her, much less to greet me. As I make my way toward her, there is the faintest flicker of a smile on her face. She is small and wan, subdued as death. Probably drugged. The fading hair is wild, a tangled halo, and her feet are bare and filthy.

"What the hell are you doing here?" I shout.

"The policemen brought me here."

"What the hell were you doing?"

"Have you brought the ciggies?"

I hand her the bag with the cartons of ciggies. Ciggies, indeed! She rips at the box, and then at the package she tears from it.

She waves a cigarette over her head, and soon one of the matrons comes to light it. "Thank you," she says with dignity, as though to a maître d' in a first-class restaurant. The first puff visibly relaxes her. I hand her the slippers, black felt with gold brocade, something for a harem dweller, but all I could find in her size on such short notice. She regards them with a shudder of disapproval.

"Think of them with irony," I say, "but put them on. Your feet are filthy, and under the filth they're blue with cold." She obeys me. I give her copies of the *Daily News* and the *National Enquirer* I've brought for her. She never reads the *Times*. These are the newspapers that tell you what is really happening. They are full of little stories.

"Thank you, Rachel," she says. "You are ex-*treme*ly thoughtful, an angel, really."

"Why did the police bring you here? What were you doing?"

"Nothing. *Tempus* sent for them. I was sitting in the ladies'."

"What were you *doing* there?"

"There is a leather sofa. I was sitting on it. Staring into space, I think."

"Why there?"

"I'd slept there, Rachel. I had nowhere else to go."

"Dammit, Deirdre, they told you not to come back. I think they're afraid of you."

She laughs mirthlessly. She's right, of course. She's so small, so frail.

"Did you read in the *Enquirer* last week about the woman who divorced one Siamese twin because she'd fallen in love with the other?"

"They tried to do everything they could for you, but you're impossible. It's your own fault, you know."

"Try to imagine what there could be to choose between one Siamese twin and the other," she says. "D'you know what the woman said? She said she'd fallen in love with her brother-in-law when she found out he was the wittier of the two."

"You *did* break a window the last time," I persist.

"Wittier. Imagine. Yes, with a wooden chair." She says this with mischievous pleasure. "I could hardly lift it. But I did, and I smashed it against the glass. It was a window in a door, however. I needed to get into the office, and it was locked."

"It wasn't even your office."

"I no longer have my office. It was Marcus's office. He has some papers I need, to do with my pension. They won't give it to me, you know."

"Deirdre, Marcus is not your enemy. He's one of the last of your friends who hasn't given up on you."

"Wrong. The last time I was with him, I looked into his eyes and there was nothing there."

"Oh, shit, Deirdre."

"Rachel. Don't talk like that. I hate it."

"How long will they keep you here?"

"Not long. This is just a holding pen."

A beautiful young woman has been waltzing past us, back and forth, back and forth, a dreamy look on her face, her head held very high on a long, graceful, soiled neck. She is wearing a dirty hospital gown, and in her arms, cradled as though it is a baby, are a dozen fading red roses. Spots of blood, where thorns have pricked her, stain the coarse cloth of her gown. She is crooning a lullaby.

"You can't stay here," I say. "I'll have to do something to get you out."

"I keep thinking about the husband. They say he was heartbroken."

"What husband?"

"The Siamese twin. The duller one. Imagine his situation."

"Have you been seen by a doctor here?"

"For approximately one second. A Dr. Sylvan."

"*Sylvan!* I'll go and see him."

"What will you tell him?"

What, indeed? "That you're an important writer. That you're *supposed* to be crazy."

The corners of her mouth twitch in her version of a smile. "I am *not* an important writer, Rachel. I am not a writer at all. And where will I go?"

Where *will* she go? I am absolutely not going to take her in.

"I'll talk to Marcus. Maybe his doctor can arrange . . ."

"You will *not* talk to Marcus. He is part of the conspiracy. I have all the proof I need. I found it in the apartment. It's one of the reasons I had to leave."

"Tell me another."

"All right, I will." She lowers her voice. "Marcus had a friend living in the very next apartment. He is a countertenor!" She says this triumphantly, then sees the blankness on my face. "Ah, I forget. You couldn't possibly know the significance of his being a countertenor."

"Is it like being a counterspy? And why is the plot musical?"

"There's no point talking to you," she is the one to say. And there isn't. And though I know it is true, I still can't believe it.

"One other thing," she says. "Did you know that the incinerator was right next to the door of that apartment?"

"Some people would appreciate the convenience."

"You're hopelessly dense, Rachel."

For a moment, I try to put myself inside her head, try to think of the incinerator as sinister. My sister's sinister incinerator. A little application and I will have a lovely tongue twister. It is impossible to keep my mind on the conspiracy. Maybe there is one, and I am too dull and ordinary to do anything but insist on reason, even though I know how much there is in life that is irrational. Maybe hanging on to sanity with such persistence, such smugness, is symptomatic of a grave deficiency, a lack of perception, hopeless stupidity. Maybe when the blinders fall off, what Deirdre sees is what is there.

"Unable to hide from anything that passes between them," she says. "In the same bed, moving to his brother's rhythm, hearing her little cries."

"Are you eating? You don't look as if you're eating."

"The food is slime."

"Would they let me bring you something?"

"What would you bring?"

"Anything. What would appeal to you?"

She looks off. I have lost her attention again.

"He can't even murder his brother without committing suicide." She giggles. "Who was it said that murder is just an extroverted form of suicide?"

She is no longer interested in my presence. She has her ciggies. Her slippers. She is anxious to get back inside her head, where her obsession clamors for her full attention.

I get up to leave. "Call me if there's anything you need," I say.

"Have you got any quarters?" Her voice has gone dull. "For the telephone."

I hand her all the change I have. On my way out, I give my name and phone number to the head nurse.

"Just in case," I say.

"You her next of kin?"

"Yes. I'm her Jewish sister."

"Rachel Levin, please."

"Speaking."

"Hi! This is Harvey."

"Harvey?"

"Candleman."

"Oh, how are you, Harvey? How'd the palimony suit go?"

"I lost. She got my house and my car."

"No kidding."

"I only lived with the broad two years. She had a good job, and she never gave it up all the time we were together. She wasn't entitled to a nickel."

My inclination in matters of this nature is always to side with the woman, even if it seems unfair. There is so much past injustice to women that needs to be redressed. It's the same equation I use with blacks—that huge balance sheet in the sky. However, I hold my tongue.

"We're gonna appeal," he says.

"Does she get to use the car and the house in the meantime?" I ask. She could wreck the car and burn down the house, though they're probably insured.

"Yeah. She's been living in the house. She has a kid. I was the one who had to move out, even though it's my house, in my name. How could I throw them out on the street?"

"I don't know. How did it happen?"

"I had to come to New York on business. When I got back, she had changed all the locks."

Naturally, this is only part of the story, his part, and because he and I are in the cheap-story business together, my mind begins to sketch in the rest. She was a woman spurned. The kid is his. He had met someone new, a New York woman. They met at a party in LA. She was flying back East in the morning. He persuaded her to stay another day. Then another. And another. They spent three days in bed, and if he weighed three hundred pounds then, what a bill they ran up for room service! Finally, she absolutely had to go back. He took her to the airport, and they held hands all the way. When he went back home, he told his live-in woman that it was *finito*, she would have to pack up and leave. How come? she asked. I feel we're not filling each other's needs. We gave it a good try. It was terrific while it lasted, but nothing lasts forever. You don't say? she said. Listen, he told her, I have nothing but good feelings for you. Part of me will always love you. Yeah? she said. We'll see about that!

"It's gonna cost me my shirt," he says. "I'm already on the verge of in hock. But I gotta fight this, not just for myself but for the principle."

"Everyone should have a cause," I agree.

"Listen, we gotta make a bundle. Did you give any thought to those story ideas?"

All the while we've been talking, I've been preparing my answer to this question. My answer is: I just can't see myself writing that sort of thing. I'm really sorry. But when I open my mouth to say it, something else comes out.

"I think I've worked out a scenario for the Santa Claus story,"

· 149 ·

I say. "It's not going to be a tear-jerker, though. It's a comedy."

"A comedy? I can't think of it that way. In the *Post* it was a really sad story."

"That's one of the things that's funny about it," I say. "What the papers do with the story." A feature story, human interest. Young newspaperman, first job, fresh out of school, acts tough but actually wide-eyed, idealistic, trusting, naive. Writes with tabloid-style bathos, anything for a tear. Pleads for reconciliation for sake of story. Ticks off husband's wonderful qualities. Streep and Garner find this hysterically droll, can't believe it, take him out for drinks to cheer him up. Streep fond of him, so downy-cheeked and sweet. In bar, cigarette dangling clumsily from corner of mouth, he tries to drink tough, falls down drunk almost at once. Streep gets him home, holds his head in bathroom, puts him to bed, tucks him in. Motherly. He falls in love with her, and when reconciliation does happen, he is heartbroken, tries to dissuade her, recounts husband's vile traits.

I tell Harvey this story, which I have been making up right here on the phone. "A light Christmas special," I say. "It's still just a treatment, a story outline, though I've done a little of the dialogue to give some idea of the flavor."

Pure lie. I haven't written a word. Until now, I never gave it a thought.

"Maybe you're right," he says. "Maybe it should be a comedy. When can we get together?"

"Give me a couple of days. I have to retype it, polish it. Call me Wednesday morning?"

As we disconnect, I hear a key turning in the door to my apartment. Lisa, although she has never actually lived with me, has always had a key. She has a key to my car, too, and keys to all the locks in the rented house. I have the key to her studio apartment, but I rarely use it. It's on the top floor, no elevator, 147 steps, and the entire building smells of disinfectant. When I finally stagger into Lisa's apartment, I am gasping for breath, filling my lungs with that dismally permeated air, and it takes me a while to stop feeling nauseated. I have never told Lisa this. She loves her little nest, and it would hurt her. The place is furnished largely with items gleaned from gutters, which Lisa is proud to have rescued from oblivion in the garbage dumps where they belong. I can barely bring myself to touch them.

Since my marriage, I have never had a lover who lived in a proper place like a grown-up person. Not, at any rate, during my sojourn in their lives. One of the things that attracts these gypsies to me is precisely what ultimately repels them, my air of stability and maturity. I appear to be so solid. I like to make dinner, and I have inner clocks and regular habits. I brush my teeth twice a day, I pay my bills, I return borrowed books. I am nearly always on time. I never leave home without being fairly certain that I have enough money *and* my American Express card. Though it has sometimes come close, my car has never run out of gas. In whatever ways I can control the circumstances of my life to ward off unpleasantness, disharmony, or discomfort, I do. On some level requiring almost no thought, my mind works in an orderly, organized fashion. I have sometimes been made to feel ashamed of this by those drawn to me because of it, as though my priorities are misplaced, as though my virtues somehow enslave me (although in fact they free me), and are indicative of a grounded soul, mundane values, as though only slobs are truly free and truly creative. What rubbish.

The door closes behind Lisa. She stands in the entry in her red wool businesswoman's coat and black pumps, her lower lip protruding vulnerably, a little girl on the brink of tears.

"What are you doing here at this hour?" I ask, since it is Monday, midmorning.

"I was fired."

"Take off your coat."

It took Lisa six months to find her job. She has been at it nearly a year, hating every minute of it. The lawyer for whom she has been working is a sixty-year-old egomaniacal misogynist, recently divorced by his much younger wife, his first and only marriage. He has done everything in his power, from the moment he understood that Lisa was never going to sleep with him, to make her life miserable. Blinking back tears, she takes off her coat. I hang it in the closet and then put my arms around her.

"I'm sure it's all for the best," I say, the good mother. But I'm not at all sure. Part of me is thinking that she ought to have learned how to handle the bastard, that discretion and diplomacy are two things she will have to learn and probably never will. Her strengths lie elsewhere. "What happened?"

"We had a fight about a sentence. A *sentence*. I corrected his grammar. He said I didn't know what I was talking about, that I write lousy briefs. I said I was the only literate person in that office, which happens to be true, that I was a professional editor. He said maybe that's what I should be doing, then. I said that the pleasure he takes in being sadistic to me is misplaced and to kindly direct it where it really belongs. He blew his stack. He said he didn't need a fucking psychiatrist in the office any more than he needed a fucking editor, that as a lawyer I wasn't even worth the fucking pittance I'd persuaded him to pay me. God, I wish I had a drink. Would you make me a Bloody Mary?"

"Sure."

She follows me into the kitchen, tears spilling down her pale cheeks. I know they are tears of rage more than of humiliation, and that it's only a question of time until she knows it, too.

"I then pointed out that he's been on my tail ever since I made it clear that he wasn't going to get a piece of it."

"You said that?".

"Words to that effect. All the way home I've been replaying the scene, going over the things I should have said, you know how it is."

She takes a handful of ice cubes from the refrigerator and drops them into the glass into which I am squeezing the lemon juice. It's the right amount of lemon juice that makes a good Bloody Mary. "So the next thing I know, he's writing out a check and handing it to me. 'Severance,' he says. 'You can leave at the end of the day.' I took the check and told him he could take the rest of the day and blow it out his ass."

"What was the sentence?"

"It was in a letter. The very first sentence. 'Enclosed are one contract with changes highlighted and several additional.' "

I laugh.

"It wasn't even the worst sentence in that letter. I mean, I *had* to call it to his attention, didn't I?"

"How else could you have lived with yourself?"

I stir the assembled perfect Bloody Mary vigorously and hand it to her. She gulps it down as though it is medicine. Because of her mother, she is not much of a drinker.

"The fucker," she says. "I'm gonna get him."

"There, there," I say.

"I'm gonna sue him for sexual harassment, the dumb shit."
No tears now. Lisa is finding her proper groove.

"I'll take you out to lunch to celebrate," I say.

We are back in the living room, Lisa with what remains of

her drink. Though she hasn't noticed, I'm not joining her in this pre-noon libation. I have to stay awake a little longer today. I have a treatment to write.

"You just talked your way out of a job," I say, "and I think I just talked myself into one."

"I really *am* going to take him to court," she says. "And I'll win, too. What d'you mean? What kind of job?"

I tell her about my telephone conversation with Candleman. "I'm going to get Meryl into Santa Claus's lap after all." Lisa's face brightens.

"You're going to do it?" she says. "Terrific. It's about time you did something real."

Lisa doesn't think my serious writing is real. She is like my father that way and it often makes me furious. If you can't make a living from it, it doesn't count. People often ask me if I make a living from my writing, as if it's any of their business. Over the past twenty years, I figure I've averaged $3.83 a day. "Yes," I lie to those people, "but I have to live on a tight budget."

"Nothing will come of it, of course," I say.

"Don't be so negative."

"I doubt if Candleman is a winner. He lost his palimony suit."

"Do it, *do* it!"

"I'm doing it. Maybe lunch isn't such a good idea. How about dinner instead?"

She squirms. "I can't," she says. "I'm busy tonight."

"What with?"

"I have a date."

Lisa's face has closed against me. I can tell that this is not just an ordinary date with one of her friends.

"With whom?"

"What's the difference?" she says.

"What do you mean, what's the difference? Why can't you tell me?"

She looks so uncomfortable. I can see her struggling to lie, but she doesn't know how to lie. I ought to let it go, to be gentle; she has just suffered such an indignity. But I am merciless. "Would you let me get away with that kind of evasiveness?" I ask.

"It's that guy I met at the tennis club. The one who took me out for a drink afterward."

In spite of myself, unreasonably, I feel a stab of pain, of rejection, and after the first pain there opens within me that old, familiar, festering wound, a dark, foul, stinking pit of roiling grief, despair, and rage.

"The hell with lunch *or* dinner," I say.

"What do you want from me?" she asks, spreading her hands, palms up. "It isn't as if we haven't talked about this and agreed that it isn't right for either of us, that it's over. You know I love you and always will. And I don't want to lose you. But what am I supposed to do?"

"I don't care what you do. Just don't come to me with all your little problems and griefs and then go skipping off to play with your *friends*. I'm not your fucking mother."

"I know you're not."

"No you don't. I'm the first one you come to when you're feeling small and bad and needy."

"I won't anymore, Rachel. Let's not do this. It's not as though we haven't talked this to death. I've always been honest with you. You've always known I want to get married. I want a baby."

It's true, she has said it, if not always, at least from time to time, and as though she meant it.

"I never believed you," I say. "You say a lot of things. If I thought getting married and having babies was truly your goal, I'd have been the first to give my blessings. I don't think any woman should go through life feeling that she's missed Life's Most Meaningful Experience."

"I'm not a lesbian," she whispers, and, cruelly, mirthlessly, I laugh.

"How would you know?" I ask. "Anyone who wants to be a poet, a lawyer, a copy editor, a singer, a professional softball player, a tennis champ, an entrepreneur, a lover of women, a femme fatale, a grown-up in the real world and a kid sitting on the stoop schmoozing with the neighbors and strumming a guitar can't begin to know what she's not."

"Oh, shit," she says, beginning to cry. "You'd think this was all me. You've been pushing me away for months."

Her crying makes me feel better. My rage begins to abate. But not my cruelty. I am relentless, though not without shame.

"Why don't you go home before I reduce you to a shambles? This is clearly not your day."

"You really are a shit."

"I know. Go away. I have to write something funny today."

She blows her nose, wriggles her feet back into her pumps, sets her mouth. Her nose is red, her hair in her eyes. She looks ugly to me, a stranger, someone I could never have wanted. There is a faint, unpleasant smell of her apartment in her clothing. What am I doing? She is at the door in her red coat. She turns to look at me, waiting for something. Anything.

"Try not to come back," I say, and she slams out. But I notice that she has not returned my keys. Always before, after scenes, though few of them have been this disgusting, she has offered to return my keys. Occasionally I have taken them, but never for very long. Her not thinking to return them is serious.

"Life is made up of interruptions."
  —W. S. Gilbert, Pinafore, *H.M.S. Pinafore*

For three days, my messages from the stars have been frantically concerned with my career. *Teammates may badmouth you to the higher-ups,* I was warned on Wednesday. *It's ambitious to get teammates on your side and accomplish a lot. That shows what a fine group leader you are.* On Thursday: *Put more effort into your job if you want to impress superiors. They might see you as a flash in the pan.* Today: *There are opportunities for progress if you're sensitive to the needs of co-workers.*

I am sitting at my typewriter feeling lonely and wondering who is living my life, since clearly I am not. Maybe it's Henry, also a Leo, who has a job with teammates, higher-ups, superiors, co-workers. Then whose life am I living? Or have I vacated it? Am I living only the lives of my friends, Margo's, Deirdre's? I am worried about Deirdre. To think of Deirdre at all is to worry about her. When I went back to the hospital to see her, she was gone. "Discharged," they said. But discharged where, into what? No, not another institution, not transferred, but set free, through the gates and back into the world. She has not appeared at *Tempus*, nor has Marcus heard from her. There is nowhere else for me to inquire and nothing I can do except wait for her to telephone me or show up at my door.

I have begun what I hope will be a new book. I don't want to get too excited about it yet because it may not take hold. But what a relief—no, relief is too mild a word—to find words forming, characters beginning to have some shape. I already have the first few pages. " 'Art is long,' Barbara thought, examining all 6'5" of him. 'Too long for this bed.' His feet extended far beyond it. While they were making love, she'd remembered reading somewhere that long-legged men made lousy lovers, long-legged women good ones. He had been slightly better than lousy."

Between yawns, I've been staring at these words for what seems like hours. This is to be a book about responsibility. I want to write about an irresponsible man like Peter, though I must make him very different from Peter, and a strong young woman's arrogant notion that she must take up his slack, bear the responsibility for both of them, and how this is not really possible, how this notion will almost destroy the woman while leaving the weak man intact. I want it to be a funny book and yet, of course, serious. But I am stopped by this idiotic beginning . Why have I named this woman Barbara? Where did she come from? Who names a character in a book Barbara? Yesterday, I read a review of a novel by a woman whose last name is Hospital, and this morning there was an obituary in the paper for a man named Isaac Paramount. I love names like these. But Barbara? I am waiting for this woman to tell me who she is and why she bears this name. Do her intimates call her Babs, Bobbie, Barb? Or is she the sort of woman who will always be called by every syllable, every letter, of her given name? These are decisions that I know must come from me, but so far I am incapable of making them. I have also been feeling uneasy about Lisa, to whom I haven't spoken since our scene three days ago. Do I owe her an apology? Of course I do. Has she not phoned me because she is angry? Hurt? Too happily involved with a new love? The tennis chap? Was that a success? Lisa's affairs with men have rarely come to much and I have often wondered why. She is attractive, and men are always giving her the eye, propositioning her. What, then? Is there some failure in bed? Is Lisa so different with men? Who is Barbara, what is she? She is certainly not Lisa, nor is she me. Should I call Lisa? If I do, will it be out of guilt or curiosity? Do I need to clarify this before I call? Nobody names their baby girl Barbara anymore. Jessicas, Stephanies, and Jennifers abound. Ellens and Susans have been used up. Three syllables are in, but not Barbara. My first summer at Camp Attica, there was a girl in my bunk named Barbara (pronounced with two syllables and only one r: Bobra). We became good friends because we were the only bad girls at camp. We were not yet aware that this camp ran on a system of honor; we were unacquainted with lofty moral fervor. I spent that summer learning it and by summer's end I was a thrillingly good girl. Not Barbara. She had integrity.

After three rings there is still no answer. Lisa's apartment is too small to require more than two rings to fetch her from its farthest reach. She picks up in the middle of the fourth ring and says hello in a furry voice.

"Did I wake you?" I ask, though it is close to noon. Ah, they've been screwing. Even as I speak, he is up there in her loft bed with its difficult vertical ladder, lying on his side, leaning on his left elbow, his head supported by his left hand, watching her naked at the phone.

"Yeah, but it's all right," she says. "I'm glad you got me up. It was dawn before I could fall asleep."

Just as I thought. I no longer feel like apologizing.

"How come?" I nonetheless ask.

"I don't know. I was up late watching television. I stayed up for Johnny Carson, but it was Joan Rivers. I love her." I wince, feeling even less like apologizing. "Oh, you," she says fondly, reading my silence. "You're such a fuddy-dud. Anyhow, after that I couldn't fall asleep. I started thinking about my life, about you, about everything. And then I was too miserable to sleep."

Feeling better, I say, "I'm sorry about the way I was. I've been feeling lousy about it."

"Oh, you were just being you. You can't help it. It doesn't mean anything."

"What do you mean, it doesn't mean anything?" I say, stung.

"I *know* you, Rachel. You seem to think I don't know you, but I do. I *really* know you. I know it's just your possessiveness. It hasn't anything to do with love."

"Yes, it does," I say. "My possessiveness has a lot to do with what I call love."

"Look, I haven't peed yet. I have to do that and have a cup of coffee before I can go into all this. Should I call you back? Or can we have dinner tonight and talk about it?"

We make arrangements for dinner, and I turn my attention back to the typewriter. Fritchie. Stanwyck. Tuchman. Walters. Barbarella. Barbie Doll. So the tennis player didn't work out. When I have more time, I must think about the relationship of possessiveness to love, particularly as it pertains to me. But the phone is ringing.

"Rachel? Harvey."

"Harvey?"

"Candleman. Jesus, Rachel. You remember me? The guy you had lunch with yesterday at the Pastrami Factory?"

"Of course. Sorry, Harvey." It was so nice of him, too, to have come downtown for lunch at four in the afternoon to my neighborhood, to which he agreed only after I assured him that there was a Jewish delicatessen nearby. This one he hadn't yet heard of, it being of recent vintage, and I don't know if it pleased him to sit in a booth beneath the varnished bagels and shellacked salamis that hang from the rafters, art deli, served by slim youths waiting for a chorus line to open up to them further uptown, instead of by rude, tired old Jews, professionals left over from Lindy's, whose careers have always been running from table to kitchen and back, their faces as sour as the pickles, but nonetheless with long-rehearsed senses of humor. I don't imagine Harvey Candleman considered the Pastrami Factory a serious delicatessen. I could have suggested the Second Avenue Deli and made him happy, but I hardened my heart. Why walk twelve blocks to please someone who needs me more than I need him, someone who loses palimony suits?

"You waiting breathlessly to hear what I have to say about the treatment?"

"Indeed I am."

"Didn't I tell you you could do it? I'm gonna sell this one. I don't see how we can miss."

I am surprised not to feel more pleased by this verdict, by this nod from the Real World. Perhaps later, if there is a fat check, I will be more seduced. I suspect it is within me to become fond of fat checks, even at this late date. But now that I am at the beginning of what may be a book, almost caught up in it, I know that one thing has nothing to do with the other. Being a short-order cook is a job, but it has nothing to do with creating a really splendid dinner. At this moment, I cannot imagine how I ever got involved in this nonsense with Candleman. It is absolutely clear to me that I will never sit with him in another delicatessen.

"You wanna work on a couple others meanwhile? I've got another half-dozen at least ideas we could kick around."

"Not right now," I say.

Furthermore, for all either Margo or I know, he is a pirate, a hit-and-run TV-treatment packager, in short, a thief. Has the word *contract* ever crossed his lips? Writers are a dime a dozen. Why split with them? Chances are they'll never know, since all they ever watch is Public Television.

"I've got one blockbuster idea that would be just right for you. I think it could work into a miniseries."

"There's this novel I'm doing, Harvey," I tell him, though it may not be true. "Maybe when I've finished it." What is true is that while I've only made it to page five, the book is becoming lodged in my head. What's more, it's sitting there on my desk, waiting for me. The thought of getting back to it makes my heart beat with both excitement and anxiety.

"A novel? What's it about?"

"Responsibility. Love and possessiveness."

"That's what it's *about*?"

"I think so."

"It doesn't sound too marketable to me," he says dubiously.

"It probably isn't. But it's what I have to do now."

He tells me he'll be back in touch in a few days.

The pride of possession, how primitive it is. I think of my father, whose original goal was to amass money, and who hated to spend any of it until he learned that it was the evidence of his wealth that gave him stature, so that he was forced, against his instincts, to spend some. His worth might have been measured by the size of his herd, the number of his wives, the length of his kingdom, the breadth of his land, his weight, his girth, anything that proved that he was a man of numbers, since it is in numbers that power lies. But dollars, themselves unseen, are too abstract, and the display becomes not the money but the symbols and the fruits of money: the Mercedes, the mansion and its furnishings, the paintings, the fine clothes, the expensive cigars. And the wife, with her jewels and furs. By these things shall ye know me.

The telephone is ringing.

"Mom? Jed. Are you working?"

"As a matter of fact . . ."

"Then I won't keep you. I just wanted to tell you that I talked to Henry and—"

"What's he doing home? Is he sick?"

"No, he's okay. You know, when I call him from the office at ten, he still hasn't left for work. The time difference."

"Right."

"He's hoping they can all come to New York this summer for a visit. Can you borrow a crib from anyone?"

"Jed! The summer is months and months away. Do we have to talk about this now?"

"Ginny and I split up."

"Oh, Jed, I'm sorry. Are you sorry?"

"I don't know. Yeah, I guess."

"Why, then?"

"She thought we were getting too intense. She said she wasn't ready for that."

"I don't blame her. It's only been a couple of months."

"Well, if she's not ready now she never will be. Why should I waste my time?"

"What do you mean, waste your time? Don't you enjoy being with her?"

"Not if she's not as serious as I am. Or as I'd like to be."

"Jed, you're impossible. Do you want to have dinner tomorrow and talk about this? I can't do it now."

"I have my poker game tomorrow. Not tonight?"

"No, I'm busy tonight. Day after tomorrow?"

"Okay."

As I hang up, the phone goes off in my hand.

"Rachel, Margo. How did you make out with Harvey yesterday?"

"He just called. He likes it."

"Good. Rachel, John has moved out."

"What do you mean, moved out?"

"He's left me." She begins to cry.

"Where did he go?"

"He rented a place on the Sound. In Connecticut. Stamford."
Long Island, on whose south shore Margo lives, juts noisily into the Atlantic Ocean, a barrier between the open sea and the mainland, creating that quieter body of water, the Long Island Sound. As the crow flies, it is no great distance across the Sound and to the south shore to Stamford, but as people must travel, in automobiles on clogged highways, John will be hours away, which is clearly his intention.

"An unfurnished place, the bastard," she sobs. "You know what that means."

"He'll have to sleep on the floor?"

"It means that at the very least he must have bought a bed,

a desk, a chair, a frying pan, a coffeepot. It means he's been doing this secretly for some time. He even moved his records out, so he must have bought a record player. He's been *planning* it. Oh, the cruel fucker, after all these years." She sobs. "I haven't slept in two nights."

"I'm sure it's temporary," I grope. "He'll miss you. He'll be back. What does he *say*?"

"What difference does it make? He'll say anything. He says he has to do it, at least for a while."

"There, you see. Margo, he really loves you. I'm sure of it."

"I know he does. Even he knows he does, some of the time. But he's British."

"What is that supposed to mean?"

"It means that having made up his mind he must go ahead with it. It's immutable. Rachel, you know how often I've said when he's been away how much I love it when he's not around, how peaceful I am, how much I can get done, what a pleasure it is that Danny and I can just have hamburgers for dinner?"

"Yes."

"How when I've been away at Woodlake for two months at a time I've never even missed him?"

"Yes."

"How often I've talked about his cruelty and how much better off I'd be without him?"

"Yes."

"Well, I can't stand it. I'm falling apart. I can't stand the pain. I want to die."

"It's pride, Margo. If you had left him . . ."

"I know, but I don't care what it is, I can't stand it. I hate myself, my dependency. I wept shamelessly when he was packing up his car. I tore at his clothing. I wailed at him. I was disgusting. I made him happy to be leaving me. I had no pride, not a shred of it."

What can one say? Time? Life is so stupid and messy?

"Do you want to come in to the city? Do you want me to come out there?"

"No. I have to work. And go to Waldbaum's. John said he'd be home for dinner."

"What do you mean?"

"It was the only way he could get away from me."

"Oh, well, then, if he's going to commute to this marriage. Maybe you could have an arrangement."

"I suggested that. I wouldn't mind his being away all week if I knew he was coming home weekends. If I knew we were *married*. But there *is* that woman."

"Is she here? There?"

"No, but she's coming. For a month."

"He told you that?"

"Last night. We'd had a lovely dinner. I made a roast duckling with apricots, it was heavenly. And we had a fire and listened to Schubert and then he told me and then we had brandy by the fire and we both cried, and then we went to bed and made love beautifully. This morning he was his usual cruel self until I said I was going to kill myself."

"He knows you'd never do that."

"Wouldn't I?"

"You're too much of a sensualist. You'd never willingly give up all those delicious little pleasures."

"Yes, I would. I just want the pain to end. But who knows, maybe it was blackmail. He got all tender and said he'd be back for dinner."

"So you can repeat the scene. And repeat it. Until it sinks

in. What are you going to do the month he's with her? How will you get through that? I don't think you should let him come home. I think you should get a lawyer."

"I can't, Rachel. Not yet. I have to grasp at any straw. I love him."

"Are you sure it's love?"

"I think so. He . . . he *defines* me."

She sobs, then apologizes for inflicting this on me and we arrange to talk again tomorrow.

I ought to disconnect this phone, I think, trying to get back to Art and Barbara. I should never have put a phone here in the first place, in this room, on my desk, next to my typewriter, next to Barbara. What was I afraid of? That I might write a page or two? She doesn't have to be Barbara. Maybe she isn't Barbara. Maybe she's Eleanor. Eleanor? No, she's definitely Barbara.

"Art stirred in his sleep, opened an eye, cocked it at her, and smiled. 'Hi,' he said, 'you know what I've been thinking?' 'You haven't been thinking, you've been sleeping.' 'What I've been thinking,' he said, 'is that you and me, we just might end up together.' End up together! The way some people think! Off into the setting sun, hand in hand, happy ending, movie over. It was his illiteracy that had drawn her to him in the first place, the very thing that made him so impossible. She was fascinated by the distancing that language made between them. He was unable to have a complicated thought because he hadn't the vocabulary for it, but when she told him one, an idea, a concept, he was stunned by her brilliance. He was far from stupid. He was shrewd, quick, direct, dishonest. He entertained her with stories for hours on end, colorful stories from his world, a world of streets, of struggle, of simple cause and effect, where one and one would usually add up to two, but not always. She marveled at how good-humored he was, and how primitive. He could not understand how someone as smart as she could know so little, could, in fact, survive from one day to the next. 'Never,' she said. 'We could never end up together. You will run out of stories. We will both lose interest.' 'What are you talking about? I'll never run out of stories, not as long as I'm breathing.' "

My fingers, flying over the keys, stumble to a halt. I look longingly at the telephone. Arthur and Barbara. What a pair! I may be stuck with them for the next two years.

My mother has come up from Florida for the weekend because it is the anniversary of my father's death. We have driven straight from La Guardia Airport to Mt. Hebron Cemetery. Not straight, exactly, because as usual I got lost. Like all New York City cemeteries, this one is huge, lodged amid a complicated webbing of highways, with their maze of connecting ingress-ways and egress-ways. For the living, just getting into the cemetery is a puzzle; it is so much easier to miss the entrance than to find it. But after a struggle, we are there. I park the car at a corner mausoleum marked ROSEN, my guidepost, and we walk along a footpath past half a dozen gravesites to one with a large gray marble stone on which is etched LEVIN, like the title page, in front of which are the smaller stones, the chapters, bearing the names of my father and of his mother and father, and my uncle Ben's first wife, Bertha. My mother stands at the foot of my father's grave and I stand beside her. We stare at his name. We have stood thus in rain and in snow, but more often it has been in sunlight, and there is a sense of tranquillity despite the constant drone of cars and trucks on the surrounding highways and the planes that fly so low, directly overhead, at regular intervals, only minutes apart. A little while ago, my mother was in one of them, flying directly over her husband, and I myself can never leave or arrive by plane without being nudged by the likelihood that I am part of a shadow cast over my father's grave.

My mother takes a small brown paperbound booklet from her purse and opens it to the page with the appropriate prayer and reads it silently, her eyes filling with tears. After a few minutes, the booklet goes back into the purse and a Kleenex comes out and my mother wipes her eyes and blows her nose. I would give almost anything to know what of their life together her memory summons to make the tears come, or whether she is weeping in a general way for the sadness of things that were and no longer are. I myself can cry about that at moments like this, but it feels like cheating. If I am going to cry at my father's grave, it ought to be about him, specific memories of him, and so I shuffle the snapshots in my memory album, searching for one that stabs with loss or wounds with tenderness, and I fail. The best I can do is recall how frightened of death he was, as powerful men and bullies are, and how puzzled and angry he was near the end of his life to have lost his faculties, and then I can pity him. Pity is entirely objective, though. That I cannot recall any moments between us that were dear can make me weep, but that is cheating, too, since it would be weeping not for him but for myself.

I cannot ask my mother what she is thinking.

So I stand, wondering at the scraps, the detritus, the leavings of a life, wondering what Henry and Jed will think when I die, if I am buried, if they ever come to my grave, and what whatever they think will have to do with me.

In the house that Lisa and I took that summer when we played at being a family, there was an enormously powerful attic fan that in hot weather was capable of cooling the house within minutes. To get to the fan switch, it was necessary to lean across a hillock of stored items carelessly stacked in front of it and around it by the owners of the house: an old rocking horse, boxes of toys, folders, a filing cabinet. On top of the filing cabinet was a shoe-polishing kit with a brush and rags stained with brown polish, and next to this was a square box neatly wrapped in heavyweight glossy paper. One night, reaching for the fan switch, I knocked the box off the cabinet. It fell with the weight and sound of a container made of metal, and what made it mysterious was that it was obviously a package that had never been opened. When I bent to retrieve it and replace it on the filing cabinet, I saw that it was labeled: ELFRIEDA WESLEY, MAY 12, 1974, POPLAR GARDENS CREMATORIUM. It was our landlord's mother I held.

Cremains. If there isn't a word for it, whatever it is, wait a minute.

"What's Bertha doing lying there next to him!" my mother says, as she always does. This plot originally belonged to Uncle Ben, my father's brother, whose first wife was Bertha. But Ben remarried after Bertha's death, and two years ago, when his second wife, Harriet, died, he bought a small plot in Miami, near where they had been living, and buried Harriet there. "I want to lie with Harriet," he told my father, and sold him what remained of the New York plot, a minor scandal, since Bertha was the mother of all his progeny.

"There's room for three more," my father told me at the time. "First come, first served."

My mother's eyes stray to the other side of my father, the place reserved for her. "There's not enough room there for me," she says. "I don't know where they're going to put me." There really doesn't seem to be any room, but they must know what they're doing. "Just see that they don't put me in there standing up. Or worse, on my head."

"I won't let them do that," I say.

"You'll probably never come here," she says, lighting a cigarette. My father must be spinning down there; he hated her smoking. "You and your goddamn cigarettes!" he is screaming. "Even *here*? I'm surprised you haven't got a scotch and soda in your other hand, fa Chrissake."

"You only come now because I need you to drive me," she says. I try to imagine myself standing here without my mother, crying over the thin strip of space on the other side of my father. Her death can't be far off, but I cannot imagine it. She has such vitality, what could kill her?

"You'll probably outlive me," I say.

"Don't say it! Don't even think it!"

"Of course I'll come," I say. "And you know David will." My brother, David, is a good and dutiful son. He would be here now except that he has to go to an office to do his work and I don't.

"Yes, David will come."

"When did you last go to Grandma's grave?" I ask. Her

parents, whom she loved, are buried in another cemetery not too far from this one, where Queens turns into Brooklyn.

"I used to go there religiously, with Uncle Phil," my mother says, sadly. Uncle Phil is her brother. "I haven't gone in years."

"Let's go there now," I say. "Do you know the way?"

"I think so. You take Queens Boulevard. I think I'll remember where to turn. There was a diner. Uncle Phil liked to stop there for coffee afterward. He loved diners. You know how he is about food, the worse the better."

My mother directs me unerringly to the other cemetery, and within half an hour we are there, standing in the sunlight, bees droning around our heads, the voices of children playing nearby. Grass and weeds grow tall on the graves, obscuring the stones, but for some reason this comforts me.

"Look at that!" my mother says. "All these years we've been paying for perpetual care. They'll hear from me!"

She does not cry for her parents, but I do. I never knew my grandfather, but I cry for Grandma. I don't have to be here to do it. Two or three times a year I wake in the night and invoke her, and invariably I cry. She has been dead for more than twenty years, but I have her so well memorized, in such detail, her earlobes, the pores in her nose, her spatulate fingers and capable arms, her long, dark hair shot with gray, knotted in a bun, her rimless eyeglasses that pinched the bridge of her nose, leaving twin marks, the way her eyes twinkled, dark and happy, and oh, she was a woman sure of herself, and even the smell of her skin I remember, and her voice. She is so well remembered that bringing her to mind brings her right into the room with me. When I die, she will truly die; there will be no one left, then, to call her back.

How stupid it suddenly seems to be standing on this rented

space just because the boxes that hold their dust and bones are planted here. If there is a spirit, a soul, and who am I to insist that there is not, it would hardly loiter here waiting for callers, in this place that had nothing at all to do with its life. If it was going to hang around somewhere on earth, it seems likely that it would choose the place that in life claimed it most, its attention, its engagement, its interest, its love. My grandmother would be in a kitchen of perpetual Passover, my father on Seventh Avenue and Fortieth Street. What would I choose to haunt? I think hard, but there is no single place that claims me, though some I have loved more than others. Perhaps it would be a person, then, and not a place, and if so, whom would I choose to tag along with? But there is no ready choice of a person, either, and this frightens me. How episodic my life has been. I have had no enduring love. Two sons, a mother, an almost-lifelong friend, Rebecca; the rest have been in and out, central during their span of years, peripheral or gone with their departures. Does Deirdre belong on my list? I don't even know where she is. No, I wouldn't choose to haunt her; it is she who haunts me.

Borges said, "We are made for art, we are made for memory, we are made for poetry, or perhaps we are made for oblivion. But something remains, and that something is history or poetry, which are not essentially different."

Standing here, I think of oblivion and of all the perished minds that dot this strange cluttered landscape, each with its unique warehouse of knowledge and memory, each with its talents and propensities, its triumphs and failures, and I wonder how much of it remains for the living, how much is lost forever, and whether all that loss is a waste or a blessing.

And then I think of the sadness of all the mildewed books

moldering in rented summer homes, books by forgotten authors whose names were familiar in their own brief time, the thirties, the forties, even the fifties, and of how little the world would have been deprived if instead of writing those books they had opened tea rooms or dry-cleaning establishments. MacKinley Kantor alone wrote about thirty books. I once mentioned this to Margo and she said, "I went to school with his son. He was the handsomest boy in twelfth grade."

Thoughts such as these make it hard to go on until I remind myself that, viewed from this long perspective, most lives are futile, and that one kind of futility is no worse than another, except that if you aim higher, you may fall farther. It takes some arrogance to write a book, to risk it.

Once, during a protracted period of low self-esteem when I was unable to work, Deirdre wrote to me. "You are all it has," she said of the work. "It has nobody else, and never had anybody else. If you deny it hands and a voice, it will continue as it is, alive, but speechless and without hands. You know it has eyes and can see, and you know how hopefully it watches you. I am speaking of a soul that is timid but that longs to be known. There is always danger fear will enter in and begin withering around."

Fear comes withering around every time I sit down at the typewriter.

"If you hate it so much," my mother once said to me when I tried to explain it to her, I forget why, "why not be a woman of leisure and just enjoy life?"

Why not, indeed?

"All right, let's go," my mother says. We have visited our dead. We have had our long and short thoughts.

The loneliest place in the world is in front of a typewriter. *Fair,* says the message for the day in this year's *Total Horoscope for Total People. Get the most out of love, sex, marriage, your career. Be ready for financial opportunities. Other key words: Plan, Get Ahead, Recognize, Know When, Success.* Yuppie words. Irresistible.

Today's message also says, *Get an early start, especially you creative people. Put more effort into work. Good for thinking up new ideas.*

Thinking up. My problem may be that I think down. Ideas, thoughts, reside in the top two inches of my head, from whence they slide into my mouth, where I taste them. If I find them palatable, though my taste is sometimes unreliable, I either speak them or send them down to my fingers to be punched out on this machine.

I try to get an early start not only in *fair* weather but in foul. *Foul* is not in the horoscopic lexicon. *Disturbing* or *disquieting* are as inclement as they get, and no matter what they tell me, so far today has been *Disturbing.* I know what I want this new book to be about, but so far this week I have thrown away seventeen beginnings and an equal number of first persons, females, all of them stick figures.

The cat jumps onto my lap, something she rarely does, and from there, after letting me feel her purring for a minute, onto the desk. She would like to be on the typewriter, since that is where I have been staring, but the stack of paper next to it is more tempting, and she settles onto that.

"You are my best friend, Colette," I tell her. There are things I say to her when we are alone that would make me sick if I heard anyone else say them. But they are not lies. Although like all cats, Colette ignores me most of the time, no day goes by without some moment when she looks at me with love, or tells me that she is happy. Her fur is soft and clean and silky, and just touching her relaxes and reassures me. I often wonder, now that she is growing old, what I will do when she dies. Most of my friends have cats, and they assure me that what I will do, and almost immediately, is replace her. But I am not sure. Colette is my first cat, and we go back thirteen years to my first visit to Woodlake Center, where I acquired her from Deirdre. Colette has aged more felicitously than Deirdre.

I'd never had a cat. I didn't like cats. Deirdre had seven of them with her at Woodlake. She tried to keep them in her studio, which was a ten-minute walk from the farmhouse where our bedrooms were, but the cats were always slipping out and pursuing her, so that she was constantly carrying them back and forth, worrying about them, feeding them, hunting the absent ones, and talking about their characters and the little dramas in their lives, not in a boring way—Deirdre could not have been boring even if she set her prodigious mind to it. Rufus, Minnie, Cedric, Hector, Sparrow, Jonquil, and Gray. Then one day, coming out of the liquor store in the new mall, she spied Colette shivering in the New England November, small and starved and abandoned.

"I tried not to see her," Deirdre told me, "but it was no use. I had already seen her. I asked in all the shops. Nobody knew her, she belonged to nobody. What could I do? I picked her up and put her inside my coat. She was a wee bit of a t'ing, she weighed nothing at all."

She was a beautiful little calico with big green eyes and a pink nose and a snowy breast and a way of sitting quietly, looking up at you with polite and infinite patience. She hardly ever spoke, and when she did it was in a nearly inaudible little voice, at least to my imperfect ears. She relied on those bright, steady, gemlike eyes, which she fixed on you, waiting, sitting with her little white feet planted so neatly.

"Aloof," Deirdre said. "She is the most aloof cat I have ever known. But she really takes to you, Rachel. She is always getting into your room, isn't she?"

I would find her asleep on the foot of my bed every night at bedtime. I would pick her up and toss her back into Deirdre's room, two doors from mine. Until one night when I was already in bed before I realized that she was there. I had grown so accustomed to seeing her there that I no longer saw her. I was too comfortable and close to sleep to get up and put her out. She slept all night on my feet, and in the morning she looked at me with something meltingly like love in her eyes and purred. How pretty she was, how soft and silent. Her fur coat was delightful to touch. She had been so still and warm and unintrusive all night, almost as though she'd been holding her breath, promising me.

"You really ought to take her, Rachel, keep her, you know. She's an excellent cat. And she has chosen you." In some small corner of my psyche, I was flattered and half in love.

"All right," I said, and I named her Colette.

"Colette!" Deirdre said, horrified. "She is *not* a Colette. She is a cold *Scandinavian* cat."

But this was after she was my cat and Deirdre knew that the

bonds were irreversibly forged, firm enough for her to confess, with her wicked smile, that she had *put* Colette in my room every night because Colette needed a person and I needed a cat. "You didn't know it, Rachel, you might have gone to your grave never knowing it, but what your life lacked was a cat, and aren't you pleased that I saved you from that? To say nothing of finding the absolutely right cat for you, even though her tail is a disgrace!"

Oh, Deirdre.

Not long after that, Cedric disappeared. He was a big, noble, dark gray tom, part Maine coon, with a proud and bushy tail. Deirdre took to walking the roads and paths that wound through the Center's hundreds of acres, crooning Cedric's name. It was winter and cold, with snow banked six feet high along the plowed roads.

"I don't want him to be cold and frightened," Deirdre said, her face lined with worry. I told her that he was such a smart, important cat that he had probably found better lodgings elsewhere, but she was not convinced. She advertised his loss on the local radio station, and soon calls began coming to the Center's office claiming that a cat fitting Cedric's description had been seen near the intersection of High and Union, or three miles north near the Turkey Glen apartments, and I would drive Deirdre there and we would both get out of the car and wander about calling "Cedric" into the snow, into the twilight, into hushed landscapes, she in her woeful Irish voice and I, self-conscious and dubious, in my New York voice. Then, one afternoon, a woman called to say that she had Cedric in her kitchen, and would we come and get him? But he wasn't Cedric. This same false Cedric began appearing in kitchens all over town until, finally, in the fourth kitchen, this false Cedric, similar to but not at all the true Cedric, made his claim on Deirdre.

"I suppose I'm meant to take him," Deirdre said. "What else can it mean, his turning up this way, waiting for me to come and fetch him?" And so the false Cedric became a member of Deirdre's collection. The real Cedric was never found. He was too smart for that. He must have sensed what was to come, what came only a few weeks later.

"Do you remember, Rachel, I think I told you, what Germaine said to me once? She said to me, 'Deirdre, you must make up your mind, are you a writer or are you a woman who keeps cats?' I have been thinking and thinking about what she said, and she was right. I am a woman who keeps cats."

"Why can't you be both?"

"I have not written more than a paragraph in six weeks." She was agitated and distant, and there were circles beneath her eyes. "I think I can no longer," she said, "go on being a woman who keeps cats."

"How can you not?"

"I've made an appointment with Dr. Fletcher for tomorrow morning at ten. The problem is, Rachel, that I cannot carry them all. I will need your help."

"What do you mean?"

"I am going to have them put away. They will be very peaceful."

I was appalled. "I won't be a party to it," I told her. "You will have to do it yourself."

"But how?"

"I don't care. It doesn't have to be a massacre. You can slaughter them piecemeal."

"Don't talk to me that way, Rachel!"

"They're living creatures, Deirdre. You can't offer them up as sacrifices to your muse, or whatever it is you think you're doing. How can you?"

"It isn't that, Rachel," she said, averting her head, her hands fidgeting nervously. "It's that I can't. Any longer. Take care of them."

It wasn't until much later, when I knew her better, that I understood her desperation, so I went on and on, saying everything I could think of to talk her out of this madness. She refused to be budged. My arguing only strengthened her resolve. "With or without your assistance, Rachel, it is going to be done. But I would really appreciate your help."

I don't know why I finally consented, what it was that convinced me. I think it was that she really might need me not just for my car, for transportation, but for something more important. And I was sure that at the last moment she would not be able to go through with it.

She had the cats packed and ready, two to a cardboard carrying case, when I came in the morning to pick her up. Her face was clenched and grim; she was a woman possessed.

"Not the false Cedric, too," I said angrily, recognizing his striped gray paw poking through one of the breathing holes. "I'm going to let him go. He was managing fine without you, and he isn't really your cat, anyway. You have no right to kill him."

"Stop that, Rachel! You don't know what you're saying. He was cold and lost and frightened, and I cannot bear the thought of it."

"Someone will take him in."

"No one will take him in."

Dr. Fletcher put them all, as the euphemism insists, to sleep. Deirdre stayed with each one in the room where they were injected until she was sure that they were dead—safe, she said, on some warm, soft cloud. And not afraid. And when we went outside to the car, she was no longer a woman who kept cats.

"Life is simply one damned thing after another."

—F. W. O'Malley

"There's someone else," Lisa says.

Surprise.

"Who is he?"

Why is that the first question? What do I care who he is? He is someone anonymous, anyone. Why must I give him shape and voice? What possible difference does it make if his name is Fred or Irwin, if he is Lisa's age or mine, if he's a doctor, sailor, certified public accountant, if his hair is brown or green? What really matters is that there is this sudden familiar sensation between my rib cage and groin, an emptiness as heavy as a medicine ball.

Whatever became of medicine balls? Does anyone still remember them besides me?

"It's not a he," Lisa says.

Along with the first blow, here is an even heavier one. During our five years together, Lisa has been telling me that she must act on what she believes she has overcome: her fear of loving men. My rational self would eventually have accepted that, in spite of my Other Self, my selfish, possessive, arrogant, jealous, hateful self, which refuses to accept any reason for me to be forsaken. To be replaced by another woman is unforgivable. There is no good practical reason for it.

A medicine ball was like an oversized basketball covered in some kind of wrinkled animal skin and filled with sand. I think it was sand. It weighed a ton. I don't know why it was called a medicine ball, except that if you managed to pick it up and throw it, or even worse had it thrown at you and you caught it, you would get a hernia, possibly a few broken ribs. Yet large, hairy men used to stand, usually on beaches, and throw this monstrous thing at each other, grunting when throwing, oofing when catching.

"Oof," I say, then struggle for words, not yet ready to drop the ball. "But I thought you wanted to have a 'meaningful relationship,' to coin a phrase, with a male person."

"I know," she says, shamefaced.

"Have you any idea how many times you've told me you weren't a lesbian?"

"As many times as you told me that neither were you. What difference does it make?"

"All the difference," I say, wanting to punch her.

"I don't see why. You and I have been over for months."

"That's no reason for you to fall in love with someone else," I say in a loud voice.

"You've been doing with me what you said you did with all the others. Pushing me away because you can't make the break yourself. Push, push, push. Then you carry on like a maniac when the person you've been pushing finally gets pushed."

Push is such an ugly word.

"Are you going to carry on like a maniac with me?"

"Why not? Is it Marlene?"

She nods. She has been mentioning Marlene, with whom she plays bridge, with increasing frequency. I have really known.

"But she's neurotic and unattractive and silly and pathetic," I say. "Also penniless."

"Oh, stop it!" she says. "I love her."

Oof.

"What's there to love about her?" I am honestly incredulous, truly curious.

"She's *really* smart." She manages to say this both emphatically and feebly. "Really smart" is something Lisa is always assuring me everyone she knows is, and it isn't always true. Marlene is quick of tongue, but it took only an hour in her company for me to know that her quick tongue would never say anything to stretch my mind in any direction. In that hour, she mentioned her "shrink" six times and talked mainly about her lousy luck with lovers. She wore baggy green and khaki camouflage trousers, calling attention to what it was she was hoping to hide. We were at Madison Square Garden, watching women's tennis. Marlene was there with a date, a tall, thin married woman who was bored with the tennis and wandered off with a woman named Dutch, a third member of Lisa's bridge group and an old friend of both hers and Marlene's.

"Damn that Dutch!" Marlene kept muttering, certain of Dutch's perfidy, her eyes glinting behind the thick lenses of her glasses, her eyebrows beetling. "She always does this. She's such a shit."

I felt like an idiot being there at my age, or at any age, in the middle of such silliness, actually saying to Marlene, "This is Madison Square Garden, where could they go? They're probably getting a Coke." Peripherally, I was aware that Lisa was showing off for Marlene. We had brought picnic suppers, and Lisa was a little high on the good white wine she'd supplied. She was growing more and more raucous. "Way to go," she kept shouting whenever someone made a good shot. I am of the school that believes you don't shout at tennis matches. If you want to shout, go to Shea Stadium.

"Good, I'm glad you've finally found someone smart," I say.

"Oh, all right, she's not as smart as you," Lisa says angrily.

"Nobody is, right?"

"Plenty of people are, but not Marlene. I suppose she's better in bed?"

"Maybe," Lisa says, and I can tell from the way her eyes light at the thought of Marlene in bed that it's true. Lisa and I went stale months ago, quit entirely weeks ago. So why am I carrying on, as she says? I simply can't bear to be supplanted, especially by someone like Marlene. I think of Margo and John and all my good advice to her about love and jealousy. Is this pain I feel jealousy? Or is it simply rejection, wounded vanity, my poor, tiny, crumbling ego? Or the way I cannot bear to have anything change? End, yes, but not change. Lisa and I have been so intimate, intimate enough to have had vicious battles, though far fewer and less violent than those with her predecessors. Lisa's strength is her ability to see to the heart of my confused anger or despair and to say exactly the right words so that I will have to see it, too, and become rational. In my regressive emotional states, she knows me better than anyone else ever has, except for Dr. Dresher all those years ago, during my breakdown.

But she knows me less well in my mature, perhaps more subtle states. Soon after Lisa and I began, I awoke one night crying for my father, who had died a few months earlier. I cried, watching him die, after watching his struggle not to die. This was only the second time I cried for him, and perhaps it would be the last. I had told Lisa so many stories about how he had dominated my childhood with his tyranny, about his bullying and anger, his arrogance and overweening egocentricity, his obsessive pursuit of money and his cruel use of it, his selfishness, his cutting attempts at humor that never failed to wound, and his rare moments of charm that had nothing to do with anyone else, or any feeling for anyone else, but were extensions of himself and his vanity—he was always at the center of his life. All this I had told her, but perhaps I failed to tell her the rest. I tried to that night, explaining ambivalence, how it was possible also to love such a man, even while you feared and hated him, if he happened to be your father and so much of your life had been entwined with his, albeit blighted, perhaps irretrievably, by him. I talked about habit, and how, when he was dying and I was watching him do it, for the first time I could pity him, and how shocking that was for me. It was a lion dying there, a lion who had always been true to his nature. He was in a coma, gasping for breath, and he did not look like an old man, or a lion; he looked like a little boy, desperate and bewildered, and I understood what I never before knew in my gut: what his childhood had been and how he had had to fight and claw his way into the only kind of manhood and survival he could forge for himself.

But there was no way to explain these nuances to Lisa, and I gave up, suspecting even then, in that beginning, that there were places where we would never be able to meet. She thought his death should be a relief to me, as in so many ways it was. But in the night I saw him unconnected to me even as I saw how much of him there was in me. Because it was finished, I held his whole life in my hands and saw it complete, all its struggle, its ugliness, its triumphs and successes, the self-pity, the self-indulgence, the meanness of spirit. Yet once he had played the violin, and occasionally there was a word he loved and savored for its own sake. "Mellifluous," he would say, rolling the word slowly over his tongue, like the honey it described. "That's a good word. Mellifluous, a mellifluous word." He was intelligent and ignorant, and who knows what he might have been if he could have been other than he was, if his father had not been ineffectual, a *schlemiel*, and his mother had not been a virago, a shrewd, illiterate peasant; if he had not been small and frightened once, and lived in a mean ghetto, and been the eldest son and had had to work and earn money from the moment he could walk. Oh then, that night, my heart broke for him, and how I wept.

"But you came out of the same thing," Lisa said, "only in reverse. Your mother so passive and ineffectual, your father the tyrant. And you're not like that. Only a little."

"There was more available to me," I said, "because of his money. I read." Money allowed me time, freedom from chores and struggle. The books came from the library and gave me other worlds, other possibilities, choices. They gave me heroes to identify with, an occasional heroine, though there were too few heroines, and those found their fulfillment usually in marriage, or in death at the stake. It was the heroes I identified with, because they vanquished enemies, they triumphed over the forces of nature and evil, they completed cattle drives, they became great pianists. They had power, like my father, and did not have to submit, like my mother.

But all this is past. In this present, Lisa is trying to explain why she loves Marlene, and I am foolishly trying to understand.

Marlene, when I first heard about her, was presented to me as an "independent" filmmaker. Later I learned that what she makes are porno flicks with all women players. For feminists. There can't be too much of an audience for feminist porn, because Marlene is always broke. Lisa says this is because Marlene won't compromise, will only do what she believes in. It was once even suggested that I try writing scripts for Marlene.

"Watching her direct, seeing what she can do with lighting, how she handles the actors," Lisa says, "something happens to me. Her authority. She's so sure of herself when she's working. She's a real pro."

"Then why at age forty is she doing such shit?"

"At least *she's* working! It's a living. And she does it very well, as you couldn't be expected to know since you're too snobbish to see any of her films."

"It's not snobbishness," I say, too proud to tell her that I *am* working.

"And it's expensive to make films. It's not like writing books. If she had financing, she'd make more serious stuff, but she refuses to spend her time groveling for funding."

"All right, that's enough," I say. "You've convinced me." I want her to stop before she tells me that Marlene is an artist. If Lisa is such a fool, then what am I? How stupid falling in love is. It's done with trick mirrors, a sideshow attraction in a carnival; it has nothing to do with love, which should be un-alloyed, which should be true. Falling in love is embarrassing and shameful, and I vow that I will never do it again unless I can do it without illusion, with honesty. If I ever do fall in love again, I promise myself, it won't be with someone I am instantly attracted to. It will be with someone I've known for a long time, someone I *like*.

"Well, I just wanted you to know," Lisa says.

"Okay, I know. Good-bye."

"What do you mean, good-bye?"

"I mean I'm leaving now. Good-bye."

"I suppose you think you're never going to see me again, the way you never saw Dibbs again."

"Why would I want to see you again?"

"Because we love each other, and that's for life."

Ah. She sees us settling comfortably into one of those younger woman/older woman friendships. She will take care of my legal affairs, drive me to airports, carry my luggage if my back goes. I will invite her to an occasional party with my more glamorous friends, lend her money in a pinch, supply her with an occasional dollop of the questionable wisdom gleaned from all my years, be a surrogate mother to her.

But now that we are no longer lovers, I am not going to want to hear about her life with Marlene and all its problems, which I know will be unremitting. As for my life, I cannot imagine that there will be anything in it that I will want to discuss with her. I know that if we meet for occasional lunches, there will be less and less to say to each other until the struggle to find a subject is not worth the bother.

So I shrug and say, "We'll see," and I leave, still carrying the medicine ball.

"I don't know why I go on seeing this woman," Margo says, "except that she's kind and decent."

"Not the worst qualities to find in an analyst."

"She's not an analyst, she's a therapist." Margo has been seeing her for almost two weeks. "She doesn't understand a word I say to her. She thinks writing is a harmless little hobby, something to keep me busy and out of mischief."

The burning stub of a cigarette lies among the remains of all the others Margo has smoked during this visit. The smell is vile. I get up to empty the ashtray.

"She told me to squeeze ice cubes when the pain gets really bad."

"Squeeze ice cubes? What did she mean?"

"I think she meant that I should hold some ice cubes in my hand and squeeze them."

It isn't nice to laugh at someone's analyst, especially someone as desperate as Margo, but how can I help it? Soon Margo is laughing, too.

"She sounds more like a witch than an analyst," I say.

"Therapist. Displacement, I imagine. An outer pain for an inner. Why can't I just talk to you? Isn't that what you're for?"

"You do talk to me. Endlessly."

"The worst part is the sexual jealousy."

"I know," I say though I'm not sure that's the very worst part. It's bad enough, though. "When Dibbs fell in love with someone else, I almost drowned in jealousy. Despite the fact that I was trying to rearrange my life in a less destructive way." I've been feeling a little of that with Lisa, too.

But with Dibbs it was more than sexual jealousy. It was a jealousy that encompassed nearly everything: the loss of the beloved as object and the loss of my loved self as subject, and especially of finding myself replaced by a total stranger, edited out and left to wander in some solitary void with all the other extraneous material that hadn't quite worked out.

"The worst of it is that I know just how you are when you're making love with her," I even said to Dibbs the last time I saw her, "what in the heat of passion you say in that extreme way reticent people like you tend to speak, and in that marvelous breathy voice of yours."

"I don't have a marvelous voice," Dibbs said, frowning at my invasion of their bedroom. "It has no range."

"You gasp," I persisted, "and then you moan, 'I've never been in love before.' "

She blinked and gave a startled little jump. "I *never*," she said, "said that to *you*."

She had plunged a dagger through my heart. I was desolated, annihilated. *I never said that to you*, and the look, almost of hatred, when she said it, said that she had never said it. What a theft! The jewel in the crown of our love affair, one of the rare, truly precious treasures in my memory chest.

"Oh, Indian giver," I wailed. "Go away. I'll never be able to see you again. Go."

It did not take too much persuasion, since that was what she had come to tell me she was doing. Still, tears came to her eyes. She, too, wanted us to be friends, but I knew we could never be friends, and I truly did not want to see her again, not like that, not unless she were to come back one day and say, Ah, it's you I love and have always loved and there can never again be anyone else and I have stopped drinking. She told me that she would miss me, she said it with convincing anguish, but I am sure she never missed me; she had already forgotten me. That sad farewell left me infinitely sadder, infinitesimally wiser.

How often have I brooded on *I never said that to you*. It reminded me once again that what we think we share with another is rarely the same for both of us, not truly shared. I may keep a memory like a snapshot to be taken out, fondled, gazed upon, recreating the emotions and sensations of the original so that I can relive it, repeat it, prevent the moment from dying. Yet you may have thrown the memory completely away, as indeed you did, Dibbs. And there am I, intricately bound to you in my memory and your inextricable role in it, while in your life, your mind, that memory, the me-with-you of that past, does not, even with alterations, any longer exist. And what a fool I feel, and how lonely!

"Sexual jealousy is a disease," I say to Margo, "but what's worse is finding out how replaceable we are."

Margo considers this for a moment. "*I'm* not replaceable," she says indignantly. "There's only this one unique me."

I smile, envious of that part of her ego that seems so substantial.

"Well, various people have replaced me in the course of my long life."

"That's your sad little conception of what they've done. They may have changed the cast of characters in their little dramas, but they haven't replaced *you*. You're irreplaceable."

"Thanks," I say, unconvinced. "The worst part for me is how memory is betrayed."

Margo stabs out a cigarette and instantly lights another. No matter which side of her I'm sitting on, the smoke blows my way, as if I magnetize the air currents, and I've begun to feel as I did when I was smoking my own cigarettes, every breath a labor. The windows are all open; there is nothing I can do. I can't even comment, she looks so bad. Her eyes are smudged with sleeplessness, her hair is a mess, the dark roots showing. She has lost weight, and her arms are so thin you can see her skeleton lying in wait. I have a moment of fear.

"It would be the worst stupidity to die for John," I say. "You don't even like him."

"It's true, there's a lot I don't like about him. But then he can be so wonderful. *You* know."

"It's not having him that you can't bear. You need him like a good, flattering mirror, to help you stay in love with yourself."

"What's the difference," she moans, "as long as I need him?"

"He's not the object of your love, you are. He's the instrument. You can always get another instrument."

Her eyes light up, considering, then darken. "I'm too old," she says.

"You're not too old. At forty-six I was having the time of my life."

"Besides, it can't be just anyone."

"No, of course not."

"An inferior lover just won't do." She sighs. "And an equal man is hard to find."

"At least you'll settle for equality," I say. "I've always wanted my lover to be someone I could rise to."

"Who, Lisa?" Margo asks, lifting her eyebrows. "Peter?"

"No, they were different, something else."

"Peter bored you. And Lisa, too, sometimes."

"Not too often. Anyway, as any good witch will tell you, nobody is ever good enough when you can't love yourself properly."

Margo sighs. She doesn't want to talk about me. Neither do

I. I don't much want to talk about her, either. We've been having this conversation over and over and I'm sick of it and of the role I always have in it, so sententious, so understanding, so platitudinous. But I can sympathize with Margo's obsessiveness. She's sick with it. As with any sickness, we must go through it.

"Part of the problem," I say, "is that he's still coming in and out of the marriage, at his convenience. And being alternately loving and tender, or cruel and angry. You don't do anything but respond to him. You're a yo-yo. Christ, Margo, where's your rage? How can you go on playing the poor starving waif begging a crust of kindness?"

"I have no choice."

"Where are all those other men you're always finding?"

"Nobody looks at me twice anymore. They're only attracted to me when I'm happy. I'm only happy when I *feel* attractive. And I only feel attractive and happy when *John is in place!*"

Mercifully, the phone rings. I snatch it up and, impatient with Margo, bark into it. Someone says hello.

"Who is this?" I say.

"What do you mean who is this? It's your mother."

"Why are you calling now?" Her time to call is Saturday morning at ten o'clock. "Is anything wrong?"

"It's a wise child who knows her own mother's voice. Nothing's wrong. I just felt like talking to you. Are you busy? Am I interrupting anything?"

"No. My friend Margo is here, but I can talk."

"Who's Margo?"

I've told her a dozen times who Margo is. She never remembers who any of my friends are. "The one from Long Island,"

I say, grimacing at Margo. I mouth "my mother," and she gets up to go into the kitchen for another drink. "The one who wrote that book I gave you, *The Courting of Justice*. About the woman judge."

"Who falls in love with the Hell's Angel rapist?"

"Well, she falls in love with all the felons who come before her. Not the misdemeanors."

"That book was pure pornography," my mother says.

"It's about justice."

"So *you* say."

"What's new with you?"

"Nothing. What could be new at my age?"

"Are you getting out? Have you been able to get to the club?"

"I played golf a couple of times this week with Frieda. But Tuesday she had an accident."

"What happened?"

"I was shooting out of a sand trap, and the idiot went up on the green to hold the flag for me. I had a perfect straight shot, though too long, right at her, and she twisted to get out of the way and fell and broke her hip."

I remind myself that my mother's eighty-fourth birthday is coming up, and knock wood.

"Poor thing," she says, "they don't know how long she'll have to be in the hospital. They had so much trouble putting in the pin, she's so brittle."

"I hope you're not feeling guilty."

"Why should I feel guilty? Who asked her to hold the flag? Am I Arnie Palmer? She shouldn't have been on the green at all. Of course I feel terrible, but not responsible."

"How's Uncle Phil?" I ask.

Uncle Phil lives two condominiums away and has been one of our topics for the last few months, since his wife, Geraldine, left him.

"I'm leaving on account of my blood pressure," Geraldine told my mother.

"What? Phil elevates it?"

"He's impossible. He never wants to do anything, see anybody. All he does is go through boxes of yellow papers a hundred years old, straightening out what he calls his affairs. When did he ever have affairs? I'm leaving him to save my life."

"What can you expect of second marriages?" my mother said to me, ignoring all the successful ones she has known. I reminded her that they were married for at least twenty years.

"Twenty-two," my mother said.

"I think he's relieved Geraldine is gone," she tells me, "if he notices at all."

"She must have nagged him," I say.

"Apart from the nagging, it's probably years since they said a word to each other. Especially Phil." My uncle is a small, dry, taciturn man. He is color-blind and wears hideous race-track-tout clothes.

"He keeps his pens in the dishwasher now," my mother says.

Uncle Phil has had a lifelong passion for pens, fountain pens, ballpoint pens, felt-tip pens, something called X-ray pens, grosses of them tied in bundles with rubber bands and kept on closet shelves in shoe boxes. I don't know where he got them, or why, but in recent years those he has thrust upon me have all been inscribed with the names of local banks, so perhaps he steals them. They rarely work.

"Why in the dishwasher?"

"Why not? He doesn't use it for anything else. What do you think? Will you be coming down for my birthday?"

"Of course."

"I want to give a party."

"Who's left to invite?"

"What do you mean?" she says indignantly. "I've got over thirty people on the list. That includes Frieda, if she's out of the hospital."

"A dinner party?"

"Of course."

"I'll cook," I offer, dreading the thought. Her kitchen equipment is the least adequate I have ever encountered, and that includes all the summer rentals I've been in. Her notion of cooking is to throw a boilable bag of something frozen into a thin saucepan that was once lined with Teflon and is now, like her other pot and her frying pan, scorched and mauled. What occupies her ample kitchen cabinets is an abundance of used aluminum-foil frozen-food containers from days when she took a little more trouble and bought frozen dinners that had to be heated in the oven.

"Nonsense. I'll have it catered. Unless I decide to go on a cruise, instead. There's a lovely cruise I'd like to take. It starts in Athens and ends in Venice, and in between it goes to Turkey and Yugoslavia and Russia and a few of the Greek islands, I forget which. How does that sound to you?"

"Where in Russia?"

"The Black Sea. Odessa and Yalta. It's only a two-week cruise. On a very good ship, small but five stars. And it doesn't go into oceans, just seas. The Sea of Ulysses, the Black, the Adriatic. What do you think?"

"Sounds good."

"You're interested?"

"You mean you want me to go?"

"Of course."

How tempting. I love ships. I've never been to any of those places, except Venice. And Russia is my motherland. My grandmotherland.

"It's an awful lot of countries for two weeks," I say. "They probably give you about a minute in each port."

"You know cruises, they're all appetizers, no main course. But better than nothing."

After our summer in trains and buses, my mother vowed never to travel in any other way but on ships. A cruise ship is a floating womb. All your needs are taken care of, and in style. The only effort required is to change your clothes and choose from the menu.

Margo, sitting across from me, rolls her eyes impatiently, consulting her watch, smoking, drinking. Will this conversation never end? she asks me wordlessly. I tell my mother that it is her birthday and to decide what she wants to do, but I already know that she has decided. She will do both, have the party, book the cruise a week or two later. Why not? Money is no problem, but time is. If each year may be your last, why not live it up? Living it up makes it interesting enough almost to ensure that it will not be the last. She says she will call me at the usual time Saturday and we hang up.

"Sorry, Margo," I say. "My mother was giving me previews of coming attractions. Would you like to hear what's in store for us if we live long enough and are lucky enough to be in reasonable health and wealth? Or would you rather just go on worrying about now?"

"Now," Margo says. "It's probably all I'll ever have."

Where is Deirdre? The last time I saw her was three months ago. First, she telephoned.

"I've been so worried about you," I said. "Where have you been?"

"Where, indeed."

"Are you all right?"

"Yes, I'm fine. Rachel, could you lend me a bit of money?"

"Of course."

"I hate to ask you," she said cheerfully.

"Don't hate to ask me."

"Is it all right if I come round right away? I won't be interrupting anything?"

"No, it's fine. I'm here."

She looked pale and soiled, and she smoked and coughed. She told me that the checks from *Tempus* had stopped. When I questioned her about the pension money, she told me that she had won her long battle to make them give it to her all at once instead of doling it out to her as if she were a child on an allowance. When I asked her what she had done with it, she was vague. I doubt if she herself knew.

She refused tea, lunch, even a drink, so we walked to the corner to my bank where I punched out the hundred dollars in cash she requested.

"Au-to-ma-tion," she said, enunciating every syllable with equal emphasis, going up an octave on the *ma*. "It's like play money coming out of a toy, not real money at all. But thank you anyway, Rachel. You're a lifesaver." She stuffed the bills inside her ruined black purse in such a careless way that I knew they would evaporate within the hour.

"Will I ever see you again?" I asked.

"Of course. But I'm going away for a bit."

"Oh? Where?"

"To my brother in Oshkosh."

"Really, Deirdre!"

"It's the truth, I swear it. He has a lovely big house in the middle of the town where I can walk to everything."

I wanted to ask her what "everything" was.

"Oshkosh," I said again, instead.

"His wife and I get along very well, and the children are all grown up."

"But Oshkosh?"

"Please stop saying Oshkosh as though it were Afghanistan."

"What will you *do* there?"

"I will get a little job with the Salvation Army," she improvised. "Just enough to keep me in money for ciggies. When I'm settled, Rachel, I'll call you up on the telephone."

"Will you?"

"I just said I would. Good-bye, Ray-chelle. Oh, and I'll send you a check as soon as I can."

"Don't give it a thought," I said unnecessarily, reminded of a friend of Deirdre's I once met in Vermont who told me that she never loaned money to any of her friends. If they needed money enough to ask for it, she gave it to them and made it clear that it was not a loan but a gift, and that they were never to think of it again in connection with her. Once it had passed from her hand to theirs, it was theirs. I knew it would be pointless and redundant to say anything like that to Deirdre. The money I had just given her was no more mine than it was hers.

In the blink of an eye, she hailed a cab, stepped into it like a queen and, as the cab pulled away, she leered at me mockingly, with hatred, through the dirty glass of the window. Good-bye, Deirdre. I will miss you. But in fact I had been missing her for some time.

Margo and I are dining in my neighborhood continental eatery, a restaurant with an air of improvisation, a little too serious about itself, a place in which it is hard to have much confidence. It is the kind of place where you feel the proprietor or his wife, in all innocence, one day said to the other, "I've got an idea. Let's open a restaurant."

We are dining here because it is so near my apartment and we are both too drunk to go further afield. We are drunk because last night I felt a lump in my breast and I have spent all of this day, easily the worst of my life, dragging myself from my internist to the laboratory for X rays, to the surgeon, to be told by the latter, a man with the most benign of faces, and without any softening prelude, "You have cancer. You have to have a mastectomy."

The doctor was sitting down when he told me this. I was standing, having just come through the door. I did not sit down. I have lived through scenarios like this countless times in my powerful imagination since the age of nine, when I first became obsessed with dying and death. And here it was, and all I could think while the fear washed over me, engulfed me, was: is this you, my death? Is this you? Death, death, death.

But maybe there was some mistake, because it was never going to be a breast. Not mine. It took me forever to grow them, and then they didn't amount to so much. Surely mastectomies were unspeakable horrors visited on large-breasted women from a line of women prone to cancer, women with a history of cysts. None of this was true of me. I wanted to faint, but I have never fainted. I wished I could vomit, spew out my insides, but there was nothing there. I hadn't eaten all day.

I don't know what my face was doing while I recoiled from the doctor's news, but it hardly mattered, since he wasn't looking at it. I suspect that he was feeling sorry for himself, having to be the bearer of such tidings, the really difficult part of a surgeon's job. I know I felt the breath go out of me, so I must have been holding it.

"Are you sure?" I said, stupidly.

Of course he was sure. Why else would he tell me something like that? Also, he informed me, my own doctor, Dr. Ludwig, had seen the X rays and mammogram and confirmed the diagnosis.

"Why not a lumpectomy?"

There was no way, he said, to do a lumpectomy given the location of this growth. But now for the good news.

"We're not going to do a radical mastectomy. It will be a *modified* radical."

"What's the difference?"

"We take the breast and the nodes and one of the two muscles, but we leave the other muscle."

He smiled at me, waiting for my gratitude.

As I was walking from the taxi to the door of my building, a woman touched my arm and said, "What's the matter? Is something wrong?"

The woman was a neighbor, but practically a stranger. I don't know her name. I don't even know her floor. I know her face because I have passed her on the street or seen her in the lobby or the elevator perhaps half a dozen times a year in the dozen years I've been living here. That adds up, but if I stopped seeing her, if she moved away or died, I would never notice. Yet here she was, stopping me, looking concerned, emboldened by something terrible on my face, something of which I, who live inside my face, who had been roiling about in a black and hideous place, was not aware. This woman's act momentarily reconnected me to the world.

"I've just come from the doctor," I told her. "I have to have a mastectomy."

The woman's face registered all the correct things, as her voice spoke all the right words. I thanked her. I think I even managed to smile. We parted. She continued in the direction she was going, probably to do her marketing, and I to the relative safety of my apartment and my aloneness. When I got there and had hung away my coat, I sat down and tried to think clearly. I could do one of three things. I could kill myself. I could go to pieces. I could behave well. Since in my imagination I have always been so cowardly and hysterical, I decided on the third choice. Being brave would give me something to do, something conscious, something I could have control over. Almost, I began to look forward to the courage I was going to have, and I began, then, to have it.

The telephone was ringing. It was Margo, with the latest installment of her continuing marital crisis and its impact on her mental health. I cut her short and told her my news.

"I'll be right there," she said.

She arrived looking pale and stricken.

"Don't get hysterical," I said. "It doesn't necessarily mean I'm going to die. Have a drink."

"I brought my toothbrush. I'm going to stay tonight. When do you go into the hospital?"

"Tomorrow. After lunch."

"Okay, I'll go with you."

"Good. That's what friends are supposed to be for."

"And when do they . . . do it?"

"The following morning. Thursday. It will all be over by lunch."

"Oh, God, lunch again," Margo said, beginning to cry. "*Lunch!* I can't stand it. Let's have another drink."

So we are in the Montmartre Café, having yet another drink while we wait for our food. Our booth is near a little alcove where the salad bar is tucked at right angles to a spinet on which a pianist, his bald head gleaming with perspiration, has been playing an endless version of "Begin the Beguine." He is trapped in it, and so are we. I feel the same mounting desperation I always feel when I hear Ravel's "Bolero."

"He can't seem to end that beguine," I say nervously.

"Ending the Beguine," Margo ruminates. "That's a good title for a story."

"You can't have it. It's mine."

"You don't want to spend three hundred dollars a day of your own money for a private room," the admissions clerk says. "That's what they charge over what Blue Cross pays. It isn't worth it."

I look at Margo who seems to think it *is* worth it. She has style. I shrug. Nothing is going to make this a happy time. "What are the semiprivate rooms like?" I ask, feeling oddly dislocated, as though I am checking into a hotel, a resort. Only the hard knot of fear in my stomach, which has been constant since two nights ago when I first felt the lump, which may never leave me, keeps me anchored.

The woman looks through the papers and charts on her desk. She picks up the phone and dials. "Did 1511 B vacate this morning? Good." She hangs up and beams at me. She is all kindness.

"We're in luck. I have a gorgeous room for you. Only one other occupant."

It *is* a gorgeous room, but the gorgeous part of it, a rounded bay of windows with views up, down, and across the river, belongs to 1511A, a hysterectomy. Sliding curtains effectively screen off all of it and screen her off, too, along with any natural light in the room, as I learn when I have crawled into my allotted space. I have a view of her curtain, beyond which I can hear her entertaining her visitors. To my left is the bathroom door, to my right the door leading into the room. I begin to hate 1511A.

Margo makes a face. "It isn't every day you have a mortal illness," she says. "You can treat yourself better than this."

I get out of bed and we go to the nurse's station to tell the woman on duty that I want to change to a private room. There is nothing today, but there will be something available tomorrow. They can take me to it right from surgery. Good. It will give me something to look forward to.

"Go home, Margo," I say. "You've done more than anyone could be expected to do. I want to read now."

In every life there are stretches of time that are utterly useless, that are there only to be gotten through. This is one of them. I can't read; I am too busy keeping the fear down, trying not to be overwhelmed by the voice in my head that keeps moaning, *Oh shit, oh shit, oh shit.*

Alone. All those years after the divorce when my mother hoped I would remarry. "I can't bear to think of you alone," she would say, since without a husband you were alone. Was it this sort of occasion she had in mind? It's true that Peter would have been with me constantly from the moment I felt the lump, would have held me all night, gone with me the next day on that awful round, been with me in the surgeon's office. He would have touched me, held my hand, put an arm around me, not for a minute released me from physical contact. Yes, it would have made a difference. I would have broken down. I would have wept. I would not have had to be so bloody fucking brave.

Not long ago, I read about a man who for many years has been confined to a wheelchair with some dreadful nervous disease. He can't really sit in the wheelchair; he is limp and slumped in it. Until recently, he could talk, but only one close associate understood him. Now he can't talk at all. Now, when he has something to say, he feebly types the words into a computer console mounted on his wheelchair that delivers his message in the artificial voice of a synthesizer.

And what is this man whose body has completely betrayed him, who is completely helpless, thinking about, lolling there in his complicated wheelchair? Is he thinking about his impending death? About his humiliating helplessness and dependency on others? About his bodily functions and malfunctions? No. He is *thinking*! He is thinking about time. About past and future. He is thinking about his theory that if the universe were to stop expanding and begin to contract, time would run backward. He has decided that he was wrong. He is thinking about "the arrow of time," and about the Second Law of Thermodynamics, and about entropy.

I am filing my nails when Becky charges in. Her face wears an interesting expression, a mixture of no-nonsense and the vain effort to conceal what she is really feeling. She had been away, but I called her before leaving for the hospital to tell her where I would be and why.

"Goddammit, Rachel!" she says.

She takes off her coat and the blue wool helmet she is forced to wear against even the least chill in the air, since her hair is again so short that there is almost nothing between her skull and the elements. She sits in the single visitor's chair allotted to my small portion of the room.

"You cut your hair again!" I say.

"I couldn't stand it. Oh, God, it's all downhill, isn't it?" she says, then proceeds to tell me about all the women she has known or heard of who had mastectomies twelve years ago and are perfectly fine. I don't know it yet, but I am going to hear a lot of these stories in the weeks to come.

"One woman in eleven," she says. "Or maybe it's ten? What a staggering statistic."

"You mean for every woman who gets it, ten women don't?" I say, doing what victims do with statistics.

"The others are being saved for something worse. Or else they died young." She looks around at the sterile room. She loves to neaten up, make order out of chaos, not even out of chaos, out of what to the average eye already looks like order. She needs to keep busy, to be useful.

"You could rearrange my toothbrush and toothpaste, if that will make you happy," I say.

Just having her here means a lot to me. Being my closest friend, she is my closest relative. I don't know how to tell her this. But it isn't necessary to tell her. She knows. That's part of it.

"Have you told Lisa?" she asks.

"No. Why would I?" As far as I am concerned, Lisa is no longer in my life. How inappropriate to drag her back into it for something like this.

"She might want to know."

"Why would *anyone* want to know?"

"What about your mother?"

My mother. I am now more mother to her than she is to me. She is an old woman whose friends are dying, and I feel protective of her. She is so concerned with avoiding her own death, how could I present her with the possibility of mine?

"No," I tell Becky. "I'll tell her after the operation, when I know what the prognosis is. Maybe."

Becky nods. Beyond the curtains, 1511A turns on a light, so we know that evening must have arrived.

"Don't you have to go home and make dinner?" I ask.

"Paul's coming here to pick me up. We have tickets for the opera. We're going with Miriam and David." David is my brother, Miriam my sister-in-law. At some point, I'm not sure when, I called them and the newspaper delivery service and Jed, so that he could come and feed the cat.

"What are you going to see? Hear?"

"Vairter."

"Oh," I say, after a moment's reflection, "Werther."

"Under the circumstances, I'd rather not. I'd rather stay right here."

"You can't in any case. Visiting hours. You'd have to leave by eight."

"I know."

David and Miriam come through the doorway. Since my father's death, David has assumed the role of head of the family with my mother and me. He does this by composing his face in a certain indescribable way, a look, he hopes, of authority and confidence, neither of which he feels. He does this only on occasions when it is called for: family crises, financial discussions. This is the face he is wearing as he enters.

"You're going to be all right," he assures me nervously.

"I *am* all right," I say serenely. They both look relieved, as if they were expecting to find me all in pieces. They are relieved to see Becky here, too, since she is so good at keeping conversations going in any situation.

"Well," David says.

"I wish you had gotten a second opinion," Miriam says.

"I had two opinions," I say. "My doctor's and the surgeon's. My doctor saw the X rays, too. I trust her."

"I mean from another cancer specialist," Miriam says. "You could still do it."

But I can't. The adrenaline that has been fueling me and my pretense of courage is not inexhaustible. More than I want to investigate, I want this over with, I want to be on the far side of it, the cancer out, the thing done, my fate *accompli*.

I am glad they are all here. Still, I wish they would go away. I don't want to have to comfort them. And they are all standing about, since there are no chairs, holding their coats. Miriam begins to tell me about her friend Elaine, who, fourteen years ago, or was it fifteen, had a *double* mastectomy. "And she's fine. Not a bit of trouble since."

Paul comes, then Jed, who is wet. "It's raining," he says, bending to kiss me from his great height. "Oh, Mom. Are you all right? I mean, I know you're not all right, but are you all right?" He sits on the edge of the bed and puts his arms around me. How hard it is not to break down. It is the first time that my child, this grown man, is parenting me. The temptation to dissolve, to let go, is almost irresistible, but I resist it.

"I'm all right, darling," I say.

"Look what I've brought you," he says, pulling a pint of J & B and a split of soda from an overcoat pocket. "And this," he says, and like a magician produces a glass from the other pocket. There is ice in the glass.

"Oh, I'm so glad I had you," I sigh. "How did you do it?"

"Resourceful," he says. "Remember in kindergarten? A-plus in Resourcefulness?" It was nursery school and, yes, they must have made up Resourcefulness as a gradable category just for Jed. He is opening bottles, mixing my drink.

"Is it all right to drink?" Becky asks, worried. "Have you had any medication?"

"If it kills me," I say, holding the lovely amber glass aloft, *"tant pis."*

In time, they all go away. In time, the night passes. In time, time passes. In time, someone is slapping my face, telling me to wake up. I pull myself up out of a swamp of a night so dark and deep and dreamless that it can hardly be different from death. The woman who is slapping my face, though gently, not unkindly, is wearing a shower cap. Last night, in the shower, I looked down at my body, at the twins, and said farewell to Lefty, old friend, who gave me so many years of pleasure, who would be gone when next I chose to look, and told her the understatement of the year, that I would miss her, that I would never forget her. But we are not in the shower, this woman I don't know and I, we are in the recovery room, which bustles with activity, with other men and women similarly garbed, and with other bodies recovering. Or not. There is a big clock on the wall, facing me. It has a time on it, but time has lost its arrow and is meaningless.

"I'm awake," I manage to say, through the fog. "Is it over?"

"Yes, you're fine." She is taking my blood pressure. If I have blood pressure, then I must be alive. I try not to think about my chest.

Someone comes to wheel me away. Drifting in and out of sleep, or whatever it is, I watch the ceilings slide by, and I think of my father's ceilings. These are the ones he meant. He must have been complaining of the view from helpless horizontal. And then the ceilings stop moving and I am in a bed, cranked up, in the new, the private, room. Becky and Jed and David are there. I am only vaguely aware of them, of the room. Jed holds my hand. David leans over me and says, "You're *fine*. It's all out and you're absolutely *fine*. You must believe me. You're *fine*. I spoke to the surgeon and he says everything went perfectly and it's all out and you're *fine*."

And then, I can't help it, I cry. For their kindness. Because I love them. "Good," I mumble, shuffling off, "I'm fine."

All day and night I drift. In and out, in and out. Becky is there all day. It was she who moved my things from the other room, put them away, arranged the flowers as they arrived. There is a nurse, hired by David, and another in the night, who sits quietly in a chair, knitting. Margo comes and goes, and so does Jed. There are thick, soft bandages around my chest, wads and wads of cotton shielding me, and two tubes protrude from there, from me, emptying blood and whatever other liquids are inside the wound into a flat, round transparent container that is pinned to my gown. When I begin to feel the pain strongly, the nurse gives me an injection and I float off on a cloud, feeling wonderful, understanding what junkies must feel and why they would not want to feel any other way.

The surgeon appears and says, "It went very well. I've removed all the nodes and sent them to the lab."

"Were there a lot of them?" I ask, an idiotic question the doctor doesn't bother to answer.

"And if even *one* of them is affected," he says, "you will have to be seen by an oncologist for chemotherapy." He tells me this almost vindictively, threatening me. Frightened, I stare at him. I have assumed that if I was fine, I was fine; that they knew. Now it seems possible that the operation was only the beginning. I look at the surgeon, this man with his placid, sweet face, this man who does not mince words, just human flesh. He is not looking at me. He is looking beyond me, at the view out my window. He has never yet looked me in the eye.

"How long will it take to get the lab report?" I ask.

"Three or four days."

"Well. When you get it," I say, "I'd rather not hear it from you. Please call Dr. Ludwig and let her tell me."

Now, for the first time, he does look at me, then quickly looks away, his color rising. "All right," he says angrily, and strides out.

There is nothing to do but be taken care of, begin to mend, wait. My day nurse, Janette, is a dark, wiry woman, rather beautiful, from Trinidad. She has boundless energy, too much personality. She is given to thespian gestures, flashing eyes, theatrical pronouncements, broad flourishes.

"I'm hungry," I say.

"That is *wonderful!* It is a pleasure, no, it is an *honor* to be your nurse." She dances across the small room that has filled with flowers that seem like tributes to her fine performance. Almost, I expect her to take her bows before disappearing in search of the buttered roll and the cup of tea she will fetch for me. When friends come to visit, she plays to them even more intensely. She sparkles. She is full of electricity. "You look sad. You must not be sad, not for a single minute. If you are in pain, you must tell your Janette, even the slightest pain, and she will gently prick you with her magic wand and send you off to Never-Never Land. Oh, lovely Never-Never Land."

I would hate to have this woman for an enemy, but it amuses me to have her for a nurse. Probably, she is insane. When her time is up and she gives way to the sedate, taciturn Miss McClintock, it is a relief. With Miss McClintock, I can read.

"You are not to worry about the lab report," Janette says, perched on the edge of my bed, holding my hand. "Chemotherapy is not so terrible anymore. They have made so many advances. It no longer makes you feel so sick as it used to. And it is extremely effective."

Now she is playing the Nurse, and I am so grateful for her words, her reassurance, that I cannot hold back tears, playing into her hands. Now she can comfort me, tell me how brave I am.

"You are going to live to be a very old lady," she says. "I can see it in your aura."

"You can see my aura?"

"Of course. Janette is a witch. She can see such things."

Becky is there every day for three or four hours. She will go home with me, stay with me for the first week, at least. She arranges the flowers, answers the phone, allows Janette to go to lunch and take coffee breaks, straightens up the room, takes coats from my visitors. When we have the time, when my blood pressure or temperature aren't being measured, when Janette is off on some errand, when I am not giving reassurances to someone on the telephone, Becky and I talk. We reminisce, and we talk about life and death and aging, but mostly we do in-depth analyses of the people we know in common.

"People don't change as they get older," she is saying, "they just get more so."

"You mean their eccentricities?"

"Yes, and their flaws. The cranky ones become curmudgeons; the irritable become irascible. And people who used to be only slightly unconventional take to wearing capes and thrashing about with canes."

"You think age gives them license?"

"Maybe it's only that the clay hardens."

"Because they've survived so many battles, or because they care less and less about the opinion of others?"

"What do you mean 'they'?"

"We? Are we there already?"

"Of course. And I don't think it's choice. It's habit."

"What about good qualities? Do the good become angels?"

"Yes. And the angels become saints. But thank God there aren't too many of those."

The telephone rings, and she answers it. "Henry! How are you? Yes, it's Becky, how did you know my voice, it's been so long. No, she's fine. She's right here." She hands me the phone.

Henry called immediately after the operation to say, tearfully, that he wished he could be here with me, that this was one of those times he wished they didn't live so far away.

"Mom? Are you feeling better? Patti and I think you should come here to convalesce. It's beautiful here now, the weather's perfect."

I am moved by the invitation. It is so sweet, so naïve, that perhaps the idea really was Henry's. I can just imagine being left alone all day in this condition with Patti adding me to all her other burdens.

"What a lovely offer," I say. "Thank you. But I've got to stay near these doctors for a while."

We agree that we will see about my coming later, when I'm feeling stronger, surer, and I ask for news of Sherry and the baby, and thank him once more, and Patti, and hang up. The moment I do, the phone rings again.

"This is Dr. Ludwig," my doctor says in a cheerful voice. "I have good news for you. The lab report is in and it's entirely negative."

I can never get used to negative being good, positive bad. "You mean . . . ?"

"All the nodes were clear."

Once again, I let out my held breath, breath I must have been holding for three days, and I can feel relief blooming on my face like sunflowers.

"So I won't need . . . ?"

"No chemotherapy, no radiation. It's over. You *had* cancer. You don't have it anymore. As soon as the blood stops draining, you can go home."

"Thank you, Dr. Ludwig," I sing, grinning at Becky, nodding my head, and while I am thanking Dr. Ludwig again, Becky does something I have never seen her do before: she explodes into tears. I hang up and we both weep and weep, and I make her come to the bed so that we can hold each other while we weep some more.

"I *knew* it!" my mother says.

"What did you know?"

"What David told me. That you were away for the weekend birdwatching with Margo. I knew it wasn't true."

"Why? It could have been true. We've done it before."

"I just knew that something was wrong."

"David's not a good liar."

"No, he sounded normal. But I knew it in my bones."

"A mother's heart. Not bones."

"So what is it? Why are you in the hospital? You sound all right."

"I am all right."

"So what was it?"

"I had to have an operation. There was a lump in my breast. It's out now. It's *all* out."

She is silent.

"I'm perfectly all right. All the nodes were clear. I don't need chemotherapy or radiation or anything. I'll be going home in a couple of days."

"What kind of operation?" she asks in a small, choked voice. "A mastectomy?"

"Yes."

"Oh my God."

"A *modified* mastectomy."

"What does that mean?"

"Not much."

She is crying. "I'll come up," she says. "I'll be there tomorrow."

"No, come in about a week. I'll need you more then."

"Oh my God," she says again.

"It's all *right*. I'm fine. I really am."

"My baby," she says.

"To your reprieve," Margo says. She has brought to my hospital room champagne, pâté, caviar, Russian black bread, and she and Becky and I are celebrating. I am getting quite drunk, what with the relief, the drugs, the champagne, the happiness. I did not believe that my life was still so valuable to me as I now see it is, in this moment of having it given back to me.

And I think of Deirdre, for some reason, perhaps because our hold on life is so tenuous, remembering her in that darkening room with the toy locomotive hooting around the baseboards, and the Mickey Mouse watch dangling from her thin wrist, and I wonder where she is, and what, at this moment, preoccupies her.

Margo spreads pâté on bread, passing it to me, to Becky, making crumbs that Becky will enjoy cleaning up when Margo goes and our little party is over.

"And to you," Margo says, "my dearest Rachel. You've been so brave, so wonderful. I never could have gotten through this without you."

In the morning of the sixth day, the young resident who assists my surgeon and who has been coming daily to check and empty the fluid in the drainage pouch says, after measuring the day's collection, "It's ready to come out. I'll be right back."

I have been lying here trying to think about Art and Barbara locked inside my typewriter at home, waiting for me to come back and unlock them so that they can go on with whatever it is they're going to do and discover. Writing novels seems such an odd thing for a grown-up to be doing. When you are a child, you play house and you are the mother, or school and you are the teacher, or love and you are the lover. If you are an adult writer, you play God. What a game!

The resident is back. He has scissors. He snips beneath my hospital gown, around the place where the tubes come through. He puts the scissors down.

"Is it over?" I ask.

"No. I've just taken out the stitches that kept the tubes in place." This is the longest sentence he has ever spoken in my presence. If he is learning surgery from my surgeon, it is clear that he is learning his bedside manners from him, too. He is dark and handsome, with a closed face. He has been coming every day, but I have never seen him smile.

"Will it hurt?"

"It might sting for a minute."

There is a sudden wrenching, tearing, incredibly searing pain, as though he has torn off the breast I no longer have with his bare hands, pulled it out by whatever rooted it, and for the first time in my life, I scream. I clutch my breast, my late breast, and turn away, gasping, tears springing from my eyes, shocked and outraged.

The doctor is not looking at me, but at the tubes in his hand. He has no interest in me, I do not exist. He has some technical thing on his mind: are the tubes intact, perhaps, or has any of it been left inside?

"Will this ghastly pain go away?" I ask, ashamed to be begging this man for anything, which is what I am doing.

"In a few minutes."

He does not tell me, as Dr. Ludwig will a little later when she comes by to give me her daily fifty-dollar smile, that the reason it hurt so much was because I was mending so well. Scar tissue had begun to form around the tubes. The resident says nothing. He puts a bandage over the holes where the tubes were, packs up his gear, and makes ready to leave. The pain has begun to subside.

"Thank you," I say as he leaves, a habit, and then I am suffused with shame.

"You must look at it before you can leave the hospital," June, the special psychiatric nurse, says to me. She is a thin Chinese woman with a soft, sweet voice and the saddest face I have ever seen. She is sitting on the edge of my bed with an attaché case from which she has taken several prostheses to show me. I once wrote a story about impotence, powerlessness, in which the metaphor was a false breast floating in a swimming pool on a bright summer day. The false breast in the story looked nothing like these heavy, flesh-colored, multishaped contrivances. "They will choose one to match exactly the other one," she has just told me, "and they will provide you with special brassieres."

I pick one up. "Why is it so heavy?"

"There is nothing to hold it in place but its own weight. Also, it's the weight of the other, so that you will be properly balanced."

It is alarming to know that I am improperly balanced, that I will be listing to starboard. June writes down the names and addresses of two shops, mastectomy boutiques, which I will forever after think of as mastiques, and advises me to get fitted as soon as possible. She shows me a catalog. It is hard to believe that there could be such an extensive line in the breast-replacement department. One item, I see, costs $189.99, nipple extra. I think of the manufacturer of these items and his genius designer huddling over ways to increase profits. "Eureka! We'll make the nipples a separate item." I stifle my rage.

"I am also here for you to talk to me," June says. "It is better to talk about these things at once."

"What things?"

"The fears, the doubts."

"Well," I say, trying to be helpful, "the fear of chemotherapy and all that is gone, of course, since I don't need it. And Dr. Ludwig tells me that my prognosis is excellent, so for the moment I'm not fearing death." But *only* for the moment. It has already crossed my mind, as it will continue to do for a few months, that they may all be lying to me, that I am not fine and fine and fine and fine. That when they operated, they discovered that the cancer was everywhere, and then only took off the breast so that I would not suspect the truth: that it was inoperable. But, of course, this would be attributing too much kindness to my surgeon, though my brother would have told them not to tell me the truth. How many times have I said unequivocally that if I am dying, there is no reason for me to be among the first to know, that the last possible moment will be good enough? So that now, if the good news is true, I can't entirely believe it.

But June is not satisfied. There is something else she wants from me. She wants me to talk about my *sexual* fears! The moment I realize this, I rejoice. It probably means that I am not dying.

But my lips are sealed. It has occurred to me that I may never have sex again, but only because I don't expect ever to want it. I suppose that's what she wants me to tell her so that she can assure me that yes, I will.

"Men," she says, forced to volunteer the news, "are usually very good about this. They adjust, too."

Oh, men, I think, how good of them to be good about this. Those who haven't already left wives with sagging breasts, in search of younger and more upright ones, may not terribly mind their complete absence.

And women, I am tempted to ask her, what about them? How much do they mind?

"Of course, husbands, men, are affected, but in time they get used to it. Now, come with me into the bathroom." She closes her attaché case. "We are going to remove the bandages and have a look."

"I can't," I say. It's my body, the one I'll have to live in for the rest of my life. I don't feel strong enough yet for the shock.

"You can't leave the hospital until you've seen yourself."

I groan, knowing I must do it. I am terrified. I am only five years old. I could pretend to look but keep my eyes shut, or roll them up in my head. Obediently, I go with her into the bathroom and stand before the mirror while she removes the thick cotton wadding that has shielded me. When it is all off, I take a deep breath and look.

It is certainly no surprise, since I was not expecting the breast to be there. What does surprise and shock is the jarring asymmetry. The basic law of human anatomy, I now see, at least externally, is that anything of which we have only one belongs in the middle.

The left side of my chest is perfectly flat, like the chest of a young boy, only there is no nipple. Instead, there is the angry crimson scar, a smeared horizontal line. The stitches, I see, are metal staples.

"The staples will come out in a few days," June says. "And then, for a few days after that, you will have only some strips of sealing tape, like Scotch tape."

How fitting. With all these office products, I have been turned into a messy manuscript. That, and my chest that is now half man, half woman, are the story of my life.

"It's not so bad," I finally say. "I look like a Miró."

The nurse smiles, relieved. I wonder how many times she has had to do this, and how other women have reacted, and how she, the nurse, has coped. What an odd job for anyone to have, I think, marveling at the fact that wherever there is a human need, someone will come to see to it.

It's a week since I came home. Becky stayed until yesterday, when my mother arrived.

We are taking a walk, my first venture out-of-doors. It is, of necessity, a slow walk. My mother used to be a sprinter, and even with my much longer legs, I had trouble keeping pace with her. Time has slowed her down, and today we are both content to stroll, though I am trying with difficulty to swing my arms naturally and to hold myself erect.

"I don't believe you ever had it," my mother says.

"Had what?"

"You know." Her voice drops. "Cancer."

I feel a momentary rage, and then I tell myself that it is her mother's instinct. One's children are not mortal, at whatever age. I can't begin to imagine Jed or Henry's dying.

"You think they just chopped it off," I nonetheless say, "because they had nothing better to do that day?"

"It doesn't run in the family."

"What did your grandmothers die of?" I ask.

"I have no idea. I never even knew them. I think my mother's mother died in childbirth."

"Let's do the mastectomy boutique tomorrow," I say. "I think we've done enough for today."

We turn back. At the corner, waiting for the light to change, my eye is drawn to a large white truck coming down the river of traffic that has resumed its sluggish flow. It grabs my attention because it is so white, so pure, and free of any words of self-identification or advertisement. Or so I think until it goes past and I see, in small black letters in a lower corner, the word MEDIWASTE. It takes me a minute to absorb the word. I watch the truck go south on Second Avenue, away from the mammoth hospitals that are everywhere in this neighborhood, and I wonder if it contains my left mediwaste, and if it does, where it will take it?

"I wonder where all the pieces go," I mumble, and my mother gives me a sidelong look of rebuke.

"I read in this morning's *Times* that New York City's medical garbage is washing up on the Jersey shore," she says.

"Jesus, I hope not," I say, shuddering, and we both begin to laugh.

Today has conditions which warn against Leos doing anything that is not aboveboard. Journeys can have lucky endings. Postpone real-estate transactions. Those who are preparing for sporting events should give some extra time to training.

I don't know why I looked a second time, bag ladies are such a common sight.

Becky and Paul and I have been to Chinatown for an early dinner at the Very Good Restaurant. We went there because of the name, so sweetly ingenuous and direct and, as it turned out, honest. Coming home, I get off the bus at Fourteenth Street, thinking to walk the rest of the way, to walk off some of the dinner. It's spring, a lovely mid-April Sunday twilight. I feel almost human for the first time since the operation, far less fragile. The fatigue seems finally to be ebbing, and there are even occasional bursts of energy. Best of all, I'm back at work, and I've reached that point in the book where, instead of feeling that I'm pulling it along, I seem to be following it. I have no idea what's going to happen in the book tomorrow, but I can hardly wait to find out. When I'm between books, part of me always feels dead, and there is always the fear that nothing will ever come. The elation I feel at working again is part of the spring renewal. There are moments when I'm tempted to perform some pagan rite, thanking the gods of fertility.

On my walk home, I am eager to see what's blooming in the

parklike grounds that mollify the ugly institutional brick rectangles of the huge apartment complex where I live. In front of my own building, just yesterday, a large, sunny rash of daffodils erupted, and on my way out earlier, there was a magnolia tree heavy with sudden blossoms. A London plane tree in the angle of one of the buildings is home to a huge flock of pigeons who roost there each night like ornaments perched branch on branch, a sight I love because it makes the tree so festive, and because the pigeons echo those other, hidden tenants layered floor upon floor behind the bricks. Last spring, a three-foot plastic owl was hung near the top of the tree, and for a while the pigeons stayed away, but pigeons are city birds with streetsmarts. They soon learned that the owl merely swayed and did not fly, and they all came back and ignored it, though how city pigeons would have known about owls in the first place, I can't imagine. Or could it have been any strange object, any shapeless blob, hanging there, and was it only the manufacturer's whimsical ploy to give it owlshape? Ignorance fills my life with such sweet mysteries.

Because my mind is occupied with this trivia while I cross Fourteenth Street going north, I see her only peripherally, almost not seeing her at all. A number of people are crossing in four directions, and such a mix of people, on this borderline between lower-middle-class respectability and the melting pot of what has come to be called the East Village—the punks and drunks, the crazies and drifters, the crack dealers and pimps and black-leather-motorcycle gangsters, the Ukrainians and Puerto Ricans and Italians, the artists and gallery owners and gentrifiers. Across this street and a few steps north, however, it is so much another country it could as well be Kansas.

But I don't make it those few steps to Kansas. Something

just beneath the level of consciousness causes me to turn and take that second look at the small, slight bag lady. Dressed in layers of filthy rags, she is running clumsily on broken shoes in pursuit of a stray cat. I feel a clutch of terror. My impulse is to go after her, to make sure, but she has disappeared around a corner. Relieved that I won't have to know, to cope, I take the measure of this new thing that has invaded me, and just as I am giving it its name, which is cowardice, she comes back into view at the corner, her head lowered, and awkwardly descends the steps into the subway.

And now I find that I do have to know, to be sure. I go after her, fumbling in my pocket for a subway token. Really, there was nothing in that woman's appearance to evoke Deirdre except for her size and the garish sunglasses. Have I ever seen a bag lady wearing sunglasses?

It's like descending into the bowels of hell. I feel that way in all New York subway stations, but this one seems even worse. The unusual depth, the bad lighting, the smell of urine, the blobs of spittle and refuse on the steps and the platform, even the obligatory panhandler near the token booth, who looks more menacing than pitiable. Even though I am wearing jeans and a sweater, I feel overdressed here. I drop a dime in the panhandler's Dixie cup and go through the turnstile.

A thin scattering of people are waiting for the train, and I instantly spot the woman making her way to the rear of the platform. I follow, not knowing what I will say to her if she is indeed Deirdre. She seems to be stumbling, and I wonder if she's drunk, then see again that she is having trouble with her shoes. She is shuffling, taking small steps, precariously balanced between the two plastic shopping bags she carries, one in each hand. My father began to shuffle like that, I recall, when he started his long final decline. I didn't know then that it was probably a side effect of the medication he was taking, and when I first saw him walking that way I asked him why.

"How am I walking?" he asked, testily. "What's wrong with the way I'm walking?"

"You're walking like an old man," I said. I couldn't stand to see him walk like that. He had always been a strider, as aggressive in his walk as in everything else, and he did not yet look at all old or frail. "There's nothing wrong with your legs, is there?"

"No."

I took his arm and said, "Here, match your steps to mine. Let me see if you can do it." And side by side, we walked the length of the room that way, my father looking down and walking in step with me, as though we were dancing and I was the leader.

"There. You see?" I said.

But when I let go of his arm and he tried to do it alone, he couldn't. It was impossible for me to imagine what he felt, trapped in that pathetic shuffle, but I could see that he was frightened to walk any other way.

Nearly obliterated by graffiti, a train rumbles into the station. The woman, setting down one of her bags, waves at the train imperiously, calling, "Taxi, taxi!" The voice is familiar, the words even more so. The train grinds to a stop. I follow her onto the last car. She takes a seat midway between the two center sets of doors, and I sit directly opposite her, wondering why I was so quick to label her a bag lady when almost every New York City woman carries at least one shopping bag. But this woman's bags, which she has rested on the floor at her feet, are worn, wrinkled, dirty, and stuffed to bursting.

The doors slide closed and the train moves on. Without looking up, the woman begins to fuss with one of her shoes, once good leather shoes but now so past redemption that she would be better off going barefoot. The straps on both are broken, and she has tied them up with string, but the string has come all frayed and undone on the shoe that is giving her trouble, and she is struggling to find two ends to knot. I stare at her bent head, which is wrapped in a ratty kerchief from which a few gray hairs have strayed. I look at the hands at work on the shoe. The fingernails are bitten to the quick, the hands are dirty and veined, but they are Deirdre's hands, disproportionately large and strong for the rest of her. Frightened again, I look away.

The car is empty except for the two of us and a young Puerto Rican woman with two children and a sleeping baby in her lap. The children's mouths and cheeks are stained with dried ice cream, one chocolate, one vanilla, and they sit beside their mother, expressionless and patient. The mother looks tired beyond belief, almost in coma. The inside of the train is also smeared with graffiti. I count ten fucks and a couple of *mierda*s among the fierce tribal names. Pages of the *Daily News* are scattered across the floor, and a can of Sprite rolls around, leaving a damp trail. As the train pulls into the Union Square station, I look back at my bag lady, who, the knot accomplished, is sitting upright. I can't tell for sure because of the oversized sunglasses with their thick black rims, but if her eyes are not closed, she can only be looking at me. There is no sign of recognition. I study her face. The sunglasses are surely Deirdre's, but what is visible of the face seems too old. She is doing something, probably involuntary, with her mouth, her lips working in and out. Her teeth must be gone, I think, and that may be why she looks so old. Her teeth, the inky black of her hair, probably her spirit, all gone. Her small face is pinched and pale, and there is no trace of the bright daub of purple lipstick that, when I saw her last, she had been unable to keep from bleeding off the contours of her thin lips.

The woman is almost surely Deirdre, or what remains of her, and what little energy I had is gone. I feel a little sick, and terribly tired.

Three teenage boys come silently into the car, their black hair greased flat on their skulls. They look dangerous, standing in the middle of the car taking stock of us. They dismiss the mother with the children, their eyes glance quickly off Deirdre, and then linger on me. I'm not carrying a purse. My wallet is in a jeans pocket, and my eyeglasses are in the sweater pocket over my absent left breast. I rarely wear the prosthesis, not because it's uncomfortable, but because its function is merely cosmetic. Without it, I don't feel at all unbalanced, and I hate the look and feel of it. Like the plastic owl, it's an impostor, so I have begun to amass a collection of shirts and sweaters with left breast pockets into which I can tuck something for camouflage, glasses, a Kleenex. If I hadn't given up smoking, it would be a pack of cigarettes.

The boys, apparently deciding against me, move to the back of the car and stand at the windowed door looking out at the receding tracks as the train rattles on. Though I've passed the subway entrance a thousand times, I have no idea where this train goes or where it comes from. The L line. I've never been on it. It is surely the worst of all the terrible New York subway lines. It reeks of hopelessness, despair, violence. It seems fitting that Deirdre should be on it, and I wonder where it is taking her.

And again I wonder why I am here and what I am waiting for, what masochism this is, though I know I will stay as long as Deirdre is sitting there. Until I get it, whatever it is, a word, a message, an answer, something. Deirdre still has given no sign of recognition. God knows what and where her mind is now; God knows *who* she is.

The train stops and starts and stops and starts and pulls into Eighth Avenue. The doors open and everyone leaves except Deirdre. And me. It's the last stop. The doors remain open for a while and a few people come aboard, a nicely dressed black couple, a deathly pale Hasidic Jew, a young prostitute in a mini with bouffant hair that looks like a wig, a shabby man with a rusty beard and a knitted watchcap, peeling an orange. A trainman comes through and unlocks the driver's cubicle at what has now become the front of the car, disappearing within it. Deirdre makes no move to leave. The doors close and the train starts up, reversing itself, going back where it came from.

Deirdre isn't going anywhere.

The bearded man, seated a few feet from Deirdre, leans across, holding a segment of his orange out to her.

"Oh, t'ank you, John," she says, taking it, the corners of her mouth twitching in a tiny smile. "That's terribly kind of you."

"Got to get your vitamins," the man says, spitting an orange pip onto the floor. "Subways are full of other people's nasty germs."

"Oh, don't I know it!" Deirdre says, coughing by way of illustration.

I watch Deirdre slide the orange crescent into her mouth. Her jaw moves slowly up and down. I know exactly what the orange feels like, the surprise of it, what the inside of her mouth is feeling. A trickle of juice escapes and slides down her chin. She wipes it with the back of her hand, then wipes the back of her hand on the rag of her skirt.

Before Deirdre worked for *Tempus*, she wrote about fashion for *Vogue*, I think, or *Town and Country*. She loved beautiful clothes, good clothes. A wide streak of snob ran through her; in an odd way, it was part of her charm. I have a small snapshot of her that she once gave me, taken in those days long before I knew her. "Here, Rachel," she said, solemnly. "I want you to have this." I loved her doing that, saying that, wanting me to know her as she had been. Then, trying to diminish it, she said, "The reason I want you to have it, Rachel, is that I can't keep it about any longer, and if I don't give it to you, I would only throw it away." In the snapshot she is about forty, stylish, elegant, beautiful, her head held high on the long, graceful stem of her neck, not a hair out of place.

The man with the orange gets off at the Third Avenue station without another glance at Deirdre. The next stop is First Avenue, where Deirdre and I got on. I wrestle with the urge to get off and go home.

Where does this train go, anyway? I look at the window where the polar points are printed in large black letters. EIGHTH AVENUE is on top, CANARSIE below. Canarsie. When I was growing up, I thought Canarsie was a euphemism for the end of the world. "Way out in Canarsie," was the way my grandmother, with a wave of her hand, described any place that was at some distance from where we lived. It was a long time before I learned that Canarsie was a real place, and then I imagined it as barren, a swamp or a desert. I'm almost certain I've never been there.

First Avenue comes and goes. Because it's Sunday night and

nearly nine o'clock, the train is virtually empty. We are under the river. Deirdre, who has been crooning softly to herself, raises her voice, and begins to sing in a strong, throaty contralto with a quaver at the upper end of the register.

". . . the time of my childhood 'twas like a sweet dream,/To sit in the roses and hear the bird's song,/That music I'll never forget . . .' " Then, without missing a beat: "You've lost weight, Rachel."

I don't know if I've heard her right. When I decide that I have, I smile like an idiot.

"Yes," I say, unable to stop grinning. "I was ill."

"It becomes you."

"It will come back," I say, meaning the weight.

"Don't let it!" she says severely, resuming her song where she left off. " 'But oft when alone in the bloom of the year,/I think is the nightingale singin' there yet . . .' " I join her for the final line: "Are the roses still bright by the calm Bendemeer?"

"You've got a terrible singing voice, Rachel."

"I'm a listener," I say.

"Well, try not to forget it."

The train makes its first call in Brooklyn. Bedford Avenue. The three boys slink off. There is no one on the platform. The doors open and close on air, a ghost train.

"So you didn't stay in Oshkosh," I say.

"Ooooh, Oshkosh! I thought I'd go out of my mind. The winter never stopped."

She subsides into silence. Perhaps her eyes are shut, perhaps she is looking off into the past, remembering Oshkosh. There is no way of knowing.

"It's unnerving talking to you, Deirdre," I say, as I said many times in the past, "with you behind that big black glass curtain."

"I do not recall asking for your company on this voyage."

"Where *are* we going, Deirdre?"

"*We? We* are not going anywhere. *We* are making an effort not to smoke. We are trying to see how long we can go without a ciggie. I hope your sickness was nothing serious."

"I had a mastectomy."

"Ooooh, I'm soooo sorry, Rachel. What a terrible t'ing!"

"I'm all right now."

"It must have been dreadful for you."

"Yes."

Her hands fidget in her lap. The train lurches and sways, and we both bend with it. "Now, if you don't mind, I don't want to talk anymore," she says. "I have a bit of t'inking to do."

We lapse into silence. I watch the stations come and go. LORIMER STREET, GRAND STREET, MONTROSE AVENUE. I look at the advertising placards that run across the car just under the curve of the ceiling. Many of them are in Spanish. Most of them are mutilated. The woman with the cockroach that ran over her roast chicken is there again, and I smile. Someone had penciled under it, *Stingy motherfucker! How much can a cockroach eat?*

An old black man gets on at Morgan Avenue, reeking of alcohol. Deirdre and I watch as he collapses onto the cold plastic benchlike seat a little way down from us. He arranges himself carefully on his side, facing the backrest, his feet drawn up, and passes out.

"The feast of life is spread for all," Deirdre suddenly intones in a mournful, carrying voice that sends shivers through me. "But there are *ooonly* so many places at the table."

Does she mean the drunk? Herself?

"You had a place at the table, Deirdre," I say softly, tentatively.

"Never!"

She begins to rummage frantically in one of the shopping bags as though terrified that there is something missing, perhaps something forgotten, something left behind. "I never had a place at the table," she moans. "I never had a place at the table. I always looked on. I never feasted." Satisfied that whatever it is she is looking for is there, she pats the shopping bag and looks up again. "Never. I may once or twice have *appeared* to be there, at the table, but I was not. I may even have put something in my mouth, but it was always ashes."

"Ashes to ashes," the drunk calls. So he has not passed out.

"And you, poor man, never had a place at the table, either," Deirdre shouts.

"Oh, yes I did," the man says, still turned to the wall of his seat, not stirring. "I always had a place at the table. Maybe not the *head* of the table."

The train does something I was not expecting. It comes up out of the ground and transforms itself into a lumbering air creature, riding on tracks elevated to the third story of the buildings it passes. Here in the open, unwalled and untunneled, the train seems far less solid and substantial.

"No, you *didn't*," Deirdre argues. "You t'ink you did. It pleases you to t'ink you did."

"And it *was* a feast," the drunk says, his voice falling so that I strain to hear him. "What a feast it was! Chicken and ham and grits and greens, and big-breasted women with skin like silk."

"Ah, the man's a poet," Deirdre says, smiling her small,

pinched smile. "You can never tell, in the subway, who are the poets." I wish I could see her eyes. Most of her smile was always in her eyes, when you could see them.

WILSON AVENUE, BUSHWICK AVENUE, BROADWAY JUNCTION/EASTERN PARKWAY. I look out at the night, at the mean, burned-out streets the train is bisecting, trying to imagine the dark, shadowy life in them, rats prowling, hearts beating, and I shiver. Why does the train go here? Most of the windows are dark, or boarded up, though here and there a dim light punctures the emptiness, and when we near a station there is an occasional cluster of figures beneath a lamppost, boys poking each other, men rapping. SUTTER. LIVONIA.

The old man is asleep. His snores are loud and regular and peaceful, waves breaking on this barren shore.

"What do you want?" Deirdre asks. I look up, startled. She is talking to me. Her face is composed, serious. "Why are you following me? What are you doing here?"

I shrug. "Funny you should ask," I mumble.

"Is it morbid curiosity?" Then, her voice rising to a scream, really frightening me, she asks, "Am I that fate worse than death?"

I stare at her.

"Is that what it is? Are you using me to face your own fears? Or to eva-a-a-de them?"

I am too shaken to respond. *Is* it that I need to know the worst that can happen? *Is* this the worst that can happen?

"What do you want of me? For that matter, what did you ever want of me, Rachel?"

I am unable to find words.

"*Answer* me, Rachel." She spreads her arms wide, a theatrical gesture. She was never given to theatrical gestures. "I am calling to you from the black abyss that you have always known was there," she chants, like a witch, like a wraith, "the abyss that you have always skirted so glibly. Am I your demon, your doppelgänger, your dark side?"

I can feel my heart thumping in my ears. Nobody has ever spoken so directly to me before. Never. Not even, years ago, my psychoanalyst. Especially not him. "I think so. Maybe," I say. "Yes."

She sighs. "Well, I am not," she says in her normal voice. "We are not at all alike. My light side, if I had one, would never be you." She sighs again, and looks away. "Tell me," she says, sounding tired, "what did you, what *do* you, want of me?"

I struggle, not so much for words now as for truth. What *did* I want? "Friendship," I want to say. But it isn't enough; it's not quite true. Rebecca is my friend, Margo and Anna and Karla are my friends.

"In the beginning," I say, groping, "I think it was hero-worship. Because I'd known you before I ever knew you. I revered you because you did what I most valued and admired better than I believed I was ever going to be able to do it."

"Rubbish," she snorts.

"Later, I think I needed you to love me, just in an ordinary human way, you understand, so that I could feel myself forgiven for being less. And then," I say, surprised to find that I am crying, "and then I needed to keep you whole and safe. You were my . . ." But I can't find the word for that sacred thing that must not be desecrated, that consecrated thing that must not fail.

We are both silent and then Deirdre says, "You couldn't keep me whole and safe either, could you?"

"No. You couldn't redeem me. I couldn't save you. Two failures."

"They were your expectations, not mine. Your failures."

But I know that there is something I've left out. "It wasn't purely that," I say, "my wanting to save you. It wasn't only that I held you sacred." I grope for a tissue, and then I blow my nose in it and take deep breaths to stop the crying. "It made me feel strong," I say. "Just *trying* to save you made me feel in control, a little powerful, a little less at the mercy of fate."

"The forces of darkness," she says nodding. "But they are much too powerful even for you, Rachel, if you only knew!"

I can't help smiling. Deirdre's dark forces are so different from mine, so much more mysterious and imaginative and mythical, and at the same time more palpable, so much more externalized, something she has had to split her mind in two to manage. Whereas mine are so ordinary they're a cliché. My dark forces have been lodged within me since childhood; my dark forces *are* that child within me, small and frightened and helpless, the child I have struggled all my life to separate myself from, the child terrified of that abominable, noisy giant, my father. The child vowing, in some deep, wordless place, to grow up and always, always be in control.

So much in my life has been out of my control! Almost everything.

The train comes to a stop. The doors open with an air of finality as the engine quivers and falls silent. ROCKAWAY PARKWAY, the signs say. CANARSIE. I have forgotten all about the trainman in his cubicle, that upended metal coffin, only a few yards away all this time. He emerges in his dark uniform, his face gray and tired, locking the door behind him. Charon, I think.

"End of the line," he announces, making his way through the car and on into the next one.

"Cheap symbolism," Deirdre mutters, echoing my own thought. Then, brightening, she says, "Rachel, would you like a glass of wine?"

I look at her questioningly.

"I just happen to have," she says, rummaging in one of the bags at her feet, "a very nice Saint-Emilion given me by . . . by an . . . an *admirer*." She slides a bottle from the refuse at her feet, and holds it aloft triumphantly. "Are you carrying your Swiss army knife?"

I reach in the back pocket of my jeans for the knife. I don't know why I carry it, it weighs a ton and it is almost never useful. A habit, among others, left over from childhood when it made me feel strong and ready, like a scout. Like a boy. She hands me the bottle, and while I am winding the corkscrew into it, she dips back into one of her grab bags, extracting from it two plastic tumblers.

"Magic," I say.

"Not at all. Just the necessities."

I withdraw the cork and cross the aisle to sit beside her, handing her the bottle, taking one of the smudged, opaque tumblers. The wine will kill the germs, I tell myself. Deirdre pours. The rich dark red brightens the space between us.

"Isn't this illegal?" I ask, lifting my glass as the doors close and the train begins to move. "Won't we be arrested?"

"Probably," she says cheerfully, raising her glass to mine. "To your health, Rachel."

"To yours," I say. We drink. Deirdre looks over at the sleeping man, and I can see that she is aching to offer him wine, too.

"Don't wake him," I say. "He won't appreciate it."

"You think not? What a nice man."

We sip our wine, and I refrain from asking Deirdre the thousand questions that crowd my mind.

"How is Colette?" she asks. "Is she still alive?"

"Oh, yes. She's wonderful."

"Such a silly, stupid cat," Deirdre says, fondly.

"Not so stupid. She has a good life. More than can be said for most cats."

"She is a *lucky* cat. But stupid."

The wine in our tumblers goes quickly. Deirdre pours more.

"And Lisa?" she asks. I tell her about Lisa. "I think I'm no longer a slave of passion," I say.

"Someone else will come along."

"I doubt it."

"Then you must be getting some writing done," she says.

"Yes." And then I dare, stupidly, to ask, "And you?"

She doesn't answer. The stations slide by. No one at all comes aboard this car.

"Your children? How are they?"

"I'm a grandmother."

"How wonderful. A girl?" I tell her about Alexondra. I even show her a snapshot. It's a relief, this weird, polite, ordinary conversation we're having. The wine, after all that emotion, is making me tipsy.

She leans her head against the back of the seat. "Of course, I don't write anymore," she says. "There is nothing more to write about."

We are silent for a long, solemn moment. I think how much there is for her to write about. Confessions of a New York Bagperson, Living Off the Land, The Woman Who Threw It

All Away, Slouching Toward Canarsie, Waiting for Godot, Queen Lear. But for her it must go far beyond ordinary writer's block, waiting for the well to fill. It must be that nothing has interest any longer, nothing outside the vortex of her madness.

"How assiduously you worked to pare it all away," I say, recalling how efficient, how methodical she was. "Your friends, your work, your money, your 't'ings,' the cats. It was as if you were preparing to die and didn't want to leave any loose ends."

"But I *don't* die," she says, bitterly. "I go on and on, end-lessly. Death is perverse. It doesn't come when you want it, only when you don't, or when you're looking the other way."

She refills our tumblers.

"I'm not so sure," I say. "Maybe some of us do die when we know we've come to the end of things." I think of the old women on the trip I took with my mother, the women who had come to the end of things, or so I believed, and who fought so hard against knowing it.

"Rubbish. The only ones who have that power are those who are permitted the option of suicide. I, alas, am condemned to await what is called a natural death."

"Speaking of suicide, do you remember Benita Broadhurst?" I ask, referring to a poet who was at the Center when we were there. "Did I ever tell you about that phone conversation I overheard her having with her ninety-year-old mother?"

Deirdre shakes her head.

" 'No joy, Mother?' Benita asked. 'No joy at all? Not even one tiny corner of joy anywhere in your life? Well, really, Mother, there's always something you can do about that. If that were true of my life, I would certainly do something about it.' "

Deirdre nods, snickering. "She hated her mother."

"Later she told me that her mother's response was, 'Oh, Benita, I would never kill myself. That would be like going to a party to which one has not been invited.' "

The corners of Deirdre's mouth twitch in amusement. The train stops. Grand Street, though I'm no longer sure if we're coming or going. A young black couple enters the car holding hands. They look at us and then at the snoring old man, and snuggle into a corner as far away as they can get, entwined in each other's arms. Deirdre looks ruefully at the nearly empty bottle in her hand.

"Then what *do* you do, Deirdre, all day long?" I ask.

"Do?" she says witheringly, as though I've missed the point of everything. "What do I *do?*"

"Yes. How do you live? What do you do?"

"I sing," she says, and begins to do so. "And the drums, the drums, the drums begin to roll . . ."

We are under the river. Tunnels beneath bodies of water are awesome. I see the cross-section as if drawn in color on a printed page: me within the train, the train within the tunnel, the layer of earth above it, eels and garbage and crabs and dead and poisonous things strewn on the muddy surface of that earth, the river bottom, then water with fish swimming about in it, then the surface of the river with tugboats and scows on it, then air with birds and planes flying through it, and people in the boats and the planes. But I am the bottom, the lowest level, beneath all the rest, yet encapsulated in a place of air and light and movement so that it is easy to be oblivious of the incredible reality of where I am.

Meanwhile, frantically, desperately, another part of my mind is telling my blessings. Over and over, with the rolling of Deirdre's drums. The usual blessings: work, children, friends, means, appetites. Pleasures of the mind and body, simple and complex. Sanity. And I still have one breast.

Lucky, lucky me.

Deirdre has stopped singing. "And I watch and I listen," she says, "and I think about what I have seen and heard." She nods her head violently. "Yes. That is what I do. The really frightening thing in life, I think, lies in our capacity for inattentiveness to it."

Maybe she's right. Maybe that's why we do it, why we write, why we live. Because we're interested. Curious. Attentive. Because we're children who've never acquired blinders.

I feel the tears coming again, but there's nothing I can do. The tears come. No, there's nothing I can do. People who have lost the need to live die in their own way. They kill themselves deliberately or carelessly, they wither, they go mad. They leave you. They leave you with what they can.

"Do you have a place to sleep, Deirdre?" I ask.

"Of course!"

We are coming into the station where all this began, and I am going to get off and go home.

"You know where I am if you need anything," I say, knowing that I will never hear from her, that if I ever see her again, it will be an accidental meeting like this one. But it's as if I had already left. She is singing again.

"And the drums," she sings in her carrying, mournful voice, "and the drums, and the drums begin to roll . . ."

The doors close on her and her ballad, and the train pulls out of the station.

I go up the steps and back out into the world. The air feels caressingly soft and sweet and pure, and the sky is dark backdrop for the lights of the universe.

· 241 ·

About the Author

EDITH KONECKY was born in New York City and has lived there most of her life. She is the mother of grown children and has published one previous novel, *Allegra Maud Goldman*, and a number of short stories.